Hira

Xarina Akhtar

*To my good friends Ash and Paulett, for their unwavering
encouragement,
and to my children, Ejaaz, Zia and Yasmin.*

About the Author

Xarina Akhtar arrived in the UK at the age of four. Naïve, totally ethnic and carrying a box of Indian sweets on her head, she walked straight past her father, whom she had never seen before. And so began her journey in England, as a first generation Pakistani, and the family's guinea pig.

Conforming to an arranged marriage at a young age, she concentrated her efforts on raising her family and on studying. Now that her children are older, she is enjoying independence for the first time. Hira is her first novel and her short story, 'Alliances', is published in a collection of 'Unexpected Tales from the Ends of the Earth', available on Amazon kindle.

This edition published 2013 by mardibooks
www.mardibooks.com

ISBN 978-1-909227-40-8

Copyright © Xarina Akhtar 2013
Cover designed by Ejaaz Akhtar

A CIP catalogue record for this book is available from the British Library.

mardibooks has a small but growing stable of writers from around the world.
We publish in ebook format on Amazon.
To celebrate our first anniversary, mardibooks has also brought out five books in hard copy.

To find out more visit: **www.mardibooks.com**

Chapter 1

Hira woke up with a start and sat up in bed. The dream had been back to torment her and again she woke up at the exact same moment as all the times before. She watched her mother being escorted away over the rickety wooden bridge, by two women, to the green and lush fields beyond. As they crossed the bridge she knew that she would never see her mother again and her heart broke for the second time. For the bridge in her dream represented the final barrier to heaven. The two women? Angels? Perhaps? Helping her mother make that final journey; taking away all her fears and indecisions of entering the paradise she had often spoke of, to Hira as a child. Whether Hira still held onto the belief that there still was a heaven or that she would one day be reunited with her mother was up for debate. But at this moment in time she felt lost and abandoned. Her mother had left her.

She brushed away a tear and looked at the sleeping form of her husband, Aaryan. Needing reassurance and comfort she reached out to touch him, hoping for a hug in return. He grunted in his sleep and shrugged.

'Leave it, Alisha,' he murmured. She withdrew her hand. He had been quite distant with her since her arrival and she got the impression that she was more of an irritation to him. Every time he looked at her he seemed to have a permanent scowl on his face. As he uttered another woman's name she felt her heart sink. Then anger. Alisha had to be someone quite close to him.

'*What had she let herself in for?*' she thought to herself, travelling halfway across the world to the state of Ambala, not knowing a soul or a friendly face. She was at the mercy of a family that she had only known about through fleeting conversations with her mother. Lying back, she stared at the ceiling and thought about the family dynamics. There was Dada, the grandfather, Dadi, the grandmother, brothers-in-law, Aiden and Alman, their wives Sabina and Amara, and then there was Akilah, a more spoilt, rude and objectionable person there could not be. One who had decided on first sight that she did not like her newest sister-in-law, not that she liked her first two sisters-in-law. Finally, there was her husband Aaryan who treated her as if she was an irritation. She turned away and closed her eyes. Hoping for sleep but knowing that it would elude her for a few more hours to come. Tossing and turning, she rolled over onto her back and felt him move. In a flash, he loomed over her, pinning her to the bed and making her head bang against the headboard. In the darkness, she sensed that he was angry but self-preservation had taught her to fight back. She squirmed under him and tried to free herself. This earned her another shake and another bang on her head. She stopped struggling.

'What is wrong with you?' he asked through gritted teeth. 'Every night you have to play out some type of drama and make my sleeping hours difficult. Isn't it bad enough that I have to put up with you for the best part of the day?'

Indignant, she squirmed under him, trying to wriggle free from not only his grip but from the look that she imagined he had. At last, he let her free, almost throwing her aside.

'Move to the couch,' he growled. She got up and went to the small sofa, taking her pillow with her. Curled up in the darkness she played out the events of the past few months before facing the back of the couch and closing her eyes.

Her restlessness irked Aaryan. It always irked him. He was not one to keep silent when something displeased him. Time and time again he would come back to the irritation that was Hira and made no bones about his dislike for her.

'Do you have a deep psychological problem or something?' Scowling, he stared at her back. 'Tossing and turning. Every night it is the same. God only knows why I got lumbered with you.' She sighed at his insensitivity.

'All he could think about was him. How he got lumbered with her,' she thought to herself, *'never mind the things that she had to give up because the aunties had said so.'*

'I can't sleep,' she told him and as if to make a point sat up and fluffed her pillow. He looked at her through the darkness, ruing the day he went against his better judgement and allowed her to join him in the bed. If it hadn't been for a colder than normal night he was happy enough for her to sleep on the couch, even if it was too small. But she had shivered so badly that he relented. He wasn't prepared to be nursemaid to her if she fell ill. Now he stared at her, annoyed that she was disturbing his sleep yet again.

6

'Well. You know what you can do.' He rolled over, indicating that he wanted no more interruptions to his sleep pattern.

'Put a pillow over your head?' she muttered.

'What did you say?' He turned briefly to glare at her. She stared back.

'Nothing.'

She was still fast asleep when Dadi, started banging on the door.

'Hira. Wake up. Do you think you have all day to sleep? Get up and open the door.' She extracted herself from the bedding, stumbled to the door, unlocked it and stepped back as the older woman barged into the room. Surveying the bedding on the couch and the still sleeping form of her grandson she looked at Hira with disdain.

'Why are you sleeping on the couch?' Hira brushed a few strands of hair off her face. She looked from the bed to the elderly woman.

'I was having trouble sleeping,' she mumbled casting a glance at the sleeping form behind her.

'Get ready and come down. Did you forget that you have to help make breakfast? Every morning, without fail. You are not here to rest and get fat. Don't let me find you sleeping in ever again.' That said, she flounced out of the room.

***

Breakfast was always a manic affair. As was the custom in so many households, the men, elder womenfolk and the daughters of the house were fed first, waited on by the daughters-in-law until they had finished. There were two of them in the house. By good fortune they got along well, supported each other in all their trials and tribulations and had welcomed Hira with open arms. This alliance did not sit well with Dadi and the only daughter of the house, Akilah. The two never missed an opportunity to belittle them and cast aspersions on their respective families, their upbringing and their standing. Dadi was the one who ran the household with a fist of iron. She was always putting down family members with her words. This morning was no different.

She picked up a puri and tossed it at Sabina.

'You call this a puri!' She sneered at her. 'It is not fit for anyone to eat. So greasy! Did your mother not teach you properly or were you too insolent to learn?'

She put her elbows on the table and rested her chin on her hands.

'Which one is it?' Sabina looked at the ground and Hira bit her tongue, anger evident in her eyes. She had seen this type of scenario played out too often. Every morning, they would run the gauntlet of Dadi's taunts as she picked holes in everything they did and belittled their upbringing. She did not expect anything less. Hira stared open mouthed, angry that the old lady was so caustic in her behaviour. Dadi caught the look on Hira's face and was quick to admonish her.

'You can take that look off your face,' she snapped at her. 'Don't get above your station. Know your place in this household and do not lock horns with me. You will not win.' She paused, an evil glint in her eye. 'After breakfast you can take on the task of clearing the garden at the front of the house. I want all the weeds removed and the beds ready for planting.' It was the middle of summer. Hot as it could be. Hira was already feeling the difference in the climate and was sure that Dadi gave her this task to give her heatstroke.

'Dadiji?' Hira's younger brother-in-law spoke. 'It is too hot. Besides, we have workers to do things like this. A daughter-in-law of this house should not be doing such things.' Dadi glared at him.

'Do not tell me what is to be done. Just because you are now one of the main earners does not mean that you will tell me what is to be done. I have made my decision. Hira will do as she is told. If you feel aggrieved then perhaps you should also help her.' Dadi glared at Hira. 'And she knows not to disobey me. Correct?' Hira hesitated before nodding. She didn't have the will in her to fight today. However, tomorrow was another day. She was new to the family and was still trying to adjust. Half the time she felt as if she was working as bonded labour. The work assigned to her in the garden was a small snapshot of what was expected of them.

'Hira? What are you thinking?' Aaryan interrupted her thoughts. She jumped and spilt the cup of tea she was holding onto his shirt.

He shot up. 'You stupid oaf!' Grabbing a napkin he dabbed the stain while Hira looked on, shocked. 'I asked you twice to go upstairs and find a clean handkerchief for me and you do this. Now I need a clean shirt. Hurry up. I am getting late.' He did not wait; instead he turned and marched away, expecting her to follow him. When he realised that she was not following, he stood still and shouted. 'Hira, for God's sake. I have already told you that I am going to be late.' Hira jolted back to the present from her thoughts. She looked at Dadi for permission to leave her place and only then, took her leave.

'Clumsy, air headed... ' he ranted as he removed his shirt and waited for her to give him a clean one. 'Clean shirt!' he barked, rifling through the wardrobe, looking for a particular shirt. Instead he happened to come across her phone and Ipod. In a fit of rage he picked up both and threw them across the room. Hira watched as they hit the marble floor and pieces flew off and bounced in different directions. Reaching beyond him she removed a clean shirt from the wardrobe and handed it to him, then went over to where the fallen items lay. She gathered up each piece and looked mournfully at them.

'Why is it that you have to be told twice about everything?' He put the shirt on and took the handkerchief from its place in the wardrobe and put it in his pocket. 'You are definitely not right in the head.'

'I could say the same for you,' she stood and stared him angrily.

'Meaning?'

'Meaning I am not the one who is grouchy all the time. You are the one who is having tantrums.' His uttering his 'girlfriend's' name during the night had riled her, as had his complete disregard for her property. He ignored the statement, picked up his jacket and made for the door.

'Damn stupid girl. Coming over here and making my life a living hell. I am not one of your English boyfriends who will put up with your questioning. Don't wait up.' He looked back. 'I am eating out and am likely to be late.'

The need to throw something at his retreating figure was great, but she suppressed it. She would not get any brownie points for

9

it. A shy and demure person she wasn't and it was killing her to behave as such. She had been told that she would need to change herself when she got married. She had to respect her in- laws and behave in a more subservient manner. This was torture, she thought. With a sigh she arranged the bedding, grabbed some old clothes and went to change. If she had to start on the garden she may as well start early before it got too hot.

Chapter 2

Akilah was the first to spot her as she descended the stairs.

'Dadi? Since when did the daughters-in-law of this house wear jeans and a t-shirt?' She made a point of emphasising the somewhat trivial issue, ignoring the fact that she was in similar attire and was ever ready to add more drama to the situation.

'She is going to be working in the garden,' her grandfather replied, picking up the newspaper and glancing at the front page. 'Would you want to do such a job in your best clothes?' He stared at Akilah. 'Don't make a song and dance about it.'

Kind eyes looked in Hira's direction. 'Beta, make sure you wear a hat, drink plenty of water and try and stay in the shade. I will send Harilal and Uday to come out and help you.'

'Thank you Dadaji.' Hira smiled for the first time that morning and made her way to the garden, ready to tackle the job ahead. Dada turned to Akilah.

'You would do best to treat your sister-in-laws with respect. It will not be long until you too, will be a sister-in-law to someone. How would you feel if you were disrespected?' Akilah rolled her eyes then threw her head back and scoffed.

'I have no intention of getting married. In fact, I will stay here after I get married. I won't leave.' She laughed and skipped off. Dada opened up his newspaper and shook it.

'Foolish girl,' he muttered, turning to the politics section. Dadi entered and sat next to him.

'Who is a foolish girl?' she asked.

'Your grand-daughter,' he replied, peering at her over the top of the newspaper. 'She seems to have this odd notion that she will stay here after marriage. I wonder who put that idea into her head.' Dadi quickly averted her eyes and busied herself.

Along with the two manservants, Hira stood, stretched and surveyed the work. The sun had reached way past its highest point and the heat had notched up enough degrees to make it difficult to spend any more time out in it. The garden had been weeded and the beds had been turned. They had worked hard and working as a team they had finished quickly as was possible, but it had still been a back-breaking task. She was thankful that at least she did not have to spend any more time in the scorching sun. Four hours was enough. She stood her face flushed and wiped the perspiration from her face.

'Hira Bahu. Please sit in the shade now. All the work is done.' Hira shook her head.

'No Uday Kaka. I can bet that as soon as I sit down, Dadiji will be out here. I don't want to give her any more reason to be upset.' Uday nodded knowingly. Right on cue Dadi's voice could be heard on the veranda as she made her way towards them. Harilal and Uday took it upon themselves to disappear right at that moment. Dadi inspected the beds and then at the weeds piled in a heap.

'Hmm. Good. I will get Harilal to dispose of these. Go inside, get cleaned up and have something to eat. Sabina and Amara will be having theirs. After that there is more work to be done. Your sisters-in-law will tell you what to do.' Hira watched the retreating figure and suppressed an urge to bow low and scrape. If ever there was a time that Dadi resembled a mythical Grand Master, it was now. Yoda did not quite cut it, but Dungeon Master was apt. With her sari sweeping the floor, it gave the impression that the older lady was floating on air, just as the character from her childhood had done. She smiled broadly.

'Is there something tickling you?' Hira's smile disappeared. Dadi had stopped and was surveying her. Hira shook her head.

'It is nothing Dadiji. I just felt happy.'

'Hmm.' I am sure that I can find you something that will get rid of that. Now get inside.' With a sigh, Hira dusted herself down and followed behind, praying that she was not assigned another task straightaway.

***

Washed and changed, she sat in the kitchen with Sabina and Amara. The lunch of chana dhal and chapatti was reheated, spreading the aroma into the kitchen and beyond. Hira was hungry and quickly dished up the food, passed it round and tucked into her portion. Sabina and Amara laughed.

'Hira. Slow down.' Sabina giggled. 'Eat any faster and you will get the hiccups.'

Hira giggled and promptly got the hiccups. She poured herself a glass of salted lassi and drank. The hiccups continued causing laughter among them as she battled to stop.

'Hira.' Dada's stern voice was heard at the threshold of the kitchen. Hira jumped.

Chapter 3

He appeared in the doorway seconds later and glared at Hira. 'Have you forgotten what I asked you to do? I have been waiting and I am fast losing my patience.' The giggling stopped and an air of seriousness and apprehension took over. Hira stood up nervously seeing the anger on his face.

'Dadaji. I am sorry. I don't remember. Please tell me what you had asked?' She was mortified. Dada had asked something of her and she had forgotten. She sensed that another punishment was heading her way if Dadi found out.

'You have forgotten?' Dada asked her. Eyes downcast, she nodded sadly. 'No matter,' he said. 'But your hiccups are gone now.' His smile reached the corner of his eyes and he watched his three grand daughters-in-law as they realised and smiled at each other. 'Food smells good.' He looked hungrily at the table.

'Dadaji. If you sit in the dining room we will bring the food out to you,' Amara offered.

'No need,' he said, using his walking stick for support he stepped into the kitchen. 'I will sit here with you.' He pulled out a chair and sat down. Like a well-oiled machine, the girls dished up the food, got him a glass of water, placed it in front of him and then sat with him to eat.

'That hit the spot,' Dada said as he pushed away his plate. He picked up his glass. 'Is there anymore lassi?' he asked. Hira gulped down the remnants of her drink. She shook her head.

'I have just downed the last of it. Sorry.'

'I think next time we will make a lot more and I shall keep the lion's share. Hira has drunk it all.'

'I think next time I will monitor what you eat.' Dadi's voice carried into the kitchen.

Dada pulled a face. She had rumbled him.

'Soraya.' He turned and gave her a smile to mollify her. 'I came over all faint with hunger and my feet led me here.' Dadi shook her head knowingly.

'Why don't you say you were faint with greed and decided to come here for seconds?' She came over to the table. 'You could have

14

asked for more food earlier on. Why hide?'

Dada looked at the girls.

'I wanted to sit and eat with my girls,' he said. 'Every mealtime they stand and serve us and then when we are finished then they sit down and eat. Soraya? It is all wrong. We should all sit together as a family.' Dadi looked at the girls with contempt.

'You girls have got work to do. Go and make a start.' One by one they stood up, washed all the dishes and left the kitchen, each giving Dada a concerned look. 'As for you.' She berated him. 'I would appreciate if you kept out of these matters. Just as I served you all when I came to this family, so should the girls. It does them good to learn how to do household things and learn a bit of discipline. I am not going to change an age old tradition simply because you say so.' Dada pouted.

'And, therefore, I shall not sanction anymore buying of saris or jewellery simply because you say so.' He turned in his chair to face her, his face softening. 'You are too hard on these girls. Surely you remember what the first year with your in laws was like?'

'And you remember what your mother was like,' Dadi replied.

'So you decided to follow in her footsteps.' He stood up, scraping the chair back as he did so. 'Soraya. You had been blessed with a wonderful daughter-in-law and then with three lovely girls who have entered our house as our granddaughters. These are gems. Don't chase them away with your attitude. Mark my words, the girls of today will not put up with it. After all, you don't want to end up all alone one day. You will remember my words one day. I am going out for a walk. Need to make room for afters.' He smiled at her and patted her shoulder affectionately. 'Go easy on everyone.' It took Dadi all of ten minutes to keep a lid on her composure. As soon as she heard the front door shut, she allowed her anger to get the better of her and she cursed her daughters-in-law, before going in search of them.

She did not have far to search. The sitting and dining areas were immaculate. Sabina was tackling the stair case; Amara was busy on the landing. Hira appeared at the door of the prayer room, sweeping the small amount of dust into the dustpan and disposing of it. Dadi remembered Dada's words and she stopped for a while. There was some truth in his words, but she was not going to allow emotions to take over. As the trio spied on her, they stopped what they were doing and stood waiting for more orders.

'What are you standing idle for? Get on with your work. I shall be resting for a while. No slacking in the meantime.' She re-arranged her scarf and walked in the direction of her room.

'Dadi.' Akilah appeared, skipped over to her and embraced her from behind, smiling. 'My favourite Dadi.' She laughed. Dadi patted her arm and smiled.

'What is my favourite granddaughter up to?'

Akilah looked upset.

'Dadi. I am your only granddaughter.' She pouted. Dadi laughed.

'So you are. And what are you being so sweet about?'

'You know me so well, Dadi. I was in the mall and I saw a beautiful outfit. Dadi, it was to die for,' she gushed. 'I tried it on and it looked soooo good. Can I have some money to buy it?'

'Hmm. Come with me to my room. Let me see what I have.' She smiled taking Akilah in her room.

Dadi opened up her trunk and rummaged around for something. Finally she found what she was looking for. Pulling at the strings to the leather pouch, she dipped inside, taking out a wad of notes and handed them to Akilah. She took the money, counted it and looked at Dadi, puzzled.

'Dadi? There is only nine thousand rupees here. The suit costs ten thousand and then I need to buy the accessories, shoes and handbag on top.' The old woman looked at her.

'For now, this is all I have.' She saw the disappointment in the young girl's eyes, reached out and touched the top of her head. 'As soon as your grandfather comes home I will get some more money. Now will you sit here and read with me?'

Akilah backed away. 'Dadi. I just remembered that I had to be somewhere. I will be back later.' Making her excuses she beat a hasty retreat. Reading was such a bore.

***

16

In the dim light of the prayer room Hira surveyed the dozens of books that took up one side. Looking at each of the titles, she saw the familiar titles of the Hadiths, the numerous copies of the Holy Quran, including a few transliterations. She pulled out a book from the shelf and turned the pages. Reading a few pages she looked up and saw her mother deep in concentration as she read the allotted chapters that she had promised. As the last verse was read and the book closed with the reverence it deserved, Hira saw a little girl sidle up to her and place her head on the woman's lap. A hand was placed lovingly on the child's head.

'Hira. Have you had a good sleep?'

'Yes Maman. I had a dream. Why were you reading?'

'Because I had promised that I would read today.' She reached out, put the book out of harm's way on the nearby table and then gathered up Hira and sat her in her lap. 'When you are a little older you will learn to read too and then you will read to me. Now shall I make you some lunch?'

'Yes please. Can I have samosa and ice cream?' Hira's mother laughed.

'That is an odd combination. Shall we see if it will work?'

Hira stared at the book through misty eyes and lovingly caressed the cover of the book. She held it to her chest and sighed heavily. Her mother had countless books but the holy books were her solace during trying times. She realised that it had been a long time since she had sat to read. A tear rolled down her cheek and she quickly brushed it away.

'Hira? What are you doing?' Hira looked up to see Dadi standing at the door. Drying her cheeks she hastily put the book back on the shelf.

'Nothing Dadiji. I was just curious.' The old woman had seen her tears but chose to ignore them. Her features did not change or soften in the slightest.

'If you have finished in here you may go. Sabina and Amara are sitting on the veranda. Go and sit with them. When I have more work for you I shall call you.' Hira nodded, tidied the book shelf and made to leave. One of the book titles caught her eye and she picked it up, flicked through the pages and made a mental note to find time to read it. She remembered that her sisters-in-laws were waiting for her and rushed to join them.

Hira was greeted by smiles as she joined her sisters-in-law on the veranda.

'Here she comes.' Sabina smiled and poured a glass of juice and handed it to her as she took her seat. Hira sat back and downed the majority of it in one go.

'You were thirsty. The way you almost finished your juice...' Amara giggled and leant forward, placing her chin on her hands. 'Were you a drinker previously?' Hira gave an animated shocked look, causing Sabina to nearly choke while sipping her drink.

'Amara,' Hira chided. 'I have not now or ever been a drinker.' She lounged back in the chair, 'Not that I need to drink to have a good time – or get into trouble,' she added.

'So you did not drink at Uni?' Hira finished her drink and put the glass on the table.

'That is classified information. I am not going to give you any ammunition to use against me later on,' she finished, adding to the giggles. She looked up and down the veranda. 'Where is Dadiji?' she whispered.

'She is asleep,' Sabina replied. 'Whenever she has chana for lunch it does something to her. She has to sleep it off.'

'We should give her chana for lunch every day then,' Hira retorted. 'If it gives us some respite from her then I am all for it.' Sabina and Amara looked at Hira quizzically until the penny dropped. Then they burst out laughing before quickly controlling the noise level so as not to wake the old lady.

'Hira you are funny. Aren't you scared of how Dadiji will punish you?' Amara asked. Hira shook her head.

'No point in being scared. If Dadiji is going to be gunning for you, what's the use?' Sabina took Hira's hand. A sad look crossed her face.

'But she has been so nasty to you since you came here. I haven't seen one day when she has treated you without any sarcasm.'

'Yeah and she was so bad to you when you talked about your mother,' Amara jumped in, remembering the events when Hira had shed tears at the memory of her mother. Sabina shot her a warning look and shook her head. Amara backed down. But it had the desired effect as Hira's features changed.

'I don't know what mum had done to make Dadiji hate her so much.' The hurt showed on her face. Facing the concern and sympathy from her sisters-in-law, her bravado and façade fell. 'She is not even allowing me to grieve. Can someone be so callous?' Her eyes pooled with tears. Sabina reached over and hugged her. Amara got up and joined them, copying the same action. Together, they soothed Hira's tears and hugged her until she composed herself. She dried her tears and gave them a watery smile.

Amara poured some more juice for them.

'I'm sorry, Hira. I shouldn't have said anything,' she apologised shamefacedly.

'Don't worry,' Hira replied. 'Stuff happens.' She locked her emotions deep within herself and smiled.

'The garden's looking good,' Sabina said with a wink. 'You must love working with plants.' Hira saw the laughter in her eyes.

'No. I just love burying things.' She returned the wink.

'Can't you be serious?' Amara giggled.

'Umm. let me think.' Hira thought for a moment. 'No,' she added looking directly at Amara who started giggling again.

'Uni must have been a blast for you,' Sabina commented. 'So what was it like going to Uni in the UK?' Hira shrugged.

'Same as here really, studying, socialising and growing up. Although to be honest, if I knew that I would end up married here, with no career prospects, I may have thought twice.'

'The face of the woman in India is changing. It is taking time but the movement is gaining ground,' Sabina told her.

'Only time will tell,' Amara added with a tinge of sadness. 'Wish it happens and soon.'

'What are you three up to?' The old lady's voice made them all jump.

'Damn. She crops up without warning,' Hira muttered under her breath. Sabina gave her a bemused look.

'We are just having a drink, Dadiji,' Amara answered. 'We have finished all our chores.' Dadi looked at the three glasses and the jug on the table in front of them.

'In future, if you are thirsty, drink water. I haven't got money to waste to bring in juice all the time for the three of you. I take it that you have not started the evening meal yet?' They looked at each other and then shook their heads. 'Well, I suggest you make a start.' That said, Dadiji walked off.

'What do we cook today?' Hira asked. Normally Dadi would tell them what she wanted cooked.

'We will just have to decide for ourselves,' Sabina informed her. 'We may as well take the initiative.' They gathered the glasses from the table and went to make a start on the meal.

Harilal Kaka had already made a start with the food preparations. As they walked into the kitchen he looked up from what he was doing and smiled. 'Thank you Harilal Kaka. You may go.' She turned to the two and quickly made a decision.

'Hira can you make the pilau. Amara you make the okra dish and chicken curry but make it with plenty of sauce. I will make the sweet dish. Aiden really likes vermicelli pudding.' As they busied themselves, Amara looked uncertain.

'What's up?' Sabina asked, seeing her worried face. She looked sheepish as she explained.

'Di. I can make the chicken. That is no problem, but the okra? You know that I always end up ruining that.' Sabina smiled.

'Don't worry about that. You make a start. When you come to make the okra I will help you. I'll show you how to make it,' she reassured her. 'There is nothing to worry about. Let's get going.'

As they busied themselves Akilah came into the kitchen.

'Ah. The worker ants are busy working away,' she stated and picked up an apple out of the fruit bowl and took a bite out of it. Leaning on the counter she revelled in having the upper hand over them. An idea came to mind. 'Dadi said not to use any spices. She wants something really mild today.' She smiled. 'Carry on.' With a smug look she sauntered out, leaving Hira fuming.

'Ooh, that little …' she grumbled as she took out the pot and put it on the stove with some force.

Amara gathered the spices and started adding the ingredients for the main dishes.

'If Dadiji wanted mild food, then why didn't she tell us like she usually does? Our food is better when it has some flavour.' She measured out the chilli powder and threw that in for good measure. They exchanged glances, knowing that trouble was afoot, whatever they did.

Chapter 4

The aromatic smell of the food enticed the family out from all corners of the house. Aidan and Alman, Sabina and Amara's husbands quickly took their seats in anticipation and turned over their plates. Dada and Dadi arrived with Akilah as the food was being dished out, took their places, offered thanks and tucked in. Akilah looked on, smiling to herself. Dadi would soon be on the warpath. She wondered who would get the sharp end of her tongue. As they ate she looked puzzled. Surely Dadi would say something now.

'How is the food, Dadi?' she asked glancing at her sisters-in-law. Dadi nodded.

'It is passable,' she replied, making a face all the same. Akilah was puzzled. She picked up her fork and took a mouthful. Expecting to taste food that was so bland that it would have been refused, instead she got a mouthful of an excellent tasting pilau, accompanied by mouth-watering chicken. Looking for an excuse she picked up the okra dish, took a mouthful.

'There is no chapatti,' she said, looking along the table, trying to find some shortcomings to bring to the attention of her grandmother. Amara picked up the container with the chapattis and placed a couple on her plate, giving her a triumphant look.

'Is there something wrong?' Dada had noticed Akilah's fallen features. Akilah shook her head and tucked in. She shot a glance at Amara who returned her gaze without a flicker of emotion and decided that she would not let this deceit pass her by.

Towards the end of the meal Dadi used the remaining water in her glass to wash her hands.

'Once you girls have cleared up, go and eat. Hira, as Aaryan will be back late... put some food aside for him so that you can heat it up for him, in case he is hungry when he comes home.' No taunts, put downs or barbed words. Hira nodded and cleared away the dirty plates, while the other two gathered the used items and deposited them in the kitchen.

Akilah showed up while they were clearing up, her face flushed with anger. They waited for her to say her piece. However, faced with all three together, she thought better of it. Instead, she swept her arm across the worktop and sent one of the hotpots crashing to the floor.

'Oops. Sorry about that,' she said, 'I guess there is no food for you. You will have to go hungry tonight.'

'What is going on in there?' Dadi's voice carried into the kitchen.

'Nothing, Dadiji.' Amara went to the door. 'A hotpot slipped off the worktop.'

'Clumsy girl. Be careful. It had better not be damaged.'

'Yes. Clumsy girl.' Akilah's eyes twinkled with maliciousness. Hira bent to pick up the pot.

'An empty vessel makes the loudest noise.' she said, relating to the pot and glanced at Akilah who shot her a look of fury at the double meaning of those words.

'I won't forget this,' she muttered, flouncing out of the kitchen.

Hira was battling sleep when Aaryan finally arrived home. He was taken aback as he walked into the bedroom and noticed that she was still awake.

'I told you not to wait up.' He took off his jacket, threw it on the sofa and sat down to take his shoes and socks off.

'Are you hungry?' She got up and pulled on a wrap. He looked up at her.

'No, I'm good. I am just going to have a shower and then go to sleep.' She got back into bed. He stared at her for a moment. 'Are you going to have a nightmare tonight as well? Because if you are I'd like to know. Can't be having another disturbed night.' She turned over and pulled the throw over herself.

'Insensitive, arrogant, no good ... '

'What are you muttering? You are forever muttering.' He stood by the bed staring down at her. She looked at him in the dim light shining in from the hallway but did not reply. 'You aren't normal.' He shook his head and walked off in the direction of the bathroom.

'What is normal?' she asked him, raising herself on her elbow. He stopped. Turning around with unguarded irritation, she was beginning to irritate the hell out of him to the point where he was looking for a way out.

'Dadi and her decrees,' he lamented silently.

'What?'

'I asked. What is normal?' He hesitated.

'Do we have to have this discussion now?'

'As good a time as any.' He shook his head.

'Give it a rest. I haven't got the patience for this or you. I'm going for a shower.'

There was no light from the bedroom as he re-entered. Hira had extinguished all the lights and had gone to sleep. Carefully, he made his way to his side of the bed and lay down. As he pulled the blanket over him he noticed that she was not there. He sighed heavily. His eyes grew accustomed to the darkness and he saw that she had moved to the sofa. At first, he was puzzled. Then he remembered his words to her earlier. He shrugged, stretched out and enjoyed the vast space on the bed.

'If she sleeps on the sofa, it is her choice. I am not going to insist to her to sleep on the bed,' he thought to himself. He replayed the events of the evening and smiled. It had been a good evening. Nice food, decent venue and excellent company. He was disappointed that it had ended at all but made a mental note to arrange another evening out and soon. He was happy to spend as much time out of the house as possible. Home stressed him. Hira puzzled him. He was irritated at the way that she conducted herself. There was no life in her. She worked, she fed and she slept. Actually, she did not sleep, he reasoned. She was the living dead and Akilah? Akilah was just a younger sister who was a pain, wanting me, me, me, all the time. He rolled over onto his stomach and closed his eyes, ready for sleep.

Chapter 5

Hira opened her eyes before it got light. Feeling a bit disorientated she looked around her to get her bearings and groaned as she stretched.

'How did I end up here?' she muttered to herself, before remembering that she had taken it upon herself to sleep on the sofa. She shook her head, annoyed with herself. 'Hira. You are an idiot. You gave up a comfy bed for no reason.' She continued muttering as she gathered the bedclothes, dumped them on the bed, grabbed a towel, her clothes and went to get ready. It would be in her best interests if she was bright and early, ready to prepare breakfast rather than be roused, chided and scolded all the way to the kitchen.

She stood under the flowing water, allowing it to ease away the stiffness from the night spent on the sofa. Closing her eyes against the flow, she revelled in its soothing massage. The sound of the bathroom door being opened caused her eyes to snap open and a feeling of dread overtook her. She jumped as Aaryan's voice resonated in the bathroom.

'Hira, for goodness sake. Can't you lock the door when you are in here?' He quickly turned his back to her. Hira quickly grabbed the towel and wrapped it around her.

'And can't you learn to knock or better still not come in. Surely the sound of water was evident?'

'Just lock it next time,' he ordered and beat a hasty retreat, shutting the door behind him.

'Just lock it next time,' she mimicked and continued with the remainder of her shower. Only when she was done and had turned off the water did she realise that she would have to face Aaryan. Her cheeks burned at the thought of the state that he had seen her in. She took a deep breath and stepped out. At this stage, she was more concerned to get ready and get to the kitchen.

She marched out of the bathroom, quickly dressed, stood in front of the dresser, combed her hair and left the room. In her haste, she did not realise that Aaryan was not there.

The chai was simmering away on the hob, eggs scrambled, with the toast almost ready and the hot parathas placed in the ever useful hotpot. Hira had been joined by Amara. Together they brought the food to the dining room and set the table. Sabina rushed down the stairs and into the dining room.

'I am so sorry,' she apologised. 'What shall I do?'

'It is all done,' Amara replied. 'Hira did most of it.' She glanced her way and smiled. Just then they heard Dadi making her way towards them. They took their places at the table and waited for everyone to arrive.

Midway through breakfast, there was a clattering at the door and a voice called at the main door. Aaryan wiped his mouth, put down his napkin and got up.

'Sounds like post. I'll go and check.' He returned with a few envelopes. 'This one is for Dada.' He handed it over. 'One for me.' He put that under his arm. 'And this...' He looked at the addressee, '...is for Hira.' He passed it over.

'Why is someone sending things to Hira?' Akilah spoke in a peeved voice. 'Is she special?'

Hira took the envelope and scrutinised it.

'It must be something from the UK,' Dadi muttered.

'Can I be excused?' she asked for permission. Dadi nodded. As she left the dining room she opened the envelope, took out the contents and stopped. Her eyes could not focus as she looked at the photos of her mother's last resting place, the final photo that had been taken during what felt like a long time gone by. She reached her bedroom, looked around for somewhere to store them, then decided to put them in the wardrobe for now. She caressed them lovingly and placed the photos in the drawer of the wardrobe and closed it. To protect herself from any further scolding, she dried her tears and hurried back to the dining room.

'Are you done with your sentiments?' Akilah's voice was icy. 'While you were in your room, other people had to do your share of the work.' Hira was confused for a moment. Sabina and Amara would not begrudge her a few moments. Then she caught Sabina's eye and understood. Akilah's attitude was solely down to having to help clear away the breakfast dishes.

Dada sat back and perused down the length of the table. He stroked his chin. Deep in thought, he worried Dadi. When he was in thinking mode, he would always come up with some mad suggestion.

Today was no different.

'What are you thinking?' she asked him.

'I thought it would be nice if we went into town. You can go and visit my sister Zehra, I can go and visit my friends and the girls can go and do some shopping. What do you say?' Dadi mulled it over for a while. It had been some time since she had seen his sister. Apart from her, there was no one else from his side of the family who gave her the time of day. Sabina, Amara and Hira looked on expectantly.

'It would be nice to see Zehra. I haven't seen her since we met for Eid two years ago and I should go, especially as she has just come back from Haj,' she said. She shot the girls a sharp look. 'I see the excitement in you. I suppose I can let you go.' Smiles lit up on their faces. 'But I want all the chores to be done before we go.'

'What chores?' Dada asked and then answered his own question. 'The breakfast things won't take long and there is nothing much to be done elsewhere. Lunch and dinner will not be a problem as we will eat out.' Aaryan and his brothers rose from the table.

'Well, we had better leave for work.' Aidan smiled at Sabina. He pulled out his wallet and handed over a wad of notes. 'Buy something nice for yourself.' Alman took his brother's lead and handed Amara money too. Aaryan stood motionless. Hira saw his hesitance and turned towards the kitchen. His reluctance to have any interaction with her was all too evident. She wasn't going to stay there like a spare part. His brothers stared at him, indicating silently that he, too, should give her some money. After a few glances between them and a glare from Dada, he acted.

'Hira,' he called sternly after her. He took out all the notes from his wallet and thrust the money at her. 'Take this,' he said gruffly. She took the money with some awkwardness and looked at him.

'Thank you.' He shrugged, picked up his briefcase and made for the door.

Akilah watched the interaction between her brothers and sisters-in-law. Jealous eyes beseeched her grandmother. Dadi saw and acted upon it.

'Aren't any of you going to give Akilah any money?' She stopped the boys in their tracks. 'Akilah needs money too.' They turned at the door. Feeling awkward that none of them had given their sister any money. Amara looked at the money in her hand and began to speak.

'The boys are not responsible for Akilah's upkeep. They have wives to think of. If they choose to give her anything it is up to them.' The newspaper rustled and Dada peered over the edge at her and then Dadi. 'Akilah gets an allowance, which is more than anyone else gets. If she cannot budget then that is her problem. I will not give a rupee more or a rupee less.'

'Dada, please.' Akilah pouted.

'Well you know where I stand on this matter,' he retreated behind the newspaper. Akilah's eyes moistened. She looked at Dadi beseeching her to say something. Dadi shook her head, silently concluding, that asking her grandfather was not going to change his mind. Dada indicated to the boys that they should go. He delved into his pocket and took out some money and handed it to her.

'Take this but bear in mind, I'll take it off your allowance next month,' he told her. 'Managing your money will leave you in good stead when you get married and have to deal with the household expenses.' He did not miss Akilah's look of disappointment as she saw how much she was given. 'Is there a problem?' he asked.

'Actually, Dada. This is only a small amount. I will need more.'

'It is enough,' Dada replied. 'Go on and get ready. We will leave in an hour.'

Chapter 6

Dada sat in the front seat of the people carrier. Dadi and Akilah sat behind, while the others chose to sit together at the back. She gave them a disapproving look.

'I don't want any horseplay going on back there,' she warned them, settling back in her seat.

'Soraya,' Dada called from the front. He turned slightly. 'Remember to do your seatbelt this time. We don't want you sliding off the seat like last time.' This elicited shocked giggles from the back as the image flashed through Hira's mind, causing her features to change and the other two to giggle. One stern look from their grandmother and very quickly they quietened down. Dadi grabbed the seatbelt and struggled to get strapped in.

'Akilah,' she said with obvious displeasure and awkwardness. 'I can't get this to connect. Do it up for me.' Akilah grabbed hold of the belt, snapped it in place and sat back.

'Can we go now?' she whined.

The journey into town was an hour and a half away. Hira sat back and watched as they made their way past quiet roads lined with trees into the hub of the city. The driver skilfully negotiated the car through the city streets. They stopped at some traffic lights, when Hira heard a tapping on the window. Outside stood a woman dressed in rags. With a babe in arms, she held her hand out asking for money. Just as Hira put her hand out to wind down the window, Sabina stopped her. She shook her head, silently making it known to Hira that she mustn't. The car moved on. Hira marvelled at the number of street sellers plying their wares at the side of the road, the gaudy hoardings advertising the latest films. The scenery gave way to a more cosmopolitan part of the city. One featuring high rise apartments expensive cars and a more affluent resident. All this was new to Hira. As luck had it, Hira did not get to see the sights and sounds of the big city. She had been whisked from the airport late at night. Since her arrival she did not have a chance to make the journey.

The driver manoeuvred the car through a set of gates and up the drive to a beautifully maintained house. They got out of the car and stood taking in the sights. An elderly woman came out to greet them. Bent over, cane in hand, wearing the thickest glasses you would ever see, she made painful progress walking towards them. They all held their breath. Dadi gasped and looked on sadly. Coming alongside she stopped next to Hira and surveyed her, first looking at her this way and that. Hira thought perhaps she should present her teeth for inspection or do something, she found the whole thing hilarious and smiled. Aunt Zehra reached out a bony hand and gripped Hira tightly. Assigning her the respect that was due to an elder, Hira didn't flinch. With a cute nod of her head the woman smiled, straightened up slightly, adjusted her glasses and let go of her cane. With a cheeky laugh she opened her arms and hugged her and then Sabina and Amara.

'My girls.' She tried to embrace them all. 'How lovely to see you.'

Dadi was not amused.

'Zehra, how could you do that to me?' She chastised her. 'I honestly thought that you had aged terribly in the short time we have been apart.' Grand Aunt laughed.

'Appa. Life is too short to be all serious.' She looked at the four girls and winked. 'Besides, if you can't enjoy yourself at this stage of life, what can you do? I am not going to sit and wait for the Almighty to take me. I want to have fun now. Not in the afterlife. Well, don't just stand there. Come in.' She grabbed Hira and started to drag her into the house.

'Zehra. The girls are going shopping. They will come back after a while and then you can spend some time with them.' Grand Aunt's face clouded with disappointment. Hira saw this and turned to Dada.

'Can we spend a short time here? We can go after a while.' He only had enough time to nod before Grand Aunt reacted.

'What an excellent idea,' Grand Aunt agreed. 'I like this one,' she said to Dadi. 'I like all of them. Can I keep them?'

'Humph,' Dadi answered disapprovingly. As much as she was fond of Zehra, she found her behaviour very unbecoming.

The house sprang into life as they entered the main seating area. Five women appeared, dressed in brightly coloured shalwar kameez, smiling broadly and laden with trays of refreshments. Grand Aunt introduced them to her daughters-in-law.

'Amma. Let Hira go. She is not going to run away,' one of

29

them spoke. Aunt Zehra released her grip and Hira surreptitiously massaged her wrist. The youngest of the five noticed.

'You got off lucky.' Her eyes twinkled. 'Next door's cat has not been the same since Amma lured it in here and played with it all afternoon. Now every time it sees Amma, it runs for dear life.' Laughter ensued as Grand Aunt smiled. She looked at Dadi.

'Isn't the sound of laughter wonderful?' she said to her. 'Anyway, sit, sit.' She led her visitors to the plush sofas. Dadi scowled as they sat down but Dada coughed, indirectly telling her that she was not in her own house now so not to cause any friction.

'Amma says that you girls are going shopping? Which mall will you go?' the youngest of Grand Aunt's daughters-in-law asked. All four looked at each other.

'We actually haven't decided,' Sabina told her. 'Perhaps we should have planned before we came out.'

'Not necessarily,' the woman continued, 'It depends on what you need. There are a few markets on the way to the shopping centre. They have lovely bangles, saris, dupattas. You can pick up some really good bargains there.'

'I am not in the habit of buying bargains.' Akilah scoffed. 'Only the best for me.'

'When it is someone else's money, you will say that,' Dada muttered. Dadi shot him an angry look.

'Well before you set off on your expedition you will eat.' The smells emanating from the kitchen made their mouths water, making them wrestle with themselves to either stay and eat or to go and enjoy their shopping expedition. Dadi for once appeared to read their minds.

'Zehra. They will eat when they will return.' She looked at them. 'If you go now, without fuss, you will be back in good time. I don't want you spending all day out of the house.'

'Soraya.' Dada was already at the kitchen door, appreciating the aroma of the cooking. 'For once just relax. They will come back when they have run out of money. It is what you used to do.' Dadi glared at him. He shooed the girls out. 'Enjoy your shopping spree.'

Chapter 7

They stood at the entrance of the grandest shopping mall that the city could offer. Akilah barged past them.

'You idiots can stand there and gawp. I'm off.' She shot them a look and disappeared amongst the throng of people already milling around.

'Let her go where she pleases,' Sabina said. 'Where shall we start?'

'Clothes,' Hira decided. 'Always the first port of call when shopping.'

'Clothes? Have you got anything in mind?' Amara slipped her arm through hers and Sabina's arms and entered the mall.

An hour and a half later they entered yet another clothes shop. As they looked through the racks of clothing, they were approached by the sales assistants, eager to make a sale.

'Hello. You have picked the right shop to come into.' He went into his spiel. 'We have just taken delivery of the latest collection from the House of Rani.' Hira looked confused. She knew only of western designers. The assistant mistook the confusion for lack of interest. 'No, no, Miss. It is not your day to day clothing. This is high end. I will give you the best prices.'

'Show us what you have got,' Hira conceded. Sabina hid her smile. Hira would no doubt end up with a nice outfit at a decent price if she was guided correctly. They were led to a rack of clothes, which the assistant waxed lyrical. They were shown outfit after outfit. Amara took a shine to a particular suit and stroked it lovingly. The sales assistant saw that he was close to making a sale and his eyes twinkled. He moved in only to hear Hira take in a deep breath.

'How much?' She had caught sight of the price tag. She looked at him, aghast. *'The monetary rates were different and the conversion rate may be comparable,'* she thought. *'But those figures on the dress looked scary.'* The assistant became more amenable.

'Miss. You don't worry about the price. I will give you a good deal.' Hira looked at Sabina in total confusion and was met with a shake of her head, an indication that she was doing okay.' All of a sudden she understood.

An emerald blue green lehnga outfit caught her eye: floor length skirt, with a short blouse and an eye catching chunni for draping over the outfit, breath taking. It shimmered in the artificial light of the shop.

'*I wonder how much that would cost,*' she mused to herself. The assistant had wittered away and was now revealing prices. Amara looked on as Hira narrowed her eyes.

'Miss. I tell you what I will do. You can have any suit from this range, twenty five per cent off and I will throw in the accessories needed. How is that?' Sabina beamed. Hira, in her confusion and naivety had got them an absolute bargain.

'That is excellent.' Sabina stepped up. 'We will make our choices and give you a shout. Thank you.' She dismissed him and started to rifle through the clothing. At last they made their choices, tried them on, decided on their accessories, and got them all packed and ready for payment at the till. The sales assistant beamed at them as they collected their purchases, followed them to the entrance and held the door open for them.

'Thank you very much ladies. Hope to see you again.'

Outside the store, armed with their bags they beamed at their purchases.

'What shall we do now?' Hira looked around her. 'There are so many shops.'

'I just need to get some make up,' Amara said. 'After that, perhaps we can get something to eat?'

'A perfect idea,' concluded Sabina.

'And eating sounds good.' Hira laughed. 'My stomach feels like my throat has been cut.' That phrase earned her a quizzical look. 'Come on.' She gathered them up. 'I will explain it to you as we walk.'

'Finally.' Hira placed her bags on the chair next to her and sank into her seat. 'My stomach is beginning to rumble. I hope that the food here won't take long,' she said and looked hungrily at the food being prepared. Sabina and Amara collapsed into the two seats next to her and followed her gaze.

'It shouldn't. The place is not as busy as before so we will eat soon,' Sabina said kicking off her sandals and wriggling her toes. 'It is so good to sit for a while.' Hira looked at Sabina's wriggling toes.

'It is good but your sandals will be killing when you put them back on.' Sabina pulled a face.

'Why do you have to be right?' She put them back on just as the food arrived. Samosa, chaat, bhajia, juice and tea. They tucked in savouring the food.

'This tastes so good,' raved Amara. Hira agreed.

'But all food tastes good when you are hungry.'

There was a bit of a commotion not far from them, followed by lots of screaming and shouting. However, they chose to ignore the goings on. Within minutes the mall's security guards appeared with four policemen who were accompanied by two female officers and they made their way to where the disturbance was. Shoppers looked on as they entered the shop where the girls had been not more than a half hour ago.

'Wonder what is happening there?' Hira asked, indicating towards the store.

'Looks like somebody has been caught shoplifting. It is a regular occurrence now,' Sabina answered, stacking up the plates and cups.

'You get them here too?' Hira asked somewhat naively. Sabina nodded.

'We should make a move. I'll call the driver.' She took out her mobile phone and placed the call, speaking only briefly. 'The driver will be a little while,' she said. 'He is on his break at the moment but will come as soon as he can. We are to wait here for him. He won't be long.' Amara and Hira did not catch the last part of Sabina's message. Their attention was taken with something else. The police appeared. In their midst, shielded from the inquisitive eyes of the other shoppers, was the alleged shoplifter, who was not going quietly. She berated, cribbed and insulted the police, the shop assistant and made a grab for her shopping bags, which was held by one of the guards. For a brief moment, the thief came into view. Akilah looked in their direction, recognised them and threw them a woeful look.

'Oh my god. That is Akilah! They have arrested Akilah! That is so shameful for the family. Dadaji will be so embarrassed.' Amara shot the other two a worried look.

'Is there anything we can do?' Hira asked.

'I suppose we have to try?' Sabina replied, gathered up her bags and headed off towards the little group. Hira and Amara quickly followed.

33

'Excuse me. Excuse me, Sir,' Sabina called after one of the men. The policeman, who appeared to be in charge, turned and gave her a curious look,

'Can I help you?'

'Yes, please,' she replied. She indicated towards Akilah. 'That is our sister-in-law. What has happened?'

'Your sister-in-law,' he enunciated the connection, 'has been caught stealing from this shop.' Akilah, watched her sisters-in-law and put on a pitiful face.

'Bhabhi. They are lying. I did not do anything. I am being blamed unnecessarily,' she protested. Tears ran down her cheeks.

'Are you sure that she stole? What evidence do you have?' Hira asked.

'We have evidence. If you come with us to the security offices we will show you.'

'They are lying,' Akilah wailed. 'It is just their word against mine.' She shot the shop owner a dismissive look. 'You have nothing against me.' Hira looked at Sabina, who nodded her agreement. They followed the troupe to the security offices.

They sat in the office, waiting for the evidence to be revealed. Akilah's sniffling was all the more audible as she sat in a corner, trying to garner any sympathy from the officers, absolutely convinced that there was nothing incriminating against her, she played the wronged, hapless shopper with gusto. There was a slight tap on the door. One of the officers walked over and opened it. The shop owner came in and handed over a disk.

Akilah sat in the far corner and wept.

'I did not do anything wrong.'

Hira identified the man in charge and took him to one side.

'If she is guilty of stealing,' she asked him, 'can we not resolve this without going to the station?'

The police officer was taken aback. Keeping his voice level he looked over at Akilah.

'I am sorry Miss. The store has a strict policy to prosecute shoplifters… '

'I am not a thief,' Akilah retorted, 'I was set up by these three.' She spat, implying that her sisters-in-law were responsible for her predicament. Hira kept her anger in check. She wanted to tell Akilah a few home truths but thought better of it.

'I think,' the security officer spoke, 'and before you start throwing accusations you have a look at this first.' He played the disk from the store's CCTV. It showed the image of a young girl, her back to the camera, rifling through a rack of clothes and throwing furtive glances in the direction of the till. In one move, she grabbed an outfit from the rail, bent down and put it in the bag at her feet. She then proceeded to leave the store. The camera had followed the thief as she exited the store. It was there that the shop assistant, in animated conversation with another customer, touched her shoulder. The thief turned, her face caught clearly by the CCTV as she lashed out at the hapless assistant.

'You can't prove that it is me.' Akilah pouted. Sabina glared at her. The police officer picked up the bag and took out the same outfit that was shown earlier. At the same time, the security officer homed in on the shoplifter's face. He looked at Akilah for an explanation. She shrugged insolently and refused to make eye contact. Hira sighed heavily.

'What happens now?' she asked.

'The decision at the end of the day is up to the store how they wish to proceed. The fact that we were called means that if the store wishes to prosecute then it will be dealt with in a criminal court.' He looked at the store owner. 'It is your decision.' The man thought for a while. He looked from one girl to the other, mulling something over in his mind. Eventually he spoke.

'In this instance, I am willing to let the matter go. But on one condition.' They looked expectantly at him. 'That you take your sister-in-law away from here immediately. We have recovered the outfit. If she wants it that badly, she pays for it. Otherwise, we will put it back on the racks. The other issue is the injury to my sales assistant. Compensate him and we will not pursue charges.' He turned to the officer. 'I am sorry that it has been a wasted journey for you,' he apologised.

The policeman accepted the apology. 'I would also advise that you are not to come anywhere near the store. If I see you again or catch you stealing then it is… ' he clicked his fingers, 'straight down to the station and charged with theft.'

'How much compensation?' Amara asked timidly, afraid of the figure that the man would say. He thought for a while.

'Twenty thousand rupees,' he said finally.

'Twenty thousand?'

'A problem ladies?' He came closer to them, leaned forward and leered. 'Of course, you can come back later and we can settle this in a different way.' He whispered and then winked. The girls balked. They checked their purses and pooled the money together. They were short by five thousand rupees.

'Akilah. Have you got any money on you?' Sabina snapped at her. Akilah shook her head. 'Are you sure?' Akilah opened her purse and pretended to scrabble around for some loose change. Hira's sharp eyes saw a wad of notes.

'You have notes,' she said. Akilah shot her a look of pure avarice. She pulled out five thousand rupees and handed them over reluctantly. Sabina grabbed them from her and put them with the rest. She passed them over. The policeman took the payment and passed it to the storekeeper. He looked at Sabina, pityingly and then at the others.

'Can we have a receipt or something to say what we are paying for?' Hira asked. At first he hesitated. 'If you we are going to pay you a sum of money, then we need something to show our family where it has been spent. After all,' she looked at Sabina and Amara, 'we haven't done anything wrong. Is it too much to ask?' The manager looked at the police officer who nodded at him. Finally, he fished in his pocket, pulled out a notebook, wrote out a receipt and handed it to Hira. She scrutinised it, thankful that it was written in English and held it out to him. 'That is exactly what we have paid out for. Can you verify it?' The manager asked the security guard to use the store's stamp to authenticate the document and eventually handed it to Hira. She took the paperwork.

'Hang on.' The cogs in her mind starting to turn. 'Why settle the compensation here and not down at the station?' Sabina touched her arm and shook her head, indicating to her not to say anything.

'You may go. Take her with you and make sure that she is kept away from here.' Akilah stood up and picked up the bag.

'What do you think you are doing?' The bag was removed from her grasp. Akilah bristled and took a step towards him. She was held back by one of the policewomen.

'You have taken twenty thousand rupees from us. Surely, the clothes belong to me now?' Stern looks greeted her.

'Young lady.' The store owner replied. 'Were you not listening? That twenty thousand is compensation for the injuries my assistant suffered under your onslaught. He is bruised and scratched. That is your fine for your actions. We have recovered the stolen item and therefore we have decided not to proceed further. It's a pity that your sisters-in-law had to bail you out. You should consider yourself lucky. Now go.'

They made their way to the foyer where they were supposed to meet the driver. As they emerged from the corridor leading from the offices, they bumped into him. He smiled.

'Good evening. Shall I take your bags?' Hira shook her head.

'No thank you, Sayed. We can manage.' Walking to the car, they whispered among themselves. This was not a small issue that had occurred. First of all they will have to explain to their husbands as to how they had spent all the money that was given to them and how to deal with the events of the past hour. There was every possibility that if found out, they would be in trouble. They sat in the car, sinking into the seats. Damned if they revealed. Damned if they kept quiet. Akilah looked back at them through the head rests.

'Just in case you think that I am grateful to you. You can think again. I am not going to be all sweetness to you because of this. You are fools.' With a smirk she turned around. 'Sayed. Hurry to Aunt Zehra's. I am starving.'

Chapter 8

'Ah, the shoppers have returned.' Grand Aunt smiled upon seeing the girls enter. She patted the seat next to her. 'Come and sit by me and show me what you have bought.' The trio came and sat by her. She oooh'd and aaah'd as she saw each of the outfits. 'Beautiful, beautiful,' she commented as she stroked. 'Appa. Look at these wonderful suits, such lovely colours. And this ...' She pulled out the emerald green lehnga. 'I will fight Hira for this. If I were to get married again, this is the colour I want to wear.' Hira sat back and smiled. 'Now you must all put them on and show me how they look on you.' Akilah skulked at the edge of the group. Grand Aunt noticed. 'Akilah,' she called to her. 'Your sisters-in-law have brought such lovely things. Are you not going to show us what you have got for yourself?' Akilah balked.

'I did not buy anything,' she quickly replied, looking away from her.

'Not bought anything? How can you go to such a place and come away empty handed?' Akilah shot a pained look at Dadi

'Zehra. We haven't got time for this. We have got to make a move. My grandsons will be on their way home and they will need to have their dinner.' Dadi started to get up.

'Nonsense,' Grand Aunt Zehra replied. 'You will have dinner at our house today. Everything is practically ready. You call those grandsons of yours and tell them that they are to come here. It has been a while since we have all sat and spent some time together.'

'Another time, Zehra.' Dadi tried to make her excuses. Grand Aunt shook her head vigorously.

'No. I won't hear another word.' She turned to the trio. 'Call your husbands.' Three pairs of eyes looked at Dada and Dadi for permission. Dada smiled and nodded. While Sabina and Amara dialled their husband's numbers Hira looked awkward. She did not have Aaryan's number. Sabina noticed and held her hand reassuringly, giving it a squeeze.

'Oh, and if you can, will you call Aaryan and let him know. Otherwise he will get home and just fret.' She smiled as she spoke. A slight blush appeared on her cheeks. She said something inaudible and cut the call. Grand Aunt beamed.

'Excellent. Dinner will be served as soon as the menfolk

arrive. If you wish to freshen up... ' she winked at the girls, 'Fatima will show you to the guest bathroom.'

No sooner had they gone out of earshot Grand Aunt leaned forward.

'Is Hira the one you used to talk about?' she whispered. Dadi gave her a warning look, angry that Zehra had broached the subject. 'I take that as a 'yes' and in my opinion, what you have done and are doing is not right. She seems like a sweet child.' She looked at Dadi with sad eyes. 'How can you live with yourself?'

'Do not utter a word, Zehra. I do not wish to talk about the matter,' Grand Aunt Zehra sighed sadly. She shook her head.

'You are a cruel woman, Appa. How many lives have you ruined with your stubbornness?' Tears glistened in her eyes. She got up and walked over to the dining table. 'The food will be served shortly,' she said without looking back. She was truly upset.

It was late when the family said their final goodbyes and headed for home. Sabina and Amara decided to drive home with their spouses, Dada, Dadi and Akilah took the people carrier leaving Aaryan and Hira to make the journey home together. They stood side by side watching the other cars drive away. Once they were out of the drive Aaryan got into the driver's seat and started up the car. He stared straight ahead not making eye contact with Hira. The moment that he began to fume Hira opened the rear door, deposited her shopping bags then got into the front passenger seat. Belting herself in, she looked at him expectantly. He didn't say a word. Instead, he put the car in gear and pulled away from the house. Hira concentrated on the family waving their goodbyes, she did the same until they exited the gates and turned onto the road home.

The silence was becoming awkward. Aaryan was not likely to speak anytime soon.

'Do you mind if I switch the radio on?' she asked, looking over at him expectantly.

'What?' He glanced at her quickly before training his eyes back onto the road.

'I asked if I could put the radio on.' He waved his hand dismissively. She reached out, pressed a button and the car filled with the sound of strumming of sitars, drumming of the tablas and the singer's tortured voice, telling a sad tale. She jumped animatedly and quickly scrabbled at the console lowering the volume and switched channels until she could find something more melodious. Aaryan stifled a laugh at her comical reaction. He glanced at the radio, then at her. She continued fiddling with the dial until she found something that she liked and sat back.

Aaryan nodded appreciatively at the choice of music.

'Nice,' he commented.

'It is,' she agreed, sat back and stared out of the window. Throughout the rest of the journey not a word was said. This suited Aaryan perfectly but it irked Hira. She sighed despondently, put her head against the glass and watched the city lights go past at a quick fire pace. She closed her eyes for a moment.

She was shaken awake. Rubbing her eyes she looked around her. They were home. Aaryan was leaning over and shaking her awake. She sat stiffly in her seat.

'Did I sleep the whole way?' she said, more or less asking herself. She didn't hold any hopes of Aaryan answering.

'Yes you did.'

Hira looked sheepish. 'I'm sorry.'

He shrugged.

'I wasn't saying much.' He got out of the car, walked over to the passenger side and helped Hira out. She collected her bags from the back and swayed slightly. She grabbed the edge of the car door and steadied herself. He looked at her, eyes narrowed. 'Are you alright?' She nodded.

'Yes, just not properly awake.' He acknowledged the fact, walked up to the heavy front door and fished for his keys. Upon opening it, he held it open for her.

'Best get to bed before Dadi gets home.' He did not make any eye contact with her and followed her inside.

They had reached their bedroom when they heard the rest of the family come in. Akilah could be heard griping about the day but Hira shut it out. She grabbed her nightclothes, changed and got into bed. She closed her eyes and was soon asleep. He stood at the foot of the bed and stared at her. Tonight she looked so different. He had tried hard not to look and had given the impression that he was not interested. It was the first time since she arrived just over a month ago, that he took some notice. She had smiled shyly at Grand Aunt's comments, laughed at her little digs and her face shone with joy as she chatted with everyone. Definitely, she wasn't his choice as a life partner but perhaps he should get to know her as a person. So far, all he had seen of her was that of a housemaid and a helplessly bad sleeper. But there were moments when parts of her personality came through but he had been too grumpy to take any notice.

'Maybe it wouldn't be such a bad idea,' he shrugged, banishing the thought and collected his nightwear. He did not feel particularly bothered to know more. As he opened the drawer to put away his wallet his eyes rested on the envelope that had arrived earlier in the day. He took out the contents, looked at the photos, then at Hira. Afraid of invading her privacy, he quickly put the photos away. He spied her phone in the drawer too. Accidentally, he nudged it and it came on. The screen was cracked, as was the casing, mostly likely caused when he had thrown it earlier. The casing was taped together. He picked it up and looked at the home screen which was a photo of Hira with her mother. Noticing that it was not protected by a code, he shook his head at Hira's naivety. Out of curiosity he navigated within her phone and opened up the photos file. There were more photos, obscured by the cracked screen, of a smiling Hira in happier times with her friends and quite a lot with her mother. It was all she had on the phone. No numbers, no texts, no history, just memories. Aaryan's face burned with shame. In anger he had thrown the phone, damaging it, without a second thought for her feelings or any respect for her memories. Quickly he returned back to the home screen, picked up his night clothes, headed for the bathroom, washed, dressed and slipped into bed. He faced her for the first time since she had arrived and felt it strange that he bore her no hate. He was just indifferent to her. She was probably caught up in this mess of a relationship just as much as he. Eventually, he turned on his side, shut off the bedside lamp and closed his eyes.

Chapter 9

The following morning, after breakfast had been eaten and everyone had gone off to do their own things, Akilah stomped around in a bad mood. She was rude to the manservants, banged doors, pulled at curtains and ignored all of Dadi's attempts to settle her down. She tore through the house as if on a mission and stopped outside Hira's bedroom. Without knocking she pushed the door, hard, making it bang into the wall behind. Hira looked up from her book.

'You owe me five thousand rupees,' she snarled at her. Hira put down her book and got up.

'How do you work that out? We all paid out five thousand rupees each to bail you out. If anyone is to be paid back I figured that it would be us.' Akilah stood in front of her with fire in her eyes.

'Don't get smart with me. You know you gave me no choice.'

'We weren't the ones who were stealing. You got caught and you would have been taken to the police station. Dada and Dadi would have been called and you would have been charged.'

'I don't care. You owe me five thousand rupees. I want them by this afternoon. Or else... '

'Or else, what?' Hira's temper was beginning to fray. If Dadi was going to punish her for arguing, so be it. Akilah gave her an evil look.

'Or else I can make life difficult for you. Now you don't want that to happen, do you?'

Hira shrugged and thought twice about confronting her nemesis. Instead she gave her an indifferent look which only served to stoke Akilah's anger even more.

'By this afternoon....' She pointed at her, shot her a final look and stomped out. Hira watched her go, picked up her book, put it away and sat on the bed. A timid knock on the door caught her attention.

'Come in,' she called out. Uday Kaka stood in the doorway, wringing his scarf in his hands. He looked uncomfortable. The manservants were not normally seen on the first floor and the awkwardness was evident in his features. 'What is it Uday Kaka?' She came towards him, concern showed on her face.

'Hira bahu. Please come quick. Amara bahu is crying downstairs. We have asked her what the matter is but she just keeps on crying.' Hira nodded.

'Thank you Uday Kaka. Where is she?' She shut the door behind her.

'She is in the study.' He replied, following her. Hira nodded her thanks and hurried to the ground floor.

Amara sat quietly weeping. Hira and Sabina got to the study at the same time. They encased her with a hug, soothing her till she calmed down.

'Amara?' Sabina's concern came through as her voice wavered. 'Why?'

'Akilah,' was all Amara could utter before she started to cry again. Obviously, she had done the rounds, demanding money from Amara as well. Hira knelt in front of her and took Amara's hands in hers and tried to get her to look at her.

'Amara. She came to me as well. Try not to let her get to you. If she does anything, we will face it together. Amara shook her head.

'I'm not like you,' she wept. 'You have no fear. If she gets me thrown out my family will disown me.' She looked at Hira and then at Sabina. 'I won't be able to face them. It will be such dishonour and my family would not forgive me.' Hira looked aghast.

'This still happens in the 21st century?' she asked herself and then mentally face palmed herself. *'Who was she to talk? Look what had happened with her recently? Uprooted and sent halfway across the world. She had been taken advantage at a vulnerable time when she was not able to think straight. Yes,'* she concluded. *'She had been sold out by her mother's so called friends.'*

'Listen to me.' Hira's voice was level but firm. 'Do not worry about Akilah or what she will do. She will not have you thrown out. She won't be able to say anything without dropping herself into trouble too.'

'Hira is right.' Sabina reassured her. 'You and I know Akilah well enough. Since when has she disclosed anything about us which would indirectly lead to her antics being uncovered? Now dry your eyes and don't worry. Should anything happen, then we are here for you.' Amara nodded, wiped her eyes. 'Now you go to your bedroom and rest for a while. Don't let Akilah see you like this.'

'She already knows. She was laughing when I started crying.' Amara replied sadly.

'Don't worry.' Hira reassured her. 'We did what we had to do. We stuck together then and we shall support each other now. Oh, I forgot to do something. Meet you on the veranda later.' She gave Amara a hug and rushed up the staircase.

In the bedroom Hira picked up the bag from where she had left it last night in her sleep. She took the outfits out and hung them up, folded the bag and put it at the back of the wardrobe. She then closed it and went to join Sabina and Amara on the veranda.

She reached as far as the door to the veranda when she remembered that she had left something upstairs. Cursing, she returned to her bedroom. Upon approaching the room she noticed that the door was slightly ajar. Her brow furrowed. She was sure that she had closed the door when she left. As she moved closer, she heard the wardrobe door banging and the clattering of coat hangers as the contents were strewn on the floor. She stood for a while and watched. Akilah was deep in her task. She pulled item upon item out of the wardrobe, held it up before throwing it to the floor.

'What do you think you are doing?'

Akilah turned round. Her eyes darkened with anger. 'It does not matter what I am doing here,' she retorted. 'This is my house and I will do what I want. The question is what are you doing here?' They squared up against each other.

'This is my room. I don't have to answer to you if I choose to come to my room.'

Akilah moved closer to her. She had an evil look on her face.

'I didn't mean that,' she sneered. 'I meant what are you doing in this house? It is clear that my brother does not consider you as his wife. Hell, even your wedding vows were carried out over the phone. All you are is a convenience. Someone to cook, clean, wash his clothes and warm his bed.' She looked her up and down. 'Although, I have my doubts if you can even do that. Why don't you just do everyone a favour and run away. Free him from the life of misery that you are causing just by being here.'

Hira looked her up and down. 'Are you finished?' She kept her voice steady, even when her dearest wish was to slap some manners into her and leave her sobbing on the floor. Hira's calm demeanour irked her.

44

'What?' She was puzzled.

'I said. Have you finished?' She looked past her to the mess of clothes that had been dumped on the floor. 'It appears either you have lost something or you just wanted to play dress up.'

'Shut up,' shrieked Akilah rushing up to Hira. 'You have no right to talk to me like that. I am the daughter of the family. I have a position here. Not like you.'

'I am not contesting that.' Again, the calm voice. Akilah's face contorted with anger.

'All I asked was what were you doing in my room? Surely I deserve an answer.' Behind her Sabina and Amara appeared, followed closely by Dadi.

'You will wait till hell freezes over. Dadi laments the day she brought you here,' she spat. 'At least the other two brought a decent dowry with them. You! You are just a charity case. She pushed Hira. Hira grabbed her by the arm and held on tightly.

'You keep out of my personal space,' she warned her. Akilah raised her hand, palm open. Hira readied herself to take action, anticipating stopping the slap if all else failed.

'What is going on here?' Dadi cut in. Akilah quickly dropped her arm. Hira stepped back. Dadi pushed past Hira and surveyed the room before rounding on her. 'Is this the way you keep your room? Get it cleared at once. Your mother is not going to come in and clear up after you. After that go down and scrub the store room and do it properly. I don't want any ants coming into the house. I will come and inspect it,' she warned before grabbing Akilah by the arm and marched her out.

Hira sighed and started to pick up the discarded clothing. Sabina and Amara gave her a hand and put the clothing back on the hangers and back in the wardrobe.

'Spoilt little madam,' Sabina muttered, putting away another outfit. 'What was she playing at?'

'She was looking for something by the looks of it.' Hira put the last of her clothing away. 'Oh dear.' She held Aaryan's best white shirt in her hands. It had been thrown out along with her clothes and had been trampled underfoot and it looked grimy along with a few missing buttons.

***

*'Mamma. My shirt got dirty.' Hira held up the stained school
shirt up for inspection. Her mother took the shirt and sighed.*

*'Hira. Why didn't you give me this earlier? I will never get it
washed and dried in time'. She looked outside. The rain had not
stopped all evening. Sad eyes looked down at her.*

*'Sorry Mamma. I was playing and forgot to tell you earlier.'
Hira watched as her mother took the shirt and began to wash it. After
she had washed and rinsed it, she got the ironing table out and
proceeded to iron dry as much of the shirt as possible. She looked so
tired. She worked a full day and now she had added to her tasks. Hira
felt as if she wanted to cry. Slowly she inched towards her mother as
she hung up the shirt so that any wet patches would dry overnight and
hugged her. Silent tears coursed down her cheeks as she held her. She
had troubled her mother so much today and yet she had washed and
dried her shirt without admonishing her. She felt a hand stroke her
shoulder, as if telling her that it was alright and she didn't mind.*

***

'Hira. Don't fret. We will get the shirt washed. The sun is out
and it will dry in no time.' Sabina had placed her hand on her shoulder,
snapping her out of her reverie. She took the shirt from her and gave it
to Amara, and indicated towards the bathroom. Amara understood and
set about washing the said shirt. 'There is no need to get upset. Aaryan
won't even notice that anything had happened to it.' Hira found that
she had tears in her eyes. She blinked them away. Sabina looked on
concerned.

'Thanks. Damn memories,' she said rationalising her
thoughts.

'It's alright.' Sabina assured her. 'You are allowed to.' Amara
appeared with the shirt.

'One shirt cleaned.' She smiled. 'I shall hang it on the terrace.
When it dries I will iron it for you and sew the buttons back on.' She
skipped out of the room.

'You are too nice.' Hira smiled. 'You both are.'

'We are each other's' strengths and weaknesses.' She hugged her.

Chapter 10

Aaryan threw down the file he had been reading, lurched forward and hit the speak button on the phone.

'Alisha,' he barked. 'Get me Dayal on the phone,' and hung up before she had a chance to acknowledge his request. He went back to reading the report and muttering at the same time. A sharp knock drew his attention. 'Enter.' He did not look up.

'Mr Dayal for you.' Alisha led the older man into the office.

'Thank you Alisha.' Aaryan continued reading. She smiled, nodded and closed the door behind her.

Aaryan handed the file to Mr Dayal. 'This is the report on the water storage and purification plant we wanted to build in Bhuj. Do you notice anything wrong?' Mr Dayal opened the file and went through the pages. Eventually he looked up.

'On the surface everything looks okay. But looking closer there is a number of discrepancies in a number of places which lead me to think...'

'That everything is not above board.' Aaryan finished his sentence for him. 'First of all, the materials are wrong and the design? It has enough holes in it that it will not hold water.' Dayal gave him an amused look. Aaryan saw it. 'Yeah, yeah. I know. Can you look into this? Scrap it if you have to, but I want a water tight plan in front of me by the end of next week.' Dayal smiled again.

'Aaryan, I will go through this with a fine tooth comb. I might just test the water too.' He was greeted with a stern look.

'I am the one who makes the lame jokes round here. Now get to it.' He dismissed him with a wave of his hand. Dayal laughed. He and Aaryan had known each other for some time and was very perceptive to his friends various moods and reacted as required. Dayal put his hand into his jacket pocket and pulled out an envelope.

'My sister graduated with full honours last month,' he said. 'We are holding a party for her to celebrate her success and her engagement. I would like to invite you and Bhabhi as my guests.' He handed over the card. Aaryan opened it, read the details.

'Who else is going?'

'I have invited all the members of your family and people from the office.' He replied. 'I will be honoured if you can make it.' Aaryan nodded, absent minded.

48

'We'll be there.'

The day finished, Aaryan shut off his computer and gathered his things. He stepped out of the office to see Alisha packing her things and smiled.

'Can I give you a lift home?' She looked up and shook her head.

'Thank you but no.' He looked put out. 'I am meeting my father to do some last minute shopping before our holiday.' She added.

'OK.' He perched on the edge of her workstation.

'Have you been invited to Dayal's sister's party?' she asked. He nodded. 'Are you bringing her with you?' He nodded. She frowned and quickly looked away.

'What was that for?'

'What?'

'That look you just gave.' Alisha snapped her bag shut.

'Well look at you playing happy families.' She looked up at him. 'Aren't you taking the dutiful husband part too seriously?'

'Why wouldn't I? After all, I am married. I am a husband. What has brought this on?' She began to worry him.

'I thought that one day we would be together.'

'What? Are you serious? You are telling me this now?' He was aghast. He shook his head. 'You and I have a good working relationship. I never even considered...I mean I didn't... ' He trailed off. *This was not good.* He thought. She didn't answer him. Instead she walked out. 'Alisha. We need to talk and sort this out,' he called after her.

'My father will be waiting,' she replied without turning round. Aaryan slammed his case on the desk, put his hands on his hips and scowled. He was finding the female psyche difficult to crack. He had the spaced out one who was always in dreamland at home and here he had one who thought he could read minds.

Chapter 11

The slamming of the main door drew Hira's attention that Aaryan was home. As usual, he was late. Judging by the sound of his footsteps she figured that he was not in a good mood. She laid out a change of clothes for him on the bed, pulled back the sheets and left the room. If he was angry, she would stay clear until he had calmed down. There was no point in both of them being upset. She would return after a while and ask if he wanted to eat.

She returned after a time and found him sat on the bed deep in thought.
'Are you hungry?'
'What?' He looked up. She saw the confused look on his face and wondered what the reason was.
'I asked if you were hungry. Can I get you something to eat?'
'No I am okay. I picked up something on the way home.' He looked at her sharply. 'Have you eaten?' She nodded. He got into bed. 'Oh, there is an invite to an engagement party. It is the day after tomorrow. You are invited also.'He reached behind his head and snapped off the overhead light. 'The card is on the table. Familiarise yourself with the names. I don't want to be babysitting and chaperoning you all evening.' Hira picked up the card and frowned.
'He was bristly tonight,' she thought. *'What did he mean by babysitting?'* That statement had puzzled her. Opening the card, she read the invite, took in the names, the occasion and made a mental note to buy a nice gift.
'Babysitting,' she said out loud and quickly looked in his direction. He slept on. Then it dawned on her. She was still a stranger to him. They had not met or spoken before the wedding. The wedding vows were carried out via phone. Theirs was the arranged marriage in the true sense of the word. He knew nothing about her and her perception of him was sketchy. She had spent the last month in a semi-confused state. Everything was new to her and it was taking time to adjust. She sighed. He would be happy elsewhere, as he had already indicated, while she joined the family as additional unpaid labour. What was her future? She got into bed and massaged her forehead.
'Babysitting,' she said to herself. 'He must think that I am wishy washy and need to be monitored all the time. What a change

50

from London.' She slipped lower into the bed, drew the sheets over her head and fell asleep.

Yawning, she came out of the bathroom, dripping wet, she slammed into Aaryan. He jumped back, making sure that she did not wet his fresh clothes completely.

'Watch it.' He admonished her, giving her a warning look.

'What did I do?' The agitated words came out before she could check herself. He was bemused for a moment but brushed it aside. He was already late and if he did not hurry then a deal would be lost.

'You walk around in a confused state all the time. Are you even on this planet?' He picked up his jacket, went to the dresser and picked up his wallet. 'I won't have breakfast. I'll have something at work. Not sure what time I'll be home tonight.' Hira suppressed a sigh. 'What was that sigh for?'

'Sigh? There was no sigh.'

'You sighed.'

'So shoot me,' she muttered, picking up the discarded night clothes from the end of the bed. He glanced at her through the mirror. He turned around. *Did she really say that?* he thought and then shook his head. He stared at her for a while. She looked directly at him, a gaze that was almost insolent, making him stop what he was doing. The ringing of his phone broke the moment, directing his attention to it. He looked at the caller information and quickly answered it.

'Yes Alisha.' He pocketed the wallet, picked up his jacket and left the room. 'I know Alisha. I am leaving right now.' The door slammed as he shut it behind him.

Hira piled the clothes in a heap and got ready.

'Hira.' The shout came from the landing. Dadi was on the prowl again. 'Hurry up. Breakfast won't make itself.' This time Hira did sigh deeply. A face bereft of any make up, she put her hair in a ponytail and rushed out.

'Coming Dadiji.'

Akilah skulked around in the kitchen, annoying everyone and getting in their way.

'Akilah. Stop obstructing us. Breakfast will be late at this rate.' Sabina was fast losing patience.

51

Akilah picked up a puri and dropped it on the floor.

'Oops.' She smirked.

'Will you please leave from here?' Hira moved her aside as she put on the pot to make chai. 'You don't help, so I have no idea what you are doing here.' Akilah tutted.

'So rude.' She picked up the paring knife, twirling it in her hand. 'I am still waiting for my money. I gave you till yesterday afternoon but I see that I am still waiting. Now I am a generous type of person,' she fiddled a bit more. 'I want that money and no excuses.'

'I told you earlier, that you won't get your money.' Hira reached beyond her and grabbed the canister of loose tea. 'We bailed you out else you would have been down the police station.'

'Yeah, yeah. What do you want me to do? Grovel at your feet. You will be waiting a long time. Don't get too smart here. It is not worth it. There is a reason why Dadi chose you as wives for my dear brothers. She just wanted cows. Cows that would do her bidding and not talk back. Just look at her with big eyes, shedding giant tears every time something went wrong.' She shook her head. 'So stupid.' She scoffed. 'I want my money.' Hira grabbed the milk

'What don't you get, Akilah?' She poured it angrily, spilling some. 'You stole, got caught, arrested, we helped you. Get some humility and be grateful.' Akilah brushed past Hira and stood by the door.

'I did not steal... '

'Liar. You were caught thieving.' Hira was in no mood for Akilah's antics and stood her ground.

Akilah invaded her personal space again.

'I did not steal,' she reiterated.

'Who did not steal?' Dadi's voice was heard from beyond the door. She came into view. Akilah gulped, hid her look of dread and composed herself. She went and took Dadi's arm and led her away.

'No one stole.' She shot back a look of pure malice. 'We were just talking about something that happened the other day.' Dadi glared at the trio.

'I will talk to you about this later.' Three sets of shoulders sank. They looked at each other, silently supporting each other. The sound of the chai overflowing brought them to their senses. Hira quickly turned off the gas and lifted the pot with the help of her dupatta.

'Ouch, ouch, ouch.' She quickly put the pot down, looked at her hand and quickly put it under cold water. Amara grabbed Hira's dupatta and held it up. It had a big tear. Hira hadn't noticed it when she picked up the pot.

'The evil little... ' Sabina stepped forward. 'How bad is your hand?' Hira continued with the cold water.

'Just a small scald. It will be fine.' She dismissed it. Amara looked worried.

'We have got to be wary.' Her eyes grew big with fear. 'Akilah will make things difficult.'

'Dadiji has got wind of something. Let's see how our dear sister-in-law behaves. She won't want to draw attention to herself.' Sabina soothed Amara. 'You shouldn't worry too much. Just don't get in her way.'

'The whole thing is just too stupid for words.' Hira turned angrily. 'She should be told a few home truths.' Sabina walked over to her.

'Things are not as easy, Hira. If we say anything Dadiji will stand by her and as you know our parents will be informed and insulted. The shame they would feel keeps us quiet,' she explained. 'Here it is a bad thing if a girl is returned to her parents' house. It means that the family is disgraced. We can't do that. Our parents would die of shame.'

Chapter 12

Dadi had decided that she wanted the verandah and the outdoor furniture cleaned. Hira scrubbed away at one of the rattan chairs. She stopped momentarily and wiped her forehead. She looked at the other two as they shifted the furniture already washed into the sunshine.

'Are you tired already?' Dadi appeared out of nowhere. 'Gather round.' Hira stood up and took her place with Sabina and Amara. The old woman viewed them through narrowed eyes. 'I am hearing a lot of shouting and arguing these past couple of days?' Akilah appeared behind her. She wore a worried look and gestured at them to not say anything. Hira just managed to hold her composure. It wasn't that long ago that she was demanding money with menaces. Dadi droned on for a bit longer. Hira's attention snapped back to her.

She found Dadi staring directly at her. 'Do I make myself clear?'

She nodded. Totally at a loss with what Dadi had said in that brief moment when her mind had wandered.

'Good.' Dadi turned and went back into the house. Akilah stood for a while before she darted behind her grandmother. Hira turned.

'Have I just signed my life away?' she asked in a shocked voice. Amara shook her head.

'No. Dadiji just warned us not to cause friction in the house. What happened to you?' Hira looked shamefaced and she blushed.

'I was tearing Akilah apart limb from limb,' she replied. Sabina laughed loud.

'Hira. You are a breath of fresh air. Don't ever change.' She turned to Amara. 'Come let's hurry. We only have the furniture to wash and it can go out in the sun to dry. Then we can have a little free time and rest before the next lot of orders come through. Dadi will not be leaving us alone for long.' Hira finished cleaning the last piece of furniture and placed it on the grass to dry. 'I am so happy that we have finished. Hira, did Aaryan mention the party that we have been invited to tomorrow night?'

Hira nodded. Sabina breathed a sigh of relief. 'Oh, I am so glad. I worried for a moment.'

'Have you thought about a gift? I mean, we can't go empty

handed.'

'Yes,' Amara agreed. 'We do need to buy a gift.' Hira sat down on the top step and leaned back against the post.

'I used the rest of my money to help bail out you know who. I can't ask Aaryan for more money. He wasn't happy to give me any in the first place. What if he asks where I spent it?'

'Don't worry about that. I will put a call through to Aiden. He will organise Jayantbhai to come to the house with a collection of saris. We can each choose that as a gift and he will invoice us.' Hira stood up, brushed off the dust from her dress.

'That sounds painless. I am dreading saying anything to Aaryan if he starts asking questions as to where the money was spent,' Sabina reassured her.

'He won't ask, Hira,' she said. 'For two reasons one is that they never normally ask and two, the look on your face as the assistant was running away with the sales pitch. He was so eager to make a sale that he pulled out all the stops. You managed to mesmerise him somehow and got us some really good deals. It is unfortunate that the money we saved there had to be spent on little Miss Klepto,' Sabina continued.

'But it is wrong not to tell them.' Hira felt uncomfortable. 'The longer we keep quiet the worse the situation could become.' She looked at the two. 'We could get into big trouble.' An uncomfortable silence hung over them. While Hira was not wrong, they did not want to think of the consequences of them keeping silent.

Hira's eyes caught the furthest corner of the garden, flanked by trees. It was overgrown and unkempt. Unloved, neglected. It cried out to Hira for attention.

'Why is that part of the garden in such a state?' she asked. They shrugged their shoulders. Hira thought for a moment and remembered how much her mother loved tending her garden. She had tried to get her involved when she was a lot younger but then all she wanted to do was play and pick the flowers and eat the mud! She chuckled to herself. Yes. She had been no more than a toddler at that time and her mother took great delight in reminding her of her antics as soon as she was old enough to be embarrassed. Her mother had great dreams for Hira.

'What is so funny?' Amara had noticed the giggle. Hira shook her head.

'Nothing much something I remembered from when I was younger. Come let's go inside. I could murder a coffee.'

'That is a good idea. Coffee then we can sort out our outfits for tomorrow.' Sabina led the way. 'What colour are you intending to wear?' She turned back and looked at them both. They thought for a while.

'Pale pink sari,' decided Amara. Hira hesitated.

'I think I shall wear one of my shalwaar suits,' Sabina said then thought for a while. 'Hira if you want I can lend you one of my suits. I have a lovely sapphire one that will look perfect on you. You can leave the new suit for another time.' Hira smiled.

'Thank you.'

'We can all get dressed in my room. It will be fun and we can help each other with our hair and makeup. Come. Let's go for that coffee before we lose any time.'

Hira stood outside Dadi's room. Her arm raised in mid-air to knock on the open door.

'What do you want, Hira?' She peered, over her glasses, at her and scowled. Her tone was so unwelcoming that Hira almost thought twice about her request. But she was at the opening to the lion's den to speak and to back away now would not be right.

'Dadi. Why is there a part of the garden that is neglected?' Dadi put down her book.

'You are here to question me on this? What business is it of yours?'

'It is none of my business and I didn't mean to question you in a bad way. I am curious. The rest of the grounds are neat and tidy. It looks out of place. That's all.' Dadi got up from the bed and walked over to her.

'What is the reason for this line of questioning?' She looked up at Hira. 'Are there no more chores to be done that you have to stand in front of me and ruin my day.'

'I wanted to ask if I can take over that part.' Dadi stared at her. She mulled things over in her mind and weighed up the pros and cons. Hira was not like the other two wives. She had spirit and an attitude, much like her mother had and that did not sit well with her. While she had to be kept under control at the same time, she needed her. In the short time since her arrival she had meted out more

56

punishments to Hira than the other two but it did not have much effect of Hira. She always bounced back.

'No.' She turned and walked back to her bed. Hira followed her.

'Why not, Dadiji? It is not doing anything.' Dadi swung round, not entirely happy at her insistence.

'Did I say that you could come in? Such insolence.' Hira quickly took a step back. 'You have no manners whatsoever. What did I do to get such a manner less girl? Did your mother not teach you the basics?' She saw that Hira was about to say something. 'Not a word. Don't even think of arguing with me. Now get out of my sight.' Hira stood just inside the threshold and stared at the old woman. She had never come across anyone so cantankerous. She turned on her heel and walked out. Disappointed, Hira headed for the kitchen to make that welcome cup of coffee.

Chapter 13

The house was shrouded in darkness. Hira opened the doors leading on to the balcony, grabbed a blanket and settled down to wait for Aaryan. She drew her knees up to her chest and looked to the end of the driveway, waiting for his car. Why she waited up for him when all he did was treat her like an irritation she did not know. Sadness engulfed her as she saw the type of life that was ahead of her. She had lost her identity, her independence and slowly, her personality. Her thoughts went back to her conversations with her mother and how she laughed when Hira had voiced that as her only reasons for her reluctance to get married.

Headlights beamed straight at her and the car drove up along the drive and came to a stop. As she stood up Aaryan came out of the car made eye contact with her. She picked up the blanket, deposited it on the bed and went down to open the door.

'Why are you still up?' The words that greeted her were terse as she opened the door. She chose to ignore the question.

'Are you hungry?' She asked instead. he nodded. 'I will make you something. You can go up and wash.' He shook his head.

'That is you all over isn't it?' he taunted. 'Just like a broken record. Do you have anything else to say or do? There is more to life than asking me if I am hungry all the time.'

Hira looked on silently.

'Never mind,' he sighed. 'I'll use the washroom here.'

She went to the kitchen, got food out of the fridge and started to heat it up. She made fresh chapattis for him. He joined her in the kitchen and sat at the table. She placed the food in front of him and waited.

'You can go.' He dismissed her with a wave of his hand and began eating. Hira stood and watched him for a while. At last she moved and headed for the bedroom. He continued eating, pointedly ignoring her. He finished eating, rinsed the dirty dishes and flicked on the kettle. One cup of tea later he was ready to go to bed.

He flicked on the switch, bathing the room in bright light. Hira groaned and blinked against the intrusion.

'Be ready to leave for the party at 7pm. Don't do the female thing and take forever getting ready.' He told her. 'I will wear my navy suit with the white shirt. Where are my nightclothes?'

'On the chair,' Hira indicated, rolling onto her stomach pulled the pillow over her head and closed her eyes.

Chapter 14

It was 6pm. Hira dressed and put Aaryan's clothes out on the bed ready for him when he returned from work. She collected her makeup and made for Sabina's room. Aiden had already been banished, leaving the girls to finish getting ready. By 6.30pm they were all ready.

Dada smiled as he watched the three girls make their way to the seated area. His face shone with pride.

'You all look beautiful.' he said. 'My boys had better watch out. Every eye will be on you tonight.' Aiden and Alman looked on appreciatively.

'Shall we go?' they asked. Sabina turned to Hira.

'It is not too late to come with us. Aaryan can join up with us later.' Hira shook her head.

'I will wait here,' she said. 'Hopefully he won't be too long. You go on ahead. I'll see you there.'

'He'll be here soon,' Alman assured her. 'If not, give me a call and I will come back for you.' After assuring Hira they left. She sat down and looked at Dada.

'My grandson is a fool,' he said. 'He has no concept of time nor can he see what he has at his feet. Stupid boy just sees things from his perspective alone.' Hira was puzzled.

'Why did Dadaji talk like this about his own grandson? Did he know something about Aaryan and Alisha?'

Twenty minutes passed and still no sign of him. Hira sat and inspected her nails then fidgeted with her hair. She wondered if he would come anytime soon or should she give up and go and get changed. She waited ten more minutes before finally deciding to give the evening up as a lost cause and change.

Just as she stood up Aaryan shot through the door, his face as dark as thunder. He stopped long enough to give his apologies to Dada before rushing upstairs.

'It's not me you need to apologise to,' Dada called after him. At first Hira thought that she should go up after him, but then figured that she would be better off waiting for him downstairs. That is, if he was still intending to go. Her question was answered moments later as he appeared, buttoning his cufflinks.

'Let's go.' He did not even look at Hira. She picked up the

package and flowers which were on the seat next to her and stepped forward. 'What are those?' he asked. Hira looked at the gifts in her hand and then at him.

'Presents for Anjali.' She took Dayal's sister's name. He did a double take. In too much of a rush he had not noticed Hira in her new avatar. She looked cultured, sophisticated even. Minimal make up, hair in an up do and the colour of her outfit complimented his. She looked good.

'Did you choose that after last night?' He indicated towards the outfit. She shook her head.

'I had decided on it beforehand.' He hurriedly looked at his watch.

'Come on then. We are late enough as it is.' He walked ahead.

He watched as she put the gifts on the back seat and got in the front.

'*How ironic,*' he thought to himself. He was late tonight because Alisha had forgotten to order a gift for him to take along tonight, despite him reminding her that morning. He had shouted at her, wasted time trying to mollify her to get something before leaving it too late to get one and she had refused point blank. Yet here was his wife, who had chosen the gift, wrapped it and had not even said a word to him.

'You should have said that you got gifts. I would not have wasted time looking for one,' he lied.

'I didn't know,' Hira replied. He shook his head, turned the car around and set off to the venue.

They pulled up outside the venue, got out and Aaryan handed the keys over to the valet boy and headed for the entrance, without looking back to see if she was with him. Hira's eyes narrowed in irritation. He would leave her to make her own entrance. That told her where her place was. She rearranged her scarf, took a deep breath and walked towards the entrance. If she was to be without her husband by her side, she would have to cope as best as she could. Anger and shame burnt her cheeks. Even in public, she could not count on her husband to be with her.

Her eyes scanned the hall for the guest of honour before

61

finally seeing her on the dais. She walked through the throng of people, steeling herself for any questions.

'Where did you get to?' A voice was heard beside her. He was by her side ready to play the dutiful husband for a few moments. 'I went to say hello to a friend, looked for you and you weren't there.' Her first thoughts were to ignore him but at the same time she did not want to cause a scene.

'I think we probably got lost among the crowd of people at the door and lost sight of each other,' she replied instead.

They approached Dayal, his sister Anjali and their parents. Hira smiled at Anjali and handed over the flowers and the present.

'Congratulations.' She smiled. 'Firstly on graduating and secondly on your engagement.' Anjali beamed.

'Thank you.' Aaryan too wished her congratulations and shook the hands of Dayal, his father and Anjali's fiancée.

'I am so glad that you made it.' Dayal beamed with happiness, 'and with Bhabhi too. We were all wondering if we would get to see you today.' He directed this towards Hira. Aaryan looked uncomfortable. 'Bhabhi, you know your husband is so secretive. We did not know that he had even got married. He surprised us all.' Hira smiled magnanimously. 'Bhabhi he won't, but you have to have a reception for us. You are still the bride. Don't be kanjoos like him. Give us a chance to welcome you.' Aaryan looked at the number of people in the hall and spotted Alisha at the far side, who beckoned to him.

'Excuse me,' he spoke to Anjali and moved away from the dais, leaving Hira on her own again. Aaryan's action did not go unnoticed. Anjali and her mother looked on pityingly. She took a deep breath, made her excuses, pasted a smile on her face and circulated around the hall. She made eye contact with a woman of advancing years who smiled at her. She returned the smile and walked up to her.

'Hello.' She offered her hand and it was accepted warmly.

'Pleasure to meet you, my dear I am Mrs Bharat. You are Soraya Aunty's grand daughter-in-law aren't you?' Hira nodded.

'Yes, I am Hira, married to Aaryan.'

Mrs Bharat beamed. 'So happy to meet you Hira beta. I live a few houses away from yours. It was such a surprise when you arrived.' She leaned forward. 'So Soraya's eldest grandson finally got married. But why so quietly? What secret are you hiding? Any scandal?

Drama?' She winked. Hira was taken back for a moment, but then she realised that Mrs Bharat was speaking in jest.

'Nothing like that I am afraid.' She spoke sadly then brightened. 'But I can always make something up.' That elicited a heartfelt laugh. The woman took a glass of juice which was offered and handed it to Hira and got one for herself. 'I like you. I see that you are circulating alone. Men! They do not think of these things. Good on you for mingling. Stick with me and I shall introduce you to those I know, but first, let me give you this.' She fished in her clutch bag and handed over a business card. 'From now on, I expect you to keep in touch.' Hira took the card.

'I am afraid I don't have any such cards....' Mrs Bharat waved her hand.

'Don't worry yourself, my dear. There will be another time. Come.' She took Hira's hand and introduced her to a group of women. 'This is Mrs Desai. She helps run a refuge for abandoned and abused women. Mrs Pravin who has a few sari shops in town and Mrs Kushal whose husband has a string of restaurants from Mumbai to Kolkatta.' Hira shook hands with them all.

'You are not from here,' Mrs Kushal noted. 'Where are you from?'

'From London,' Hira told her.

'A lovely city,' Mrs Kushal appreciated. 'I went there during the summer for the Olympics and to shop. I enjoyed it immensely.'

'It is a lovely city,' Hira agreed. 'The Olympics really brought out the best for London.'

'And you left it to come here.' Mrs Pravin said sadly. 'It must be quite a wrench for you.' Hira shrugged but kept quiet on the matter.

'Oh, we have a newbie here.' A deep voice next to her drew her attention.

'I am Devendra Das.' He introduced himself. 'Welcome to India. You do realise that all eyes are on you.'

'Do I stick out like a sore thumb?' Hira asked good naturedly.

'A very welcome sore thumb,' he replied. Mrs Bharat stepped in.

'Now Devendra. Don't think that just because she is London bred that she will be taken with your sweet words. I am taking responsibility for her. Now be gone.' She playfully slapped him on the arm. Devendra Das put his hands up and laughed.

'Oh, Aunty. I guess that I should have known that you would take her under your wing.' He smiled and then winked. 'It has been nice meeting you.' Mrs Bharat gave him a stare. 'I'm going. I'm going.' He put his arms up in mock surrender, chuckled and walked away.

'That is my nephew. Be wary of him. He is a sweet talker and hanger on. No, you stick with me.' She did the rounds with Mrs Bharat and totally forgot about Aaryan for most of the evening. She found that people welcomed her warmly, appreciating her attempt to only speak in hindi but they all wanted to converse with her in English so she complied and earned herself new admirers in the process.

She made some acquaintances, provisionally accepted invites to lunches, coffees and other social events, which she was unsure if she would get permission to attend. Deep down she was hoping that she would not have to disappoint them.

She felt a tap on her shoulder.

'Looks like you have settled in well.' Sabina hugged her. 'And here I was worrying how you would cope.'

'You had doubts? I was almost wetting myself,' Hira whispered in her ear, returning the hug. 'There are some awesome people here. So many women here work for good causes. I am impressed.' Her eyes sparkled.

'Yes. There are many people here who work for various charities. They are a shining beacon to everyone else. Aiden and I are going to make a move. I have got a bit of a headache. Amara and Alman are around here somewhere. Where is Aaryan?' Hira scanned the hall. She spied him at the far side of the hall. He was making short work of the offer of drinks on tap.

'I am not sure,' she lied. 'He was at the dais a short while ago.'

'Well if you want, you can come back with us. Aiden can text Aaryan and let him know.' Hira thought for a while.

'I would like to come back with you, but it wouldn't be right. I should come back with him.' Sabina nodded.

'OK. Take care. I'll see you at home. Call if you need to,' Hira reassured her and bade her good bye.

Hira stood by the sink in the washroom, washed her hands, dried them and inspected her reflection in the mirror. She checked her lipstick and smoothed her hair. She was enjoying the evening immensely. Amara and Alman had left an hour beforehand. After bidding them farewell she went in search of Aaryan and found the washroom instead.

She was aware of a couple whispering on the other side of the door. It sounded like they had had a disagreement. Hira froze. The voice was Aaryan's. The words were hushed and angry.

'Stop hassling me. I am here aren't I? Don't give me a hard time. I have spent most of the evening with you trying to get to the bottom of this, so much so that I am getting a headache. What more do you want?' There was a pause. 'Oh please. Not the silent treatment. Speak to me. '

'I can't bear that you brought her here.' Alisha griped.

'She is my wife. What did you want me to do? Hell, I never gave you the impression that you and I are an item. We just worked together.' There was another pause. 'At least I hope I didn't.'

Hira was taking everything in. She gripped the edge of the vanity and continued listening.

'That is all you ever said. I was hoping that I could make an impression on you. But the next time I saw you, you announced you got married. You are not happy with it. You said so yourself and that this marriage was done against your wishes. Why can't you face facts? Tell her the truth.'

'Oh for god's sake Alisha! Leave this marriage thing. We had dinner a few times, a couple of drinks. Even that was with other people around. We were never exclusive. If I have to leave my wife then I will do it at a time that is right for me. Not on somebody else's say so or for you. Stop this.'

'Can't you see that I have feelings for you?' He was taken aback. The voice broke for a moment. He bit back a curse.

'Look, I think it is better to finish the conversation here and now. I cannot work around you when you are like this. I will arrange for your transfer in the morning.' He began to walk off. Alisha grabbed his arm.

'Aaryan. Please don't do this. If you do this then I shall tell your wife that you and I are an item.' A tinge of desperation could be heard in her voice.

'You would do that?' He looked at her in a different light. 'Forget the transfer. I want your resignation letter on my desk tomorrow morning. Now let go of my arm.' He said icily.

'No. Not until you accept me.'

The sound of a thud on the wall made her jump. For a moment Hira thought he had lashed out at Alisha.

The door opened and a crying Alisha barged into the washroom. She saw Hira, stopped for a moment and then dived into one of the cubicles. Aaryan caught a glimpse of Hira in the washroom. He looked angry and then surprised. Then the door shut on him. The sound of sniffling was heard from the cubicle. In two minds whether she should console the other woman or not, she stood for the briefest of moments before heading out. She had her own issues to tend to.

There was a smudge of blood on the wall Hira noticed as she went passed. It looked as if Aaryan may have punched the wall in anger. Hira felt uneasy. She had only seen his irritation towards her. *'Would he resort to violence before long?'* she shuddered.

She returned to the party and tried to find Aaryan but he seemed to have disappeared. Scanning the hall, she was spotted by Mrs Desai.

'There you are Hira beta. Come with me. There are some people I would like you to meet.' She dragged her towards a group of people. 'They are anxious to meet you and know more about London.' Hira was bemused, but deciding to take her mind off what had gone on outside the washroom, she smiled and greeted the various people waiting for her, all eager to ask her questions.

It was coming up to midnight. Sensing the need that she should find Aaryan she made her excuses and went in search of him to find out if he was ready to go home. He wasn't anywhere in the hall so she searched for him in the corridor and thought to get someone to check the men's washroom.

She spied a lone figure slumped against the wall as she walked along the corridor. She drew nearer then stopped in her tracks. Aaryan looked at her with eyes that could barely focus.

'Dear God.' He was hopelessly drunk. She looked about her helplessly. Her mind began to race. Thinking of how she could get him out of the hall without drawing attention to him or to her. There was a fire exit near them. She could get him out there into the fresh air and see if it had an effect. She supported him and led him outside. He took his jacket off, slumped to the floor and looked at her.

'Why has this happened to me? All I wanted was a simple life and instead I get caught up in family politics and you. Why? You don't seem to be a bad person. Why are you blighting my life? And Alisha,' he moaned 'she seems to see things that aren't there. Why?' She bent to help him. He flailed his arms and caught her on the cheek with the back of his hand. She flinched but didn't respond. Nor did she have an answer. Ignoring his questions, she brought herself down to his level.

'We have got to go now.' She helped him up and moved towards where the valet boys had converged. She handed over the token that had been given earlier, upon getting the car parked and waited.

The car drew to a halt in front of them. Hira opened the passenger side door and sat Aaryan in the seat. One of the boys gave her a bottle of water. She offered Aaryan a few sips until he refused. Then it dawned on her that her husband was in no state to drive home. She thought for a moment and made her decision. Aaryan was bundled into the back, strapped in and covered with his jacket. She then got in the driver's side, adjusted the seat and mirrors, acclimatised herself with the gears, took her sandals off and pulled away.

The drive home was almost an hour away. With limited knowledge of the area, Hira prayed that she was on the right route. After making a number of wrong turns and seeing the amused looks from passers-by, she stumbled upon a police check point. As the policeman made his way towards her, fear made her lock herself in the car.

'Are you okay, Miss?'

Winding down the window slightly, she explained her predicament.

'Don't worry Miss.' He leant down and gave her instructions to get to her destination. Offering her thanks, she turned the car round and headed in the direction she had been told. Finally, she was on track and breathed a sigh of relief when she found herself on the sign posted road that she vaguely remembered that led the way home. Aaryan was muttering away in his drunken stupor about Dadi, land deals, honour and throwing his life away. Most of what he said was incoherent and Hira didn't pay much heed to him but kept an eye on him through the rear view mirror. Moments later he retched and threw up over his jacket, which had been draped over him. Hira recoiled in disgust. For as long as she could remember, she found it difficult to deal with anyone who had been sick. It was one of her shortcomings. Beginning to feel nauseous herself, she opened the driver and passenger windows and let the fresh air course through. Aaryan continued to sleep. His head tilted to one side. She checked once more on him and concentrated on getting them home as soon as possible, and in one piece.

Chapter 15

Pulling up to the gates to the house Hira gestured to be allowed through. The night watchman looked puzzled but ushered her through and she came to a stop directly by the main door. She rapped on the door and then went to check on Aaryan. The door eventually opened. Dada came out, bleary eyed. He took one look at the state of Aaryan.

'Beta you wait here. I shall get Aiden and Alman to help bring the fool in.' As much as it turned her stomach to do so, she ran in, grabbed a towel and a bowl of water, came back, removed the jacket and wiped Aaryan's face. Once clean, she threw the water in the bushes and shuddered inwardly.

Dada reappeared with Aiden and Alman. They looked into the car.

'The idiot.' They both agreed and pulled him out of the car and started to drag his inebriated body upstairs to bed, with little ceremony, a lot of grunting and loud whispers. Dadi came out of the bedroom to see what the commotion was.

'What in god's name is going on here?' She demanded. Everyone stopped in their tracks. The trio slowly turned on the stairs and faced her. Aaryan came to momentarily. He slid down and sat on the step and wagged a finger at Dadi.

'God's name is Ishwar, Bhudiya. And you should not take God's name in vain.' Aaryan slurred and then started chuckling, seemingly laughing at his own joke. She gasped at the audacity and state of her eldest grandson but quickly recovered.

'What are you doing standing there? Get him to his room at once.' Aiden and Alman pulled him to his feet. She walked away in disgust and muttering under her breath about youth, irresponsibility, duty and control. She stopped and turned. 'Why did you allow him to get like this? You are supposed to look out for him. How did you get home?' she asked Hira, the trademark look of annoyance etched on her face. 'Aaryan could not have driven home. Who drove you home? Have you no manners that you do not thank the Samaritan who got you home safely? Go and bring him in.' Hira turned towards the door, locked the car, put the key on the table and made eye contact.

'I drove us home,' she stated in defiance, waiting for the lecture. If anything, Dadi was a traditionalist. She pigeon holed things as women's duties and men's duties. This would surely get her a hard time. Right on cue, Dadi took a deep breath.

'Soraya,' Dada cut in, almost taking the air out of her sails. She pursed her lips shut. 'Instead of being upset, be thankful that Hira did drive home. Otherwise they both would have either been stranded in town or worse. What if they had fallen prey to someone who could harm them? You know the state of the city at night.' He turned to Hira. 'Beta, you go upstairs. Aaryan might need some help.' Hira nodded and started up the stairs in her bare feet.

'Where are your shoes?' Dadi demanded. 'I hope you have not been walking barefoot in the street. Shameful!' Hira's mouth dropped in disbelief. 'And what happened to your face? That smart mouth of yours got you a slap?' Dada took Dadi by the arm dragged her to the bedroom. Hira raised her hand and rubbed her cheek. It would heal.

'It is time for bed. Leave Hira so that she can tend to that idiot grandson of yours.' He turned to Hira. 'Get some ice on that cheek too. I will talk to you and him in the morning.'

Hira looked on as Dadi was led away. '*Her grandson has been brought home blind drunk and she goes on about the shame of walking barefoot.*' She shook her head and trudged up the stairs, not entirely looking forward to the job waiting for her.

Aiden and Alman dropped Aaryan on the bed and looked at each other, unsure if they should just leave him there. Hira walked in.

'Thank you.' She walked to the bed. 'I suppose I should take it from here.' They did not need telling twice. With grateful yet sheepish looks they left the room.

Hira looked down at the prone figure of her husband before finally making a move. She straightened his body on the bed, bent slightly, and pulled off his shoes and socks, throwing them behind her, removed his shirt, threw that on the floor, and straightened, thinking as she thought about removing his trousers. Not entirely comfortable about removing them, she collected a flannel and some warm water and sluiced him down, properly before drying him off and covering him with the blanket, then headed off for the bathroom to sort herself out.

He was cocooned in both blankets. Pulling a quilt out from the ottoman she shook it out and settled down for the night. It had been quite an eventful night. Tomorrow would mean questions and lectures, but for now she closed her eyes. She did not have time to process the statement which she had heard earlier but she thought back to it now. From what he had said in his stupor, it appeared that he had bowed down to duty and family honour and married her. She had been thrust upon him when he had already made his own choices. No wonder he was always in a mood with her from the outset. She probably would have been too. *'Where do you go from here Hira?'* she asked herself. *'Try harder or give up now?'* Her 'aunt', in the absence of her mother, had lectured her on how to behave at the in-laws' house. Mentally she ticked off the list. Helpful, polite, respectful, demure. *'OK.'* She thought. *'That last one was going out of the window. But what am I supposed to do? I can't be something that I am not.'* She rolled over and closed her eyes and saw the image of her aunt, red faced, heavily made up and looking at her sternly.

'Men do not like women who are too smart. They like their women to obey them and take care of them. Don't go shooting your mouth off like you always do and have that attitude. That is a sure fire way to antagonise your husband.'

'But Aunt, why do I have to go? I don't know anyone over there. What is wrong with me staying here and looking after myself? I am old enough.'

'And have me responsible for you? No way. I have enough on my plate with my lot and if they see you so independent they will want the same. You will do well in India. Besides they are not strangers, they are family.'

'May as well be strangers. I still don't see why I cannot decide for myself,' she muttered, crossing her arms.

'Don't start. These are the instructions that I was left with and that it is what I am doing.'

'Instructions from whom?' Hira questioned. *'Mum would never do anything like this without telling me. I won't agree.'* Her aunt turned towards her. Her face contorted with anger.

'You will get married. You have no choice in the matter,' she hissed and left her in tears.

Tears dripped onto the pillow.

'Mum, I wish you were here. I have landed here to god knows what? I don't know what to do. Help me?' she implored.

71

Chapter 16

The tea set clattered as Hira carried the tray into the bedroom. He still slept. She placed the tray on the bedside table and poured out a cup. Still he slept. Putting the cup down on the table she thought of shaking him awake. She took a step forward, slipped on his shirt that she had thrown down the night before and landed on her bottom.

'Ow,' she shouted in surprise more than pain. He opened his eyes and focused on her with bleary eyes.

'What are you doing on the floor?'

'Looking to see if the designs on the marble tiles are the same throughout,' she replied, annoyed for slipping in the first place. 'I slipped. What did you think I was doing?' She stood up and rubbed away the pain. He did a double take.

'Are you mad?'

'No. This is normal for me.' He gave her an odd look and sat up.

'Who...?' He noticed that he was not wearing his shirt. Hira gave him a bashful look. He lifted the blanket next.

'You weren't that lucky,' she replied and handed him the cup of tea. He took a sip and grimaced.

'What is in this?' He handed the cup back to her but she refused.

'Just tea with black cardamoms it should settle your stomach. I would drink up if I were you.'

'Was I sick?' She looked at him, daring him to ask the next question. 'How bad?'

'Sick? You were sick all over the back seat. It is in such a mess. I don't know how you will make amends. I was upset. Besides I left it for you to clean. Anymore questions?' He choked then looked at her long and hard. *His mind was befuddled. She was actually speaking to him normally. No faraway look, lack of concentration. He must still be drunk.* He thought to himself. A hazy image appeared in his mind. Hira in the washroom, the look on her face that let on that she had heard everything. She had been aware of Alisha? But the look of surprise troubled him. He put the cup down and wondered whether to talk about last night. Instead he noticed the redness on her cheek.

'What ...?' He began to ask. She skirted round his question.

'Dadiji still expects you to come down for breakfast. We have made parathas.' Brown eyes twinkled as she saw his attempt to keep down the tea at the mention of food.

'Are you enjoying my discomfort?' he asked her accusingly. She stepped back.

'Umm, I have got to go.'

Aaryan looked green around the gills as he finally appeared at the breakfast table. Hira served the food and put the plate in front of him. He waved it away and reached for the tea instead.

'What have you got to say for yourself?' Dadi glowered at him from the top of the table. Aaryan pushed back the plate of food that Hira had put under his nose again.

'I went a bit overboard, Dadi.' he replied. 'No big deal.' The plate was pushed back in front of him again. He glared at Hira and pushed it back.

'No big deal? You are brought home totally senseless. Made a mess of the car and you say that is not a big deal?'

Aaryan held his head in his hands. Dadi was not going to let up.

'Dadi. Do you have to shout?'

'Why shouldn't I shout? You were being irresponsible. Also, you were in such a state that Hira took it upon herself to drive you home.' Aaryan's head snapped up and he looked at Hira. Finally he stood up, a sheen of sweat appeared above his top lip.

'I am going back to my room,' he stated. 'I am not going to work today.' He directed that to his brothers. Dadi watched him walk away.

'What is this world coming to,' she tutted. 'Boys getting drunk, girls getting above their station and driving cars.'

'Dadiji. Times have moved on. It's not a bad thing.' Aiden stood up for her. 'In fact, after last night's incident I think it is important for Sabina and Amara to learn too.'

'Absolutely not,' Dadi objected. 'I don't care what the rest of the country is doing. The daughters of this family will not learn to drive. Do I make myself clear?' She directed this at Hira, warning her in her own manner that the deed was not to be repeated again. Hira for her part kept quiet. However, it was not enough for Dadi. She interpreted her silence as confrontational and acted as such. 'I will not have you putting ideas into their heads.' She indicated at Sabina and Amara. 'This is my house and you will live and breathe according to my say so.' Hira quelled the anger that was beginning to build inside her

'The woman is such a control freak.' She sighed and realised too late that it had been audible. Dadi picked up the serving spoon and brought it down on the back of Hira's hand. Hard. The others jumped. She held her hand close to her body and nursed it. It smarted. Dadi glared at her.

From the comfort of his bed he watched as Hira moved around the room, clearing up and putting away the clean clothes she had brought up with her. He cleared his throat.

'You're awake.' She turned. 'Sorry if I woke you.' He shook his head.

'I was awake anyway.' He saw a cup of tea on the bedside table. 'Is that fresh?' he asked, reaching out and touching the cup. It was cold. 'I have a headache.' Hira poured a glass of water and handed it to him. She sat on the bed, rummaged around in the drawer of the bedside table and produced a blister pack of tablets, popped two and handed them to him. 'Thanks.' He downed the pills and the water.

'What happened to your hand?' He asked noticing the makings of a bruise on it.

'Something and nothing.' She shrugged and made to move off the bed. He looked at her.

'You know? I realise, I know nothing about you.'

Hira turned and stared.

'Is there any point?' she asked. He was taken back for a moment. 'You look blank.'

'I don't understand why you said that?' Then he thought back to the washroom when he had seen Hira as the door swung open. His stomach lurched as he remembered the look on her face. 'Set aside what you heard last night. Why?' Hira sat back on the bed.

'What I overheard outside the washroom is one thing. I always say that many a truth is uttered in a drunken stupor. I think I heard enough.' She looked down.

'I have no idea what I said. If there was anything said that hurt you then I am sorry. But can we at least keep the corridors of dialogue open? I don't like it when people freeze me out.'

'I don't know what you want me to say?' She shrugged. 'I come over here from halfway across the world and find the man that I accepted is already involved with someone else. I find it hard to fathom that you so readily accepted marriage, especially if you were involved with someone else.' It was his turn to look away.

'I was not involved with anyone. What I will say is that emotional blackmail is a horrible tool. It is used far too often here.' She nodded. It was a well-known emotion used in London too and she had seen it used often enough, mostly against her mum by her so-called aunties whenever they wanted something.

'That is all very well, but where does that leave me?' There was an awkward silence as they stared at each other for a time until she looked away. Eventually she got up from the bed.

'There is a lot that I need to know about you.' He smiled slightly to reassure her. 'Hira. Can we talk some more later? I do feel bad with how things have turned out. I would rather not be strangers.' She shrugged then nodded.

Chapter 17

Akilah was skulking along the corridor. She was bored. All her friends had gone to the city and with no one else around she wandered through the house sighing and stomping. She spied the door to Hira's room slightly ajar and smiled. Creeping up to the door, she pushed it slightly and looked inside the room. Silently she crept in and made a bee line for the wardrobe. Opening it, she smiled and pulled out the outfit that Hira had bought recently. Her eyes glinted.

'Hmm, Hira madam. I think that I will take ownership of this. You made me lose a suit so I shall take this one.' She held the suit against her and swung around.

'Akilah? What are you doing?' Throwing the outfit back into the wardrobe and slamming it shut Akilah swung round. Aaryan stood by the French windows, having stepped out to get a bit of fresh air.

'Aaryan? I didn't realise that you were still in here.'

He looked at her with questioning eyes.

'You haven't answered my question. What are you doing in my room?'

Akilah giggled nervously.

'I just came up to see how you were doing?' she lied.

'And for that you had to open my wardrobe to ask that question? What were you doing? You didn't come here to ask after me. I know you too well.' Akilah backed up.

'You always put me in the wrong,' she protested. 'I really was coming in to ask how you were.'

'OK. You haven't done that so there is no need for you to be in here. Out!' he barked. She turned on her heel and ran out of the room.

He walked over to the wardrobe and spied a piece of material hanging out. Opening the door, he picked up the outfit from the floor of the wardrobe and held it up close to him and rearranged it on the hanger properly.

'I didn't have you down as a cross dresser.' Hira burst out without thinking. She appeared from the en suite and stood in the doorway. He bit back a laugh.

'It had fallen off the rail. I was just putting it back.' He composed himself enough to face her.

'What?' It was more of a statement then a question. She stood there with such an indignant but innocent look he tried hard not to smile. He put the outfit on the rail. 'I think I should get to know you better,' he muttered to himself.

'Hira.' They both faced towards the door. Dadiji was calling and seemed to be in a mood. She stole him an almost apologetic glance before running out of the room.
'Coming Dadiji.'
'Wait,' he called after her. She skidded to a stop. 'Can I have a snack?'

Dadi was sat reading when Hira appeared at the door. She knocked and waited patiently as Dadi finished the chapter she was reading. Finally she looked up.
'You called me.' Hira said.
'Yes. I seem to be catching a cold. Do you know how to make panjiri?' She peered over the rims of her glasses.
Hira hesitated. '*Why would she be asking for something like this at this time of night?*'
'Dadiji, it is not something that I have made before but I will give it a try.' Dadi was amazed but hid her reaction.
'Go and see if there are enough ingredients for it. If not write a list and give it to Harilal. He will get them for you and you will make it tomorrow.' She nodded.
'Yes Dadiji.' She headed off in the direction of the kitchen.
Akilah watched quietly from the shadows as Hira walked away from the room.

Hira hesitated. She scanned the cupboards trying to remember what she needed.

***

'*For the basic panjiri you will need sugar, flour, ghee, chopped almonds, pistachios, walnuts and ginger. Although a lot of people don't like ginger so you can leave it out and there are other ingredients you can put in but I don't have them here.*' Her mother put *the ingredients on the table. Hira looked on. 'Was it the start of winter already?' She thought to herself. 'It was only yesterday that the summer holidays had started.' Hira sighed.*

'What was that sigh for? You will see how good this is once it is made. It will give you strength and help ward off colds and chills. You will see that it is good for you.' Hira picked up a handful of almonds and started munching on them. 'Hira. Don't eat all the almonds. There will be nothing left.'

'But mum. I thought you said that it was for nursing mothers.' She looked down at herself. 'What happens if... Why can't we just add the almonds and pistachios to warm milk like we always do?' Mum laughed as she realised what Hira was referring to.

'I think that you will find that there is more to producing milk than just eating panjiri.' She took the almonds away from her. 'This way is more fun. I will show you and when the mixture cools we will make little round balls. You can have one at breakfast every day.'

A disinterested Hira looked on as her mother put the ingredients together. Every step was explained to her but all she could think was that the park looked really enticing today.

***

Hira galvanised herself. She checked all the canisters for the ingredients she needed and wrote out a list of the items missing. Picking up a few almonds she put them in her mouth, then promptly ran to the bin and spat them out. They had gone soft.

'Definitely order more almonds,' she noted and was about to leave the list on the counter but then thought again and pocketed the paper. She would give it to Harilal at breakfast. She snapped off the light and then remembered Aaryan's request. Checking what was available she finally settled on putting together a chicken sandwich. As she put the sandwich together Akilah graced her with her presence. Hateful eyes followed her every move. Finally she spoke.

'Who said that you can make yourself a sandwich?' Hira glanced her way and continued what she was doing.

Akilah sidled up to her. 'What's your problem? Can't you even be bothered to answer me? I asked you a question?' She grabbed the sandwich from her and took it apart, dropping the filling on the floor. She stared at Hira who for her part glared at her.

'The sandwich is for Aaryan.'

'Aww. My brother wants a sandwich,' she taunted. 'And aren't you a good little wife for making it for him.' Hira took out another two slices of bread and made another sandwich. She reached in the cutlery drawer to get a knife. Akilah slammed the drawer shut and attempted to trap Hira's fingers in it. Hira pulled her hand back just in time before any further damage could be done. She glared at the girl and wished with all her heart that she could wipe the smirk off her face.

'Tsk, tsk. What happened? Trapped your fingers in the drawer?'

'Nearly,' Hira replied and slammed the knife on the counter, making Akilah jump. She opened her mouth to say something but observing her sister-in-law cutting the bread, with some attitude, she thought against it. Instead she beat a hasty retreat, almost running into the kitchen door in her hurry.

She put the sandwich and a glass of juice on a tray. She moved towards the door then jumped. Dadi stood blocking her way. She looked at the tray and then at Hira. Akilah moved from behind her.

'I told you, Dadi. I told you that she was stealing food.' She stood with Dadiji accusingly, a triumphant look on her face.

'Did I send you here to stuff your face?'

Hira looked at the items on the tray, then back at her grandmother.

'I was taking them up to Aaryan. He requested a snack.'

'Liar,' hissed Akilah, moving ahead of Dadi. 'You were taking it for yourself. You see Dadi.' She turned. 'She lies too. Butter wouldn't melt.'

'How do I know that you are not taking that for yourself?'

'I am not,' Hira protested. 'Aaryan asked for this.'

'Insolent girl.' Dadi knocked the tray out of Hira's hand, sending the contents to the floor and the juice was hurled against the cabinet. 'Not only do you lie but you act innocent as well. I rue the day I let you come here,' she grumbled. 'Treating the house like it's your own.'

79

'Hira? Are you going to bring me that snack?' Aaryan's voice was heard from upstairs. Dadi looked from Hira to Akilah. She shot her grand-daughter an angry look.

'Make sure that you clean that properly. I don't want to step in here in the morning and find ants all over the place. And you,' she turned to Akilah, 'before you come running to me, get your facts straight.' Without another word she turned and stomped out with Akilah quick on her heels.

'Dadi. I thought she was making it for herself. How would I know that it was for Aaryan?' she wailed. 'What about her pushing me? Does she not get punished for that? Dadi, she pushed me and threatened me. Before she came no one said anything to me. No one would dare, Dadi why won't you say anything to her?'

'Silence.' Barked Dadi. Akilah had worked her up into such anger that at this moment her grand-daughter was treading on shaky ground.

Hira seethed in anger as Dadi and Akilah disappeared. She pulled herself together, cleaned the food and the spilt juice, washed her hands, made yet another sandwich and took it to Aaryan before the spectre of Dadi could materialise again.

'That hit the spot.' Aaryan put the tray on the bedside table. He looked at Hira, who was standing by the French doors. 'Thank you.'

There was no response from her. Mistaking her silence for indifference he retreated from asking her any questions and headed off out.

Hira was deep in thought. She looked up into the night sky and followed the twinkling lights as they almost seemed to speak to one another. She watched a comet pass by and stood transfixed as the trajectory made its way across the night sky and thought back to her childhood when she would watch excitedly and make a wish. This time there was excitement, no wish. No need to believe in miracles. They did not happen.

She was still there when he came back. Same position, same stance. He walked up to her.

'Have you been standing there since I left?' he asked. Hira jumped and almost fell against him.

'You left? When? How?' Aaryan steadied her.

'Yes about half an hour ago and on foot.'

He could be smart too. In the darkness of the room she looked at him in silence.

'Why are you standing in the dark all this time and you are cold.' He led her toward the bed. 'I know that there are things that we need to talk about. I promise that I will take out some time to give to you soon. I have just come back from Aiden's room. We have a big project that we are going to embark on and things will be busy but we will talk.' He looked for assurance that she understood.

'It is going to be a busy few weeks.'

She lay down and pulled the blankets over herself. Before long she was asleep. While she slept, he was deep in thought.

Before Hira came along and even up to last night he had been perfectly happy with spending time with Alisha, but her behaviour yesterday distanced him from her. Was he that shallow that he was willing to change overnight? With these questions going round and round in his head he lay in the dark, staring at the ceiling unable to sleep.

The atmosphere at breakfast was as it always was, Aaryan noticed as he took his seat. Dadi scowled over her paratha and chai. Akilah had the same smirk on her face as she always did. Dada slurped his chai like a true veteran. Hira turned over his plate and proceeded to spoon some breakfast for him.

'Disgusting,' Dadi exploded. 'Use your right hand,' she shouted at Hira. 'Surely your mother taught you the difference. Use it.' Hira changed hands and reddened. The bruising had got worse. Sabina and Amara looked on concerned. Aaryan looked on speechless. He hadn't realised that it was that bad. He looked around for an explanation. Instead he saw Akilah smirk, and look in Dadi's direction.

'Don't ever let me see you using your left hand while dishing up food.' She waggled her finger at her. 'Don't forget that you are making panjiri for me,' She waited for Hira to make some excuse. Instead Hira nodded, matching Dadi eye to eye. She was not going to be cowed.

'Do you want us to help you?' Sabina asked. Aaryan looked on silently.

'No, its fine,' Hira assured her, ignoring the caustic scowls coming from Dadi.

Aaryan finished his food, wiped his mouth and stood up.

'I am off,' he declared. He picked up his jacket, glanced in Hira's direction and walked out only to come back after a moment.

'Can I catch a lift with you guys?' he asked his brothers sheepishly.

'The car has been disgraced.'

He looked over at Hira and had the grace to be embarrassed. Both his brothers laughed.

'How did you manage to find that phrase? And yes, you did disgrace it. It is going to need a good clean out. Give us five minutes.' Aiden answered.

Chapter 18

Striding through the corridor to his office Aaryan answered with the customary greeting to the office workers who asked after his health. He walked into his office deposited his case and scanned through the in tray before prioritising, sat down and worked his way through the paperwork. After an hour of solid analysing, signing and reading he felt thirsty. Not finding any water in the room he picked up the phone to request some and hesitated.

'*I want your resignation letter on my desk in the morning.*' He remembered from the night of the party and replaced it. He would find a peon to get him water. He stepped out of his office and came face to face with Alisha. They stood for a while, not speaking. Finally Aaryan broke the silence.

'Are you working out your notice?' Alisha looked surprised for a moment. Then realisation dawned on her.

'No,' she replied. 'I haven't tendered my resignation. You didn't come in yesterday. I called so many times.'

'Can you find someone to get me a jug of water? There is none in there.' He indicated to his office. She nodded. 'And can I also have the file on the Shriman project. I have a meeting with my brothers and I will need it.'

Alisha picked up the phone, instructed the recipient at the other end to bring in a jug of water, then located the file and handed it to him. 'Thank you.' She followed him into the office.

'Why didn't you return my calls? I waited all day.' She was interrupted by a knock on the door. Dayal stood in the doorway and she scowled at him. Aaryan smiled seeing him.

'Dayal. Come in. The meeting is not for another twenty minutes.' He looked at his watch, checking that he wasn't late. Dayal shook his head.

'No, no. We still have time. You did not come in yesterday so I rang the house to thank you and Bhabhi for the lovely gifts you gave to my sister. She is so happy with them and she asked me to thank you again on her behalf. 'Is your headache better?' Aaryan looked confused. 'Your grandmother answered. She said that you had a headache. Self-induced was it? Aaryan indicated that it had been. He noticed that Alisha was still standing there.

'Did you need anything, Alisha?' She glared but shook her

head and left the room. Aaryan sat down and invited Dayal to do the same. Dayal sat down and looked towards the door.

'I sense trouble brewing.' Aaryan looked at him troubled.

'Trouble indeed, I feel bad. She seems to think that she and I are an item.' Dayal looked surprised.

'You mean to say that you are not?'

Aaryan shook his head.

'Why? What's been said?' Dayal looked uncomfortable. He shifted in his seat.

'The secretaries' talk and the word is that you and Alisha have been spending a fair bit of time together and are more than just colleagues.'

Aaryan looked horrified. Dayal went on. 'In fact, there was surprise when you announced that you had married, especially as the rumour was that you two would get married. Imagine our surprise.'

Aaryan shook his head in disbelief.

'I told her on the night of your sister's party that I didn't think of her in the same way. She wasn't too happy. Did I let it get too far? What do I do?' Dayal thought for a while.

'If this is going to cause problems then maybe it might be better to transfer her to another department.' Aaryan shook his head.

'I considered that. I then asked her to hand in her resignation.' He said sheepishly. Dayal looked alarmed.

'Should you be doing that?'

'No, I guess you are right. I am just a fool. No. I think that at this stage it would be wrong to ask her to accept either of those.' He looked about him. 'It is like running away from your problems. If you don't stand up and face them they can blow up in your face.'

On the other side of the door Alisha listened to the conversation and she hung her head. She sat at her desk and wiped away her tears.

The door opened and one of the workers entered carrying refreshments and water. 'Is Alisha back?' he asked the worker. The man shook his head.

'Madam picked up her things and left the building, Sir. She left this for you.' He passed over a piece of paper. Aaryan took the note, read it and then gave the man instructions.

'Will you see if there is anyone spare who can cover for her?'

Aaryan told the man. 'Send them over. I will brief them.' The man nodded, placed the tray on the table and backed out of the office. 'Alisha has gone on sick leave. Not sure for how long. But she has asked to be transferred to another part of the company upon her return. Best thing to do under the circumstances I think.' He put the paper on the desk. 'Why do I get all these headaches?'

'Because you refuse to see what is happening in front of your eyes.' Aiden stepped into the office and gave his view. 'I am surprised. We all saw it. How could you not?'

Aaryan groaned. 'If you could see it, then why didn't you tell me? Now I feel like such an idiot.' He ran his fingers through his hair. 'I suppose I liked the attention.' He added ruefully.

'Hey, you are the elder brother. You are supposed to be worldly in all these matters. Never mind, you will learn. But first, you have to concentrate on this meeting and getting the project off the ground. We have a lot of people to convince that this is a good idea. Then you can sort out your reputation.'

Aaryan picked up his jacket, shrugged it on, picked up the file and made for the door, closely followed by his brother and his friend.

Chapter 19

Hira presented the panjiri to Dadi and waited until she had tasted it and passed judgement.

'Tea,' Dadi demanded. Amara quickly poured her a cup. She took a spoonful of the stuff, put it in her mouth and chewed. Tense moments passed for Hira as she waited for the verdict. Finally Dadi spoke.

'Not bad,' she commented. 'Put a little more sugar and you will have had it perfect for my liking. You did make this yourself didn't you?' The old lady peered over her glasses at her. Hira nodded. Dadi looked as if she was mulling things over in her mind. 'I give you permission to take care of the neglected part of the garden.'

Hira gasped and smiled.

'But make sure that all your chores are done.' She waggled the spoon at her. 'I will not tolerate any neglect of any sort.'

Hira quickly agreed. Dadi went back to eating the panjiri.

'Dadi. What are you eating? I want some too.' Akilah rushed in and took a pinch. 'Nice.' She sat down and helped herself to a spoonful.

'Dadiji likes it too,' Amara declared proudly. 'Hira made it.' Akilah stopped chewing. A look of distaste crossed her face and she spat out the remainder into the plate.

'Yuk.' Dadi looked at Akilah with disgust.

'Have you gone back to your childhood?' she admonished her grand-daughter. 'There was nothing wrong with it. Now you have ruined what is left.' She handed the plate to Hira. 'Throw this away and bring me a fresh batch. Akilah, go make yourself useful. Bring me my glasses and my books. I would like to sit on the verandah and read.' Akilah quickly got up.

'Dadi,' she cooed. 'I would love to but the thing is, I promised to meet a friend and I am already running late. Can't one of these get them for you? After all, that is what they are here for, to serve you? It is alright to go, isn't it?' Akilah rushed away before the old woman had a chance to reply and shot out of the door at lightning speed. Hira looked annoyed.

'Hira,' Dadi warned her and shook her head.

'*Hell,*' thought Hira, '*She could read minds too?*' Hira disappeared into the kitchen to do as Dadi had asked, added a little more sugar and set about moulding the mixture into little round balls.

'Well done,' Sabina whispered as she patted her on the back. 'Keep doing that and we might see a change in Dadiji yet.' She started to help. Hira smiled.

'I think that if we carry on as we have been, one day she will open her eyes.'

Amara came in with the tea set. 'Dadi has gone out to the verandah. She has asked that we make something simple for lunch and dinner. Everyone will be late, so it will just be us,' she informed them, pouring them each a cup and passing them over. Sabina took the cup offered to her and sat down at the table.

'Fine. We can organise lunch and dinner together and then have the afternoon to ourselves. Unfortunately, while this big deal is being brokered we will see less of our men.'

'Is it that intense?' Hira sat with her. Amara nodded.

'Yes.' Amara sat down. 'They will spend most of the time at the office. They will just come home to sleep.' Hira absent mindedly took out a biscuit and bit into it.

'I think Hira has gone into shock after hearing Dadiji's comment.' Sabina and Hira laughed.

'I know I am finding it hard to take in. But the plus side is that she has agreed for me to work on that area of the garden that has been neglected.'

'I am so glad you have found something to concentrate on. We were getting worried that boredom might have set in.' Hira took another bite.

'It will be a while before that sets in,' she replied. 'But if you see me going round and round in circles or walking back and forth, take me away.' She laughed.

'But until then,' she raised her cup in salutation, 'I shall pray that I will find other things to keep myself amused.' Two more cups joined hers.

'We'll second that.' They giggled.

Chapter 20

Aaryan stepped out of the house and into the garden. After having a desperately bad day at work he needed to relax. Neither bed, nor sleep was able to soothe him and he wandered around the house restlessly until his feet led him to the direction of the garden. He stood still for a moment, closed his eyes and let the sun's warming rays caress his face. It was while he was standing that he noticed that he was not alone. He heard the gentle sound of water being sprinkled over flowerbeds and headed towards the sound.

In a once secluded and over run corner of the garden Hira, straightened up and surveyed her handiwork. In the weeks since Dadi had allowed her to take over the small plot, she had planted seedlings and saw with pride that they were beginning to flourish. In time, they would bloom into an array of colours in beautiful hues of purple, yellow, red, pink, white and green. She looked forward to nurturing them to the stage where their beauty could be seen and appreciated. She had sectioned out an area for herbs and they were flourishing under her care.

He stood a short distance away transfixed by the transformation. As he stepped forward, a twig snapped underneath alerting Hira to his presence. She looked up and acknowledged him.

'Hi. Have you been home long?'

'A while,' he replied. 'It is looking so much better here.'

'There is still a little bit more to do.' She looked around her, smiled and wiped her hands on the back of her jeans. 'Are you hungry? Thirsty?' He declined. She walked over to the small fountain, which had lain defunct for a time. He stood on the other side and watched as she cleared away the debris from the bottom.

'Ouch.' She withdrew her hand and inspected it, squeezing the blood out of the cut she sustained.

'Let me see.' He was by her side in a flash, checking her finger before taking out his handkerchief, staunching the blood supply and encasing her finger with it. 'Is there anyone more accident prone than you? You should be more careful. Anything could have been in that rubbish.' He inspected the finger for any tell-tale signs should there be anything other than a thorn that had caused this injury. Luckily there was no sign that it could be anything else. Hira watched bemused as he fussed. He treated her more like a person. He was

table.

'Didn't you make a pot?' She pouted. Aaryan checked Hira's cup.

'Do you want another?' She shook her head. He picked up the empty utensils, rinsed them and put them on the side to dry. 'No. There were only two of us so there wasn't any point.' He turned to Hira. 'Are you ready to come up? We can at least start the conversation there.'

Hira nodded. Akilah scowled as they left. She picked up the kettle and slammed it down on the hob in anger. There was no way that she was going to allow her brother to bond with Hira. Even if she had to go to his room and remove his bedding to the guest room she would do it.

Hira came out of the bathroom drying her hair. She had spent too long in the shower and was only brought to her senses when Aaryan knocked on the bathroom door to ask if she was alright. He was sat watching the television. Upon seeing her, he turned it off and indicated the seat next to him. Hira sat down, feeling like a naughty child. Would he tell her off for using all the hot water, she wondered.

Aaryan picked up his case, pulled out a small package and handed it to her. Hira took it, looking surprised. She removed the paper packaging.

'My phone?' She looked at him confused. He sat next to her.

'I had the screen fixed, the casing as well.' He explained. She turned the phone over in her hand, inspecting it. 'I realised after I had thrown the phone, how precious it was to you. I saw the photographs of you with your mother. I felt extremely bad and ashamed of myself. I am sorry.' Tears glistened in Hira's eyes.

'I could not find our photo albums before I left. These are the only ones I have of us.' She looked lovingly at the photo on the home screen then looked at him. 'Thank you.' She whispered. Aaryan nodded. Finding that the time was right he thought to tackle a few things straightaway.

'We should have had this conversation a month ago.' He seemed apologetic. She sat opposite him. 'I want to clear something up first. Since you arrived, I have given you the impression that this marriage is not of my choosing. The truth is, I had no intention of getting married just yet but Dadi had told me that Dadaji was ill and might not have enough time left so I agreed.'

Hira was horrified.'Dadaji is sick?'

Aaryan, hearing the alarm in her voice quickly, allayed her fear. He shook his head.

'No, Dadaji is fine. He was sick at the time but it was a ploy to get me to agree. When I found out a week before your arrival I was mad, angry and I took it out on everyone, including you. I could not bear to be at home and I did not want to be around you so I spent a lot of time at work, in the city, anywhere but here.'

Hira continued to towel dry her hair.

'Are you listening to me?'

Hira quickly put down the towel, sat back and looked at him with wide eyed innocence.

He tried hard to suppress the smile that played on his lips but instead it came through. 'Don't give me that look. It won't wash with me.'

'Rumbled,' muttered Hira, looking away then gave him her full attention.

'As I was saying, all of what happened then was nothing to do with you. I am glad that we started talking to each other. I want to know more about you. What are your likes and dislikes, where did you study, where did you live and tell me about your family? All I know of you is that you like gardening, have a weird sense of humour and that you are a bad sleeper.'

Hira opened her mouth to reply to his questions.

'Aaryaaaan.' The wail was heard outside the door and the rapping started. An annoyed look crossed her features as she was ready to tell her life story. Aaryan got up and threw open the door.

'Akilah? What is wrong?'

She stepped into the room and cast Hira a cursory look, then turned to her brother.

'Nothing,' she replied nonchalantly. 'I just wanted to see what you were doing. I am bored.'

He grabbed her by the shoulders, turned her round and marched her out of the room.

'Is it only me you can think of when you are bored? Go. Find one of the others. I am busy.'

'Please.' She turned round. 'There is nobody downstairs except for Dadi and she is sleeping most of the time. Come and play a game of chess with me?'

'Take Hira with you. You can spend some time with her and see how she is at chess.' He looked at Hira to step in.

'I want you to keep me company, not her.' The last two words dripped ice. She would do everything in her power to ensure that Hira would be sidelined by Aaryan. She had lost interest in the other two. Hira's unhappiness was in her sights now even more so.

'Don't be a spoilt child. Go down and amuse yourself.'

'Oh come on. Just a couple of games of chess, then you can come back.'

Aaryan sighed. His sister was the world's biggest pain. He shot an apologetic look towards Hira. She nodded as if to say another time and picked up the towel and went back to drying her hair. He glared at his sister, angry that she used all the emotional tactics to get what she wanted. But he was not surprised. After all, the fruit did not fall far from the tree and she spent all her time around their grandmother. Happy that she had won in keeping her brother away from Hira, for now she beamed, grabbed Aaryan's hand and dragged him out of the room.

The evening went on forever. He continuously looked towards the landing, hoping for an end to his boredom and tried to ignore Akilah's chatter. Chess was a non-starter as all she wanted to do was to crib about the hardships of being a girl. He switched off, letting her drone on. His eyes grew heavy and he closed them for a millisecond.

He woke. Cold and disorientated. Looking around him it was clear that his bratty sister had gone off to bed without giving him a second thought.

'Spoilt brat,' he muttered, getting up from the settee and stretching. 'Went off to bed and did not even wake me.' True she was spoilt. Dadi had spoilt her. They all had. They lost dad the month before she was born and then mum had passed away due to complications. To make up for their loss she was treated with kid gloves. Only now it was coming back and biting them on the back-side. He had always been aware of her evil streak and suspected that she did not spare Sabina and Amara since they joined the family as she was the main cause to instigate Dadi against them. She was lucky that they were such angels to her he concluded. Anyone else would have left her high and dry years ago.

Moonlight streamed through the windows as he approached the bed. She had not closed the curtains. He glanced at her sleeping form and noticed that the sheets were all twisted, another one of her nightmares. He would get to the bottom of her fears one day. Today had been a perfect opportunity had it not been for Akilah. Quietly, he drew the curtains and felt his way round the room to get to his side of the bed, reached it without much ado, got in and fell asleep straightaway.

Chapter 21

Dada sat at the dining table, laughing and talking on the phone. Aaryan came up behind him, patted him on the shoulder. Dada looked up at him and smiled acknowledging him. They were the only two at the table. The others had yet to turn up. Finally, the phone conversation ended and Dada beamed.

'Oh dear god, he is smiling.' Dadi appeared in front of him. 'I wonder what calamity has befallen us now.'

'Soraya. Why is it every time I smile you immediately assume that something has gone wrong? That was Hafiz on the phone. He is in India for a few months and he is passing through here. I have invited him to stay with us for a few days.'

'Hafiz is here? When is he coming?' She bristled at the mention of his name. At every visit he managed to upset the ambience, normally hers.

'They,' he corrected. 'In a few days time. The whole family are staying with Zehra tonight. They intend to make it here for dinner. He will be coming with his sister-in-laws family.'

'We should get the spare rooms ready,' Dadi concluded. She shouted towards the kitchen, 'You three come out here.' Dada was put out at the way she called out.

'Soraya. Don't ever shout like that. They are part of the family, not your servants.' Dadi glared at him.

'You keep out of this Ji. There is much work to be done. If I don't shout then they will be on my head, telling me what to do.' Dada thought for a moment.

'I have to tell you, Soraya. They are coming to see Akilah.'

'What,' Dadi exploded. 'Really?' Dada nodded.

'Yes. Riaz finished his studies last year and now he is working in the family business. The time is right. In the absence of Riaz's father, Hafiz will be coming here to make it official.' Dadi started to get hyper. She hurried in the direction of the kitchen.

'Where have you three gone and died? I called you once already.' She was met by the procession of three, carrying breakfast. They arranged the food on the table and stood by. 'Listen to me and listen to me good.' Dadi's lecture started. 'My cousin will be arriving here with his family in a few days. I want the guestrooms cleaned, new sheets on the beds and the place spotless.' She rattled off more orders. 'I will decide on the food and I don't want any slacking. Understand?' Sabina and Amara nodded silently. Aaryan looked at Hira and wished that he could get into her head right now. Her face was a picture. Shock, confusion and amusement showed. He practically laughed out loud as he imagined what she would be thinking. She caught him looking at her and gave him a knowing look then looked down.

'Hira pay attention,' Dadi demanded. 'You will wash the floors and take the curtains down and wash them by hand.' If Hira was upset she did not show it. Instead it was almost as if she wore a mask. No emotion whatsoever.

'Dadi, what is going on?' Aidan and Alman took their places.

'Hafiz will be coming here to ask for your sister's hand in marriage for his nephew Riaz. Your grandmother is going overboard with the arrangements. Can we eat now?' Dadi sat down grumbling.

'We have got so much to do and you want to eat. I am asking you Ji. Are you taking this seriously or not?' She looked ready to cry.

'Soraya, don't misunderstand me. I am the first to be happy about my grand-daughter's impending engagement. But, I am hungry and you know how I must keep my blood sugars stable.' Almost as if those words brought her out of her state of agitation she turned over his plate, served the food for him and sat down.

'I don't know what I was thinking.' She was almost apologetic. She helped herself to tea and took a sip. 'Where is Akilah?' She asked looking up in the direction of Akilah's bedroom. 'She must still be sleeping. Amara, go and wake her up.'

'Yes Dadiji.' Amara put down the hotpot she was serving from and headed upstairs to Akilah's room.

The room was empty and the bed was made. The windows were open and the curtains were blowing in the gentle breeze. A hand appeared holding onto the ledge on the outside followed by an arm, a leg and then the body. Akilah pulled herself up and fell into the room, landing on the floor. She heard a timid knock on the door, dived into the bed, drawing the blanket over her so that only the top of her head was visible. Amara peered in.

'Akilah,' she called out. 'Everyone is at breakfast and Dadiji is calling for you.' Akilah yawned, almost sat up and stopped herself.

'You go, I shall come down soon,' she replied sleepily.

Amara left the room, shutting the door behind her.

She sprang into action. She went over to the window, scanned past the gates to the lone figure standing beyond. She waved to indicate that things were fine and gestured for them to leave. She then rushed to the bathroom, undressing on the way.

'She was still asleep Dadiji.' Amara informed her. 'She said that she would be down soon.'

'I hope she hurries. I can't wait to tell her.' Dadi smiled at Dada. 'She will be so excited.'

'She will be excited or are you taking her share of the excitement?' Dada laughed.

Breakfast was being cleared away when Akilah deigned to make an appearance.

'Someone was very sleepy.' Aiden commented as she came down the stairs. 'What happened? Didn't get enough sleep?'

Akilah looked concerned for a moment and then composed herself.

'Well I need my beauty sleep.' She sat down. 'Where is my breakfast?'

'Breakfast is where it has always been,' Dada informed her. 'This once, why not sit with your sisters in-law. But before that your Dadiji has something to tell you.' Akilah looked towards her grandmother.

'Akilah beta, I have good news. Hafiz will be visiting here in a few days and guess what?' Akilah was puzzled. Dadi continued happily. 'And he is bringing Riaz with him. Your engagement will be set this weekend if all goes well.' The air left her lungs and she paled.

'What?'

Chapter 22

'Why are you looking so shocked?' Dada asked her. 'It is not as if you weren't aware that this day would come.'

Akilah struggled to find the words. She opened and shut her mouth soundlessly.

'All girls are rendered speechless when they are told an offer of marriage comes through.' Dadi looked sternly at Dada. 'If Akilah does not speak, then there is no law to say that she has to.'

'I don't want to get married,' she said eventually. Dada looked bemused and Dadi gave her a stern look.

'Akilah. All girls must one day marry and leave their parents' home at some point.'

'But this is not my parents' home. It is yours and you said that I did not have to move out after I get married.'

'Stuff and nonsense,' retorted Dada. 'We don't and will not entertain the notion of a ghar jamai,' referring to the lesser known tradition of a son-in-law moving in with the girl's parents after marriage. He looked directly at Dadi. 'Have you been putting stupid ideas into her head?' Dadi ignored Dada and continued her breakfast. Eventually she spoke up.

'We will have to go shopping and get you a couple of new outfits. Be ready after breakfast. We will go to the mall.' Her sisters-in-law appeared from the kitchen. Akilah's eyes darted nervously. There was only one mall that Dadi preferred to go to and it was the very one that she had been banned from. She saw the look that passed from the three and looked angrily at them.

'Dadi. There is more than one mall. But I can't go today. I have got lots of work to do.' Hira coughed. Akilah glared at her then looked at her grandmother with big eyes.

'We can order the clothes and get them delivered. I will ask the jeweller to come to the house so that we may pick out a ring and a set for you.'

Akilah breathed a sigh of relief and sat down, turning her plate over and reached for the food.

'If you have served the food, move from here.' Dadi grumbled. 'You are taking the pleasure out of breakfast and the news.' The three stepped back from the table.

'Soraya!' Dada was appalled at her behaviour. 'They are not

your servants. How would you like it if Akilah was treated the same as you are treating Sabina, Hira and Amara? How would you feel?' Dadi was unrepentant and continued her breakfast silently. Dada looked at them with sad eyes.

'You go and eat your breakfast,' he said to them gently. 'The breakfast dishes will be brought into the kitchen when we are finally done.' He looked at the boys. They nodded in agreement.

'You go.' Aiden told them.

'So much work to do,' Amara moaned as they sat down. 'Dadi will want the place gleaming.'

'It is nothing new, Amara,' Sabina replied wearily. 'Every time we have visitors Dadi will go overboard. Cleaning, cooking. But at least this time it is for a good cause. I shan't be sorry to see the back of Akilah.' Hira sat next to her.

'It is not like you to moan.' She poured a cup of tea and passed it over. Sabina rubbed her forehead.

'Don't mind me. I am just feeling a bit crabby today.' She smiled reassuringly at Hira. 'I'll be fine in a while. I just need some food in my belly and this tea to soothe me.'

'Is that all it is?' Hira looked at her. Sabina laughed.

'That is all. Don't read into things that are not here.' She cradled her cup. Amara sat down with her cup and distributed aloo paranthas from the hotpot.

'At least we can count down the days till the wedding,' she said.

'Don't be too happy. I am sure that our dear sister-in-law will make sure that her presence is felt while she wiles away the hours.' Hira picked up a slice of toast. 'I don't see her mellowing any time just yet.'

'Haven't you three got anything better to do than chat away?' Dadi stood in the doorway. 'Breakfast is done. Go and collect the dishes.' Before they got the chance to put down their spoons and get up, Dada appeared carrying a couple of plates, followed by Aiden, Alman and Aaryan.

'I said that we would bring in the dishes. Let them eat,' he growled. Dadi stepped away and flounced off to her room.

Chapter 23

Hira was scrabbling inside the various trunks in the dusty store room. Under Dadi's watchful eyes she pulled out material after material and placed it in front of her. Dadi looked at the item disdainfully then finally she pointed to a small suitcase high on the shelf. Out of reach even by using the ladder, Hira scaled the high wall using each ledge as a foot hold until she was within grasping distance. Reaching out, she had almost grabbed hold of the case when Amara seeing a spider nearby, screamed as it landed on her making her dance on the spot. Startled, Hira lost her footing and fell to the floor, bringing down the case and other items. Despite herself Dadi shouted out in concern as did Sabina. The screams alerted the others and they rushed to the room, the worry and shock on their faces was evident. Sabina raised a shaky finger.

'Hira.' Sabina pointed tearfully. They quickly removed the pile of bags, baskets, assorted sheets, quilts and other sundry items to get to Hira. When the last item was removed they expected to see an injured Hira underneath, weeping. Rather than weeping, a dusty Hira emerged laughing uncontrollably.

'Hell.' Aiden was amazed. He looked up at the high top shelf where the things had been stored and then back at his sister-in-law.

'Is there anything you don't do?' Aaryan scolded her. She shook her head, trying to control herself. He held out his hands to help, pulled her to her feet and held her close to him so that she would not fall if she was injured. 'Are you hurt?' Her giggling had already set his brothers off and they tried hard to keep a straight face. Dadi's face was a mixture of concern and anger. Aaryan remained composed and authoritative as he tried to get to the root cause of Hira's giggling. 'What was so funny?' Hira wiped her face, stopped her giggles and stepped away.

'I just couldn't get the sight of Amara out of my mind. The last time I saw anything jump like that was when we turned the vacuum on behind our kitten. The poor thing jumped forever before running off.

'You just likened me to a kitten,' Amara said in a small voice. 'What could I do? That spider was massive. Are you sure you are not hurt?'

'I'm sure. I am fine,' Hira reassured her.

'Silence,' Dadi shouted bringing the laughter to an abrupt halt. 'Stop your infernal giggling and pull yourselves together. Stop wasting time. Pick up the bedding so that I can check and see if it is suitable.' Hira smothered her giggles. Each of them picked up a sheet or a quilt and showed it to Dadi for inspection. 'These will be fine. Wash them properly. Once dried, I want them ironed and placed on the beds.' She turned to Hira. 'The curtains can be washed in the machine. After your antics I don't trust you not to drown while washing them.' She turned to her grandsons. 'The three of you can put things back onto the shelves in here. And try not to drop things from the top.' That said she walked out, muttering to herself.

Hira sat on the bed, drying her hair and yawned. The day had been tough. They had washed, cleaned and dusted the place within an inch of its life. Dadi worked them like donkeys. They had all worked hard and it was all they could do to stay awake while serving dinner.

'Tiredness kicking in?' Aaryan stepped into the room. She nodded somewhat sheepishly. 'What are you like?' He admonished her. 'Do you need some painkillers? You took a leap back there.' She declined the tablets. He offered her a glass of water. Feeling thirsty she gulped it down in one go. 'Please tell me that you are not accident prone?' He leant against the wall, arms crossed. She shook her head.

'Not normally.' She replied. 'I used to get into scrapes and stuff when I was a lot younger but that was all. I was always making mum fret. She never knew what type of injury I would return from school with.' She smiled at the memory of her mother waiting for her at the end of the school day with antiseptic and cotton wool to hand. In primary school it was a daily ritual.

He handed her a brown package.

'This arrived for you.' She took it from him, opened and scanned the contents and immediately felt the tears well up. She took a deep breath.

'Can I ask you something?' She snapped out of her thoughts and nodded. He sat down on the bed. 'Every night since you have been here, you have been having nightmares. I look at your behaviour during the day and it does not tie in. Yes, you were spaced out since you got here but I put it down to the culture shock, jet lag and being away from home. You have relaxed recently but at night I still hear

101

you cry. Will you tell me why?' Hira stared at the bed sheet and thought for a while before looking him in the face. Just as she took a deep breath they were disturbed by a knock on the door. Aaryan was irritated as yet again they were disturbed.

'One minute,' he said, got up from the bed and threw the door open. 'What,' he shouted at the unwelcome visitor. Akilah was at the door, disturbing him again. He glared at her, remembering how she had taken up his time with inane chatter, complaints against her sisters-in-laws and being hard done by, by everyone in the world. She smiled at him and then sneered beyond him at Hira on the bed. 'I said. What do you want?'

'Nothing,' she muttered and walked off.

'Annoying, selfish little brat.' He shut the door and pulled the curtain across. 'She had better not come back,' he muttered. He walked back to Hira. 'You were going to say?' He sat again and watched as a myriad of emotions played on her features. For a moment he thought that she would not answer and got ready to accept that.

'I lost my mother a little while ago. During the day I have the luxury of having people around me so I can function ok. My mind is taken up with the day to day chores. But at night I feel so alone.' She looked at him. Her eyes shining, yet no tears fell.

'When did your mother die?' He asked expecting her to say a time frame over the past couple of years.

'July.'

'July of this year?' He stared at her, horrified. They were coming to the middle of October. Hira had flown over in late August. Their vows were taken a couple of weeks before her arrival. He deduced that it would have been soon after the fortieth day. The grieving period had only just ended at that point. Her distance and far-away look of the earlier days was now making sense. She looked so sad and vulnerable sat there that he wanted to take her in his arms and give her a hug. But he held back, not sure as to how the gesture would be received. Instead, he took her hands in his. He studied them and noticed the absence of the adornments that a newly wedded bride would wear. No bangles, no finery, no henna. He remembered that when she arrived she had arrived as Hira. Not as his wife or his intended, just Hira. He stared into her eyes.

'I'm sorry.' It was almost a whisper. 'I was told that your

mother had died but I didn't realise that it was so soon.' He looked embarrassed, uncomfortable even. 'I behaved insensitively towards you. You came here alone and all I did, all we did, was to treat you like an irritation.' He noticed that Hira was silent. He held on to her hands. Finally she looked around the room until her eyes rested on him and he saw that she was not in a position to say anything. He pulled the blanket back and helped her to lie down. 'I'll be right back,' he said as soon as she was comfortable. 'I am going to see Aiden.'

He met Dadi on the landing. She seemed a little flustered.

'Have you seen Akilah?' she asked him. He shook his head.

'She was at my room earlier on, being a pain. I sent her away.'

Dadi looked puzzled.

'She is not in her room,' she replied looking towards her room. 'Anyway leave that. I will find her later. It is good that I have bumped into you. I want to talk to you.' Warning bells sounded for him. Dadi never spoke to him. She always spoke at him. While he could have forgiven her all her past transgressions he could not forget the fact that she had used his grandfather like a pawn to get what she wanted from him. She shuffled off towards the staircase. When she realised that he was not following she called to him.

'Don't just stand there. Come.'

Reluctantly he followed her down the stairs and to the study. She shut the door behind her and turned to him.

'I see that Hira received some post.' He shrugged. It was Hira's post, her business. He surveyed the old woman's face. 'It looked very official. If I am correct then it is the deeds to the acres of land and property that her mother was bequeathed which has now passed on to Hira. I want you to check the papers and if it is, get her to sign the inheritance over to you.'

'Why?' He was well aware of the answer but he was finding it hard to stomach that his grandmother was thinking like this. 'As her husband it practically belongs to me. Why do you want her to sign it over to me?'

Anger flared in Dadi's eyes.

'It needs to be in your name solely. That way it saves any hassles later when you sign it over to me.' She looked at him closely with beady eyes. 'Why are you concerned with Hira all of a sudden? It

103

wasn't long ago that you protested at the mere sight of her. Are you forgetting that we took her on in the absence of a dowry? What has changed?'

'Are you forgetting that she took us on in the absence of the full wedding rituals? And don't forget, you initiated all this so don't start moaning about dowry,' he shot back. His anger taking him back to the day when she had prodded and rushed him through the nikkah ceremony over the phone, telling him that such trivial things did not matter. Her haste to complete the nikkah in record time had irked him. 'And since when have we started to ask for a dowry?' Disgusted by his grandmother's continued behaviour he had to step away from the old lady.

How much lower was she prepared to go? Wasn't it bad enough that she played with his emotions to get what she wanted? He asked himself.

'I will ask no such thing,' he eventually said. 'If she chooses to share it with me, then that is her business, but I will not push her.' Not waiting to hear any more he left her standing alone, fuming.

Hira was tossing as she slept, knowing the reason he was no longer irritated. He turned over and faced her. Tentatively he reached out, about to stroke her forehead. To somehow soothe the pain of what she was feeling. He hesitated. Instead he held her good hand, holding it close to him and watched her. The small gesture had a calming effect on her and her distress lessened somewhat. Facing her, he also fell asleep.

Chapter 24

Standing by the bed in the guest bedroom Hira yawned. Armed with clean sheets and cases her job was to make the beds. Dadi walked in as she was on her third yawn.

'Don't waste valuable time standing there and yawning. Make the beds.' She scrutinised Hira, watching her closely to see if there was a cause for her tiredness. 'Did you not sleep last night?' she asked. She mulled whether it was worth her while to separate her from her grandson for the time being. It seemed like he was getting far too close for her liking. She resolved to move Hira into another room after the guests had left.

'Sorry Dadij,' she apologised, putting the cases on the ottoman and shaking out the sheet and throwing it over the mattress, gingerly working around it as she tucked in the ends despite the pain in her hand.

'Not used to hard work,' Dadi scoffed and watched on as Hira added the top sheet, smoothed it to an almost mirror finish and put the pillow cases on. 'Hmm, do the other beds quickly. This is the list of the chores to be done.' She handed over yet another crumpled sheet of paper. Hira took it and read with a sinking heart. 'Only when you have finished all the chores on the list, can you have some time to yourself. Hafiz and his family won't be here until seven on the day. If you are going back out into that garden or yours make sure you are presentable in good time and don't lose track of time. The rest of the food will need to be cooked.'

'All these tasks?' Hira looked at Dadi. She noted that many of them had been duplicated, having been completed the day before.

'*This was inhumane,*' she thought to herself.

'Don't make such a fuss. I can always add on a few more,' Dadi threatened. With a sad nod Hira moved on to make the beds in the other rooms. It had been quite a while since she had the opportunity to work in her garden and with the list handed to her it looked like it would be even longer till she would be able to spend some time there. Silently, Hira moved away to carry out the next task. Dadi looked at her retreating figure, her features dark and brooding.

'Hello. Is anyone home?' Mrs Bharat stood at the open door and peered in. She beamed as Sabina came into view.

105

'Mrs Bharat? Greetings, please do come in.' She led her in and invited her to sit. 'It is so lovely to see you. What can we do for you?' Mrs Bharat looked around then focused back on Sabina who was joined by Hira.

'I was passing through on my way to the city and I thought that perhaps you or your sisters-in-laws would like to come with me. I met Hira the night of the party and thought that it would be nice to meet my neighbours. We hardly see any of you as it is, such a sad situation.' She tutted. 'There is a function tomorrow at the park near the school. The school children have made beautiful decorations and it is all in a good cause. We are raising money to build a shelter in the playground so that the children have some shade to play in on the hottest days. Will you come?' Their eyes lit up and they beamed, looking forward to spending some time in company.

'Absolutely not.' Dadi emerged from the corridor leading from her room. 'My granddaughters-in-law have got better things to do that waste time at your functions.'

Mrs Bharat's face showed her disappointment and her displeasure. Her previous altercations with Dadi always left her with a bad taste in her mouth. Time and time again she had extended the hand of friendship only to have the offer thrown back in her face in the most rudest of manners. But for the sake of the young girls in the house she tried to include them in the community's functions.

'Soraya Aunty, how long can you keep them in the house constantly? They are young girls and should be able to enjoy themselves at times. Not be tied to the kitchen sink all the time. It is just a function and one that is close to home. What is the harm in that?' Hira took the opportunity to try and pacify Dadi.

'Dadiji, please can we go? Mrs Bharat says that it is close to home and for a good cause.' If looks could kill Hira would have died there and then. 'If we finish all our chores then what is the harm?' Dadi continued to glare.

'I have made my decision and I will not budge. Nobody from this family is going to any function. I will not allow it.'

'Why?' Hira stood her ground. Sabina immediately put out her hand and stopped Hira from saying anything else. Mrs Bharat stood up.

'I guess it is not to be,' she said sadly. 'But if you change your mind just come along.'

'There will be no changing of minds.' Dadi re-iterated. 'I suggest you take yourself off and do some dogooding elsewhere.' Mrs Bharat shot her a look of contempt before saying goodbye to the girls.

Disappointed Sabina and Hira watched as she left.

'Hira!' Dadi shouted. 'Have you forgotten that you have plenty of work to do? While you are at it you can also scrub down the floors in all the main bathrooms. I want them gleaming.'

Hira looked at her perplexed.

'This woman had a tyrannical mentality,' she thought. *'Work, work, work and that too from other people. Her idea of relaxation must be in deciding which whip to use.'*

'Hira what are you thinking?' Dadi barked. 'The sooner you start the sooner you will finish. There will be other work too.' Before she could stop herself the words came out.

'Why do we have to work ourselves to the bone? This is not a normal existence. Why are we made to work like donkeys?"

Sabina looked on open mouthed.

Dadi, for all her lack of stature drew herself a little higher.

'Who are you to question me? If it wasn't for me you would not have a roof over your head. Instead you would be roaming around on the streets of London with nowhere to go. Your mother was never one to think ahead,' she taunted. 'Say one word and I will have your mouth washed out with soap,' she warned her. Hira backed down. Not so much for the threat of having soap put in her mouth but for the fact that her mother's memory was being disrespected.

Chapter 25

Dadaji, Aiden and Alman chatted excitedly as they arrived home. In their hands they held flyers for the gathering that Mrs Bharat had spoken of.

'I think it is a great idea,' Aiden enthused. 'We don't get a chance to do many things. This will be good.'

'And a good chance to network.' Aaryan joined them. 'For a long time we have not even met with our neighbours. We could go out after dinner. What do you say?' Dada, Aiden and Alman smiled.

'Excellent. We should tell the girls.'

Dadi glared as the family gathered at the main door. She had failed and saw it as a defeat at the hands of Hira. As the family headed off towards the school she closed the door on them. There was no way she was going to join in with the festivities.

Mrs Bharat beamed as she saw the family make their way. She rushed towards them.

'I am so happy that you could make it,' she told them. 'Mingle. Everyone is here and the children have worked hard with all the stalls. Enjoy.'

There were lots of different stalls. Some selling foodstuffs, drinks, handmade trinkets and various games one played in order to win a prize. The centrepiece of the event was the rides. Children chattered excitedly as they climbed aboard, in their minds' eyes they were embarking on a journey of a lifetime.

Aaryan picked up a plate of chaat, passed it to Hira and picked up a plate of samosas for himself and found room to sit on one of the various benches. The others had decided that they wanted to see the array stalls but Aaryan had seen Hira yawning and thought that it was better to sit. He offered her a samosa while at the same time she offered him some chaat.

'This is nice.' She looked at the crowds mingling.

'It is,' he agreed. 'Good that it is helping out the local school. Did you have anything like this in the UK?'

'Different cities had various functions. Mum and I didn't really live among the Asian community until much later. We went to a lot of theatres, museums, cinemas and stuff. Theme parks were our thing.' She smiled remembering the times they had visited places like Thorpe Park and Chessington simply to try out new rides.

'So this must be a gear down for you,' Aaryan remarked. Hira shook her head.

'Why do you say that? It is no different to the school fayres we used to attend. I remember there was one where there was a chance to do some horse riding.' Just at that moment the crowd parted and a donkey was seen giving rides to young children. 'So what did you used to get up to as a child?' Aaryan shrugged.

'Not much. Mostly things like this were discouraged but Dadaji loved them. If he went then he took us with him but it wasn't very often. Half the time we just played football in the garden or just played in the house. Friends weren't exactly welcome at home.' Hira nodded. She didn't find that strange after what she had witnessed today. They finished their snacks.

'Do you want an ice gola?' He asked her.

'A what?' She hadn't come across such a thing before.

'Come with me.' He took her by the arm. 'I'll show you.' They stopped by a stall where the vendor had a large block of ice. When requested he shaved off slivers of ice into a plastic cup, added some syrup and handed one to her.

'Oh this,' Hira exclaimed. 'You call them ice golas? We had something a little similar. I used to call them slushies.' She sucked on a corner of the ice and nodded. 'Yep. Still tastes the same.'

'You sound like you have had these a few times.'

Hira nodded. They walked, enjoying the ices as they perused the various stalls. Her eyes alighted on a pretty necklace set with green stones. Aaryan noticed.

'Do you like it?'

'It is nice.' Hira was reluctant to admit liking it. 'But I can't possibly buy it.'

Aaryan looked confused. 'Why?'

Hira felt uncomfortable. She squirmed a little before she explained.

'I don't have any money of my own. Previously I earned my keep and spent how and where I wanted. I can't buy it.'

'Nonsense,' Aaryan retorted, taking money out from his wallet and handing over the required amount. 'I should have done this earlier. From now on I will give you an allowance.'

'But I can't...' Hira protested.

'Not another word. If I am responsible for you then I am responsible for your keep.' He took the necklace. 'Do you want to put this on now?' There was something in his voice that told her that the matter was not up for negotiation. Eventually she nodded and turned round so that he could put the necklace on her. 'It suits you,' he complimented.

Before she got a chance to reply, the sound of music assailed their ears followed by an announcement that a dancing programme would soon take place and invited, nay cajoled, couples to participate. They jostled with the others reaching the edge of the throng that stood to watch the participants. From the feel good Punjabi bhangra to the various dances enacted in many sangeets and weddings. Hira stood and watched, clapping in time to the music.

'Have you taken part in any dancing before?' She turned to Aaryan and shook her head.

'Not this. My preferences went as far as the school and uni discos. I have only stood on the sidelines and watched the dancing during Navratri.' He spied dhandiyas being handed out.

'Do you want to give it a go?' Hira looked at him in surprise.

'Really, you don't seem the sort to let your hair down and dance.' He handed her the two sticks.

'What sort would that be?' He teased before leading her into the circle.

They were joined by other couples as well as Sabina and Amara with their respective husbands. Hira smiled excitedly. As the music started up she relied on her memory of the moves and soon she was in the thick of it, whirling, tapping the dhandiya in time with her partner and letting herself go.

In the midst of the dancing she felt a hand on her shoulder. As she turned she felt the sting of a slap on her face, causing her to stagger back a little. A shocked silence prevailed as the crowd took in what had just happened.

Chapter 26

Dadi stood before her. Her face so dark with anger she practically shook.

'Who gave you permission to dance? Look at you, acting like a shameless dancing girl.'

Aaryan was mortified. He stood in front of Hira. A barrier between her and his grandmother in case the woman took it upon herself to mete out some more slaps.

'I gave her permission to dance,' he told her through gritted teeth. 'If you had bothered to look around you, you will see that there are others dancing, enjoying themselves. What right do you have to behave like that?'

Dadi gasped momentarily but composed herself.

'As her elder I have every right if she is bringing disrepute to the house.'

Aaryan advanced one step.

'As her husband my rights supersede yours.'

Hira looked from one to the other. Part of her wanted to jump in and say that she had rights too but she kept silent.

'I asked her to take part and did it escape your notice that I was taking an active part too?'

Dadi backed down in the face of his questions.

'It is unislamic,' she muttered. He took a sharp intake of breath.

'Don't bring out the religion card,' he told her. 'You are in the wrong and you know it.'

She was being confronted and didn't take to it very well. Without replying, she turned on her heel and walked off leaving the crowd muttering among each other.

He turned to Hira. 'Are you okay?'

Dada pushed his way into the circle. 'What happened?' he asked, oblivious to the scene that had played out. 'I heard that there was an altercation.' Hira was still in shock. She looked beyond the crowd to where Dadi had disappeared.

'Can we go home?' she whispered, acutely aware of the looks and comments that she was getting. Aaryan sensed her discomfort and nodded.

'You have nothing to be ashamed about,' he whispered to her.

'Don't worry. I will deal with Dadi.'

'Aaryan Beta? What is wrong with your grandmother?' An elderly neighbour walked up to him as they tried to leave. 'Such anger, what did the poor child do?' He looked on in sympathy and confusion. Hira felt suffocated with the looks of pity and the attention. She faltered. Not sure whether to diffuse the situation by covering for Dadi's behaviour or make excuses for her. In the end she smiled weakly at the old man.

'It is something and nothing?' she told him. The old man looked puzzled.

'What type of an answer is that?' He moved his hands animatedly. He had not heard this phrase before. Aaryan tried his best to explain.

'Uncleji, it is the only answer that makes sense.' He took Hira by the elbow and led her away.

They walked back to the house in silence. Aaryan slowly seething, Hira slightly bemused. Then it came to her. This was payback for suggesting going along in the first place. Dadi had forbidden them but did not bank on the rest of the family agreeing unanimously to attend. Inwardly she groaned.

'What would Dadi have in store for her next?'

Aaryan seemed to sense Hira's predicament.

'Try not to worry,' he assured her. 'I will deal with Dadi.' Hira held back causing Aaryan to turn back.

'Aaryan, it will only make things worse.' He felt for her but there was a resolve within him to do what was right.

'Don't think like that.' He assured her. 'I'll sort things out and there will be no comeback for you.' He looked towards the house. 'Dadi needs us more than we need her.'

'What you did out there was disgusting, unbecoming and downright rude,' he confronted Dadi as soon as they entered.

'Shut up. Who do you think you are, behaving like such a big man thinking that you can make up your own rules!'

'Who do I think I am?' He stepped forward. 'In case you are forgetting I am the elder of the grandsons and part owner of this property.' He expanded his arms covering the vast size of the interior.

'If I choose I can extradite you from here. All I have to do is tell Dadaji what ruse you pulled to get the nikkah ceremony to take place. I am sure that he would be very interested to hear.'

Dadi gasped shocked by what she had heard. Uneasiness gripped her for she knew that if her husband ever found out what she had done then the chances were that he might disown her. For all her bluster she did care what her husband thought. While she could placate him she had no fear. In all the years Dada had reprimanded her but never said an angry word to her.

'You wouldn't dare,' she bluffed, glancing furtively towards Hira and then back at Aaryan.

'Try me.' He made for the kitchen. 'One other thing, if you single Hira out for any punishment out of spite then I won't stay silent. You don't treat another human being the way you do and expect to get away with it.'

Chapter 27

The main door clattered. Dada stood in the doorway. His face contorted with pain. He was breathless and his lips had a blue tinge to them.

'Aaryan.' Hira rushed forward. 'Dadaji doesn't look well.' Aaryan looked closer at his grandfather and he too rushed forward.

'Dadaji.' They got hold of him and led him to the sofa. Dadi came out of her mood and quickly grabbed a glass of water.

'Here drink this,' she offered. He waved it away. 'Lie him down.' She put down the glass and took his shoes off and forced him to lie down.

'No,' Hira said. 'It is better for him to be sitting up. If he lies down there would be too much pressure on his chest and his heart. Has he had this before?' she asked.

'No,' Aaryan told her. 'This is the first time.' Hira turned and grimaced at him.

'We will need to get him to the hospital,' she whispered. Aaryan understood.

'I'll get the driver.' He ran off to organise transport. In the meantime Hira rubbed his hands, turning them over and looking to see if there was any change to the blue tinge she was seeing.

'I told you to lie him down. What nonsense is this in keeping a sick man sitting up?' She put her hands on his shoulders and tried to push him back onto the sofa.

'I know what I am doing Dadiji. He needs to be sat up. Laying him flat will not help him in this instance. Let me do what I have to.'

Dadi stood back allowing Hira to take charge.

'Dadaji, listen to me. I will try and help you. On a scale of 1 to 10 how bad is your pain.'

Dada held up seven fingers.

Hira nodded. 'Where is the pain?'

Dada indicated the length of his left arm.

'In the jaw as well, chest?'

He nodded.

'Do we have any aspirin?' she asked Dadi. No reply. Dadi appeared to be in a trance. 'I said do we have any aspirin?' Hira's voice rose a decibel or two. Dadi came back to the present. She

114

hurried off in search for the medicine box bringing it back in record time and holding it out to Hira, her eyes imploring her to do her best.

Hira took the box, found the aspirin, checked the expiry date and took a tablet from the pack.

'Dadaji, I am going to give you some aspirin. Don't chew. Keep it under your tongue.'

'The car is at the front.' Aaryan rushed in. 'I have called Alman. He will let the others know and will be here soon.' Dada appeared to have calmed down a little, his breathing not as laboured as before. 'Will you come with us?' He asked her. 'You seem to know what you are doing.' Hira nodded.

'Dadaji, we are taking you to the hospital now.' Dada moved his hands as if to dismiss the need. 'Just to get you checked over.' She told him. 'Don't worry. We are coming with you.' With Aaryan on one side, they led Dada to the waiting car.

Dadi's legs felt like jelly. She sat down heavily on the sofa
'I will wait here for Alman and Aiden.' There wasn't a moment to pacify her. Time was short and the important thing was to get Dada to the hospital and in the best possible care.

They met the rest of the family as they drew up to the main gate. Aaryan leant out of the window.

'Dadi is in there. Get the other car and meet us at the hospital.' Without waiting for an answer he sped off.

At the hospital he parked at the entrance and ran in to get and orderly and a wheelchair. Within minutes Dada had been admitted and the doctors were brought up to speed on the history, events, monitoring and the medication given. He was taken to a treatment room, put on a monitor and further investigations were carried out.

Hira took her place on the hard metal chairs in the corridor and waited. Aaryan sat next to her.

'Where did you know how to do all that?' He was somewhat in awe. She had taken control of the situation so calmly.

'First Aid was a necessity Mum used to say. She enrolled me in classes since the age of 10. We covered all medical emergencies. It is a handy thing to know.' He held her hand.

'You did extremely well. Thank you.' He looked deep into her eyes and she saw the gratitude within them. She placed her other hand over his and shook her head.

'He is my grandfather too. There is no need for thanks.'

Concerned chatter filtered down the corridor, causing them to move apart. Aiden and Alman rushed in closely followed by Sabina, Amara and Dadi. Mrs Bharat and a number of other people from the fair were hot on their heels.

'Aaryan?' Aiden was the first to reach him. 'How is Dadaji? What happened? People said that he was talking with his friends one minute and the next he became quiet and breathless and walked off. We got your call as we were searching for him. We didn't realise that he had come home.' Aaryan indicated towards the treatment room.

'They are running some tests. But it is likely that this was to do with his heart.' He looked at Hira gratefully. 'Hira knew exactly what to do. She was really good.' They looked at her with the same gratitude as Aaryan. She gave them a look as if to tell them to man up, got up and walked over to the door and peered in through the window. Dada was on the bed hooked up to the heart monitor and oxygen while the doctor attended to him. She placed her hand on the glass reaching out to him.

***

'We are not quite sure as to the extent of your mother's condition,' The junior doctor informed her as she looked helplessly at her mother. 'The next 48 hours are extremely crucial. We need her to wake up. Perhaps if you sit with her she might notice your presence and come round.'

'Was it a stroke?'

She looked at the figure on the bed. He opened the door for her.

'We can't tell at this point,' he told her. 'There is some bruising which would indicate that she may have hit her head and there was a clot too. A further scan showed that she is bleeding into the brain. With all things added up we are not sure how well she will

116

recover. The prognosis does not look good.'

Hira's feet felt like lead. With difficulty she moved towards the bed. A lump rising in her throat as she saw her once strong mother reduced to a shadow of her former self. Despite her fears she sat with her and started to talk. She knew that she was not making sense and was babbling away. But she was hoping beyond hope that her mother would wake and tell her to quieten her inane chatter. But it never came. The only sounds to be heard were those of the heart monitor and the sound of other equipment fighting to keep her alive. As she held her mother's hand in hers, she kissed it and wept, pleading at the same time for her to open her eyes.

***

The door opened and Hira snapped back to the present, quickly wiping the tears from her face.

'Don't cry, Beta.' The kindly doctor smiled at her. 'Your grandfather is going to be alright. He is responding well to the treatment. By the grace of god he was blessed to have a learned person with him.' The family rushed forward. The doctor let the door close behind him. 'Your grandfather is very likely to have suffered a minor cardiac episode. We have carried out a trace of his heart rhythm and run blood tests. The trace shows an irregularity in the beginning but it is now more settled. We have given him some medication along with the aspirin you had already given and will run a blood test twelve hours after the initial onset of the pain. Either way, given his risk factors and medical history we would like to keep him in for a few days to monitor him continuously. If there is no repeat of his symptoms then we will send him home with medication and follow up appointments.'

A collective sigh of relief went up after which the emotions which had lain buried due to concern came to the fore and they all hugged and offered a prayer of thanks to god for seeing their grandfather safely through this episode after which they all piled in to see him. The nurse was removing the electrodes as she unhooked him from the machine and removed the oxygen mask.

'No too long.' She warned them. 'Mr Dajani needs to rest.'

'I thought my time was up,' He told them. 'I just felt this pain and knew that I needed to go home.' He looked at his grandchildren. They were all there. Bar one. Dadi held back. A little figure dwarfed among her grandsons. 'Where is Akilah?'

'She must be asleep,' Dadi said. 'We rushed out of the house in such a rush.' Dada nodded and closed his eyes. 'You all go home and rest. I shall be fine. The hospital will call if anything happens.'

'I'd rather that nothing happens,' Alman spoke up. 'I mean we'd rather that .....'

'I know what you meant.' Dada told him. 'Now go home. I shall see you in the morning. Go.'

They split up between the two cars. Aiden and Alman decided to go together with their respective wives. Dadi held back. Aaryan looked at her.

'I suppose you had better come with us.' He opened the back door for her, helped her in and opened the passenger side door for Hira. 'Let's go home. We should all try and get some sleep. In the morning I shall ring Grand Aunt Zehra's place and let them know what has happened. It is better to postpone the meeting for Akilah's alliance for a little while.' There was hardly a peep from Dadi. He observed her through the rear view mirror. She was shaken up. He decided that he would go easy on her.

Dadi didn't stop to speak to the family. Immediately she headed for her bedroom. Hira started to go after her. Aaryan held her back.

'Let her go Hira,' He told her. 'Dadi needs to be alone. She won't appreciate your gesture.' He walked towards the staircase. 'Are you coming?'

'Won't she need someone with her?' Hira asked. Aaryan turned back.

'It won't be you,' he told her. 'Don't drop yourself into the jaws of a wounded dog. You will only get hurt.' Hira understood what he was trying to say.

'We should sleep too. Dadaji won't want a family of zombies at his bedside. Goodnight all.' Everyone murmured their replies and headed off to bed. The heavy doors were locked and the lights in the hallway were turned off for the night.

Chapter 28

Aaryan put the call through to Grand Aunt Zehra the following morning after he had spoken to the hospital and asked after Dadaji's progress. Thankfully there was no repeat of his symptoms during the night. He relayed the message to the rest of the family. Now he walked up and down the length of the dining table and imparting the information of last night's events to Grand Aunt Zehra and updating her with the recent reports from the hospital. At long last he cut the call.

Akilah surfaced from her bedroom. Immediately she sensed the tension in the air and looked around for Dadi to try and glean from her the reason for the mood. Dadi was not to be seen. She looked at her brothers, puzzled.

'What has happened?' She looked from one to the other. 'Is there something I should be aware of?' Aiden looked surprised.

'You didn't hear anything that happened?' She shook her head.

'I was sleeping,' she muttered.

She quickly looked away knowing full well that it was a lie for she had gone out to party with her friends. She had heard the commotion last night and seen Aaryan drive out at speed. She had secreted herself amongst the shrubbery near the gate, giving thanks that she was not seen as she slipped out of the house to yet another night of merriment with her friends. Alman narrated the events of last night and watched in astonishment as his sister just nodded.

'Don't you want to know how Dadaji is doing?' he asked her. Akilah awoke from her trance like state.'

'What?' Alman sighed in exasperation and sat down, shaking his head.

'For your information he is doing well.' Akilah picked up a bowl from the table, helped herself to the food.

'OK.' She walked away with the bowl only to be confronted by Dadi.

'You will eat at the table like everyone else,' she told her, pointing her back towards the table.

The events of last night seemed to have an effect on Dadi. Although she kept her feelings well hidden, they knew that she was worried. Apart from a certain silence, she grumbled about the food. Hira decided that it would be better to give Dadi a wide berth. As it was she did not have to make any special arrangements. Dadi got up from the dining table, picked up her teacup and headed off towards her room. Aaryan saw the looks which passed through the family.

'I'll go and talk to her,' he conceded. He did not think for one moment that she would make any effort to speak to them. As always he would make the first move.

The door was ajar as always. He stood at the threshold and waited for her to acknowledge him.

'What do you want?' If he was surprised at her behaviour he did not show it.

'You have been quiet since last night. I just wanted to see that you were alright.'

She got up from the bed.

'Why would you be concerned? She walked up to him. 'It was last night that you were stood out there in that hall and told me that I was wrong, that you would tell everything to your Dadaji. Why the concern now?' She put her hand on the door. 'I don't need your words. Keep them to yourself.' She closed the door on him.

'Spiteful woman,' he muttered to himself and stomped off. 'Well two can play at that game.'

Grabbing his case he made for the door, closely followed by his brothers. He stopped for a moment and turned around.

'Shall we go to the cinema?' he asked.

'That is random,' Hira said. 'Are you sure?'

Aaryan nodded. Hira looked at the others.

'All of us?' he smiled and nodded.

'Sounds like a really good idea.' Hira replied.

'Excellent, we can pop in and see Dadaji tonight and then go onto the cinema.'

'You know? That is a nice thought?' Aiden suggested. 'As it is we haven't been anywhere like that in quite some time.'

Aaryan agreed. 'We'll make an evening of it. Be ready at five. Bye.'

Hira beamed at her sisters-in-law. They would all have a nice evening and be able to relax outside of the house. It would make such a change. The evening was worth looking forward to but before then there were still the usual chores to be done.

Dadi did not surface the whole day. Food and drink was left for her on the side table outside her room, which she took but continued to sulk the whole day. Hira actually found it quite refreshing. Not having Dadi standing over her while she carried out her chores and hearing her taunts. Akilah sensed the lighter mood and attempted to dampen their happiness until she too gave up and retired to her room. Dadi had not entertained her interruptions either.

Chapter 29

Dadaji looked up as his grandchildren trooped into his room. He pushed aside his newspaper, beamed at them and held his arms out to embrace each and every one of them.

'My wonderful children,' he greeted them. 'How are you all?' They stood around his bed and fussed over him.

'Never mind how we are? Alman told him. 'How are you? What have the doctors said?'

'I have been told that the doctors are doing their rounds now. Sooner or later they will get to me.'

Hira picked up the file from the bottom of the bed and flicked through it.

'Dadaji? What is this?' she asked him. 'You refused to do some simple exercises?'

Dada looked sheepish. 'They wrote that on there? The truth is I find them tiresome. Turn your ankle one way and then another. What use is that?'

'It is to help your circulation Mr Dajani.' The doctor entered the room with his team and took the file from Hira. 'Tiresome it is but with your medical history it is important.' He flicked through the reports. 'Well Mr Dajani. Since you were admitted there have been no further episodes of chest pain or breathlessness all a good sign.'

Dada looked at him in anticipation. He put the file back in his place and peered at him. 'We may let you go home soon but will ask that you attend our cardiac clinic for follow up appointments. However, to be on the safe side I would like to keep you in for tonight just to make sure.' He turned to Aaryan. 'Telephone the nurses' station tomorrow afternoon to check. If everything is fine we will let you know and you can take your grandfather home in the evening.' He looked at Dadaji sternly. 'Provided that he does his exercises.' Chastised Dada started to rotate his ankles.

'If this is what it takes to graduate from here then so be it.' The doctor smiled.

'If all else is fine, I will present you with your certificate myself. I shall check in again tomorrow. Good evening.'

'That is encouraging.' Aaryan turned to Dada. 'I will come by with a change of clothes for you too.'

Dada looked at the smiling faces.

'Are you all going somewhere?'

'Aaryan hit upon the idea to go to the cinema.' Aiden smiled. Dada's eyes lit up.

'So glad that you are behaving like normal couples,' he said approvingly. 'I worried that you would just be boring and work all the time.' He joked and looked at the time. 'You had better go now. You don't want to be missing the start. Go on.'

As they were leaving the hospital Aiden took Aaryan to one side.

'Aaryan, do you and Hira want to spend some time together? We can go elsewhere?'

Aaryan looked surprised. 'Idiot,' he said eventually. 'If I wanted to be alone with Hira don't you think I would have told you to make your own plans?' He had a thoughtful look on his face. 'Who knows? It might still be possible. What do you think of this as an option?' Aiden listened as Aaryan relayed his suggestion.

'Good idea. Shall we go?'

They stood in the multiplex and perused the advertisements, deciding on which film to watch.

'Do you have a preference?' Alman turned to Amara who in turn smiled shyly.

'Romance,' she stated shyly, her eyes downcast.

'I'd like to see some comedy,' Sabina suggested. 'Hira what would you like to see? Comedy or Romance?' Hira studied the banners around her.

'They are all, all singing and dancing.' She noticed. 'But I would like to see that one.' She picked out her choice. Aaryan looked pleased but, that left them with a three way split.

'So what are we going to do?' Amara asked with uncertainty.

'We will watch a movie,' Aaryan said. 'There is nothing to say we all have to watch the same one. You watch whichever movie you want. Hira and I will see this one.'

He took Hira by the hand. 'Shall we meet later?' Without stopping for their reply he walked away.

Armed with drinks and popcorn they settled themselves in their seats and waited for the movie to start.

'What made you decide on this one?' Aaryan asked her. Hira relaxed back in her seat and took a sip of her drink.

'I just fancied something a little out of the ordinary. I have not seen a lot of hindi movies with a supernatural theme. It won't bore you will it?' He shook his head.

'To tell you the truth I am just happy to be out of the house. I guess you must be too.' Before she got a chance to reply the lights went down and they settled to watch the movie.

Hira wiped her eyes as they emerged from the screening. Aaryan looked at her in wonder. He shook his head.

'You are the first woman that I have met who will sit through a serious movie such as this and still find something to laugh about.'

'I am sorry,' she apologised. 'But I wasn't the only one laughing. That movie is going to become a huge cult classic.'

'True.' He had laughed as well, as had the rest of the audience. The movie, although advertised as supernatural had unintentionally become a comedy due to below par props, mis-timing by the actors and mis-interpretation by the audience. What had started out as a b grade movie was now a hit with the audience in its new guise as a comedy.

Aaryan took out his phone and tapped out a text message.

'Let's go.' He led her out of the multiplex.

'What about the others?' She looked back.

'They will be fine,' he assured her. 'They have their own arrangements. Come on. I am starving.'

They took their places at a restaurant near the multiplex.

'This is nice,' she commented as the waiter brought along their drinks and complimentary papadoms with chutney. She encircled the glass with her hands.

'How does this fare with what you have in the UK?' He asked her. She looked at him oddly.

'Compare? Restaurants are restaurants.' She told him. 'But why do you want me to compare?' She asked him. He sat forward.

'I am just curious. In the UK you must have ample

opportunity to visit places like these.'

'And I thought you were a man of the world,' she teased. 'Is it fair to compare? I am not doing that at all, although at times I have thought to myself of where I have ended up.' Hira saw his expression change. She realised that there must be a reason for his questioning. It wasn't the first time he asked her about comparisons. She looked at him and wondered if he felt insecure with her previous life. Her aunt had told her many times of the misconceptions that many Indian men harboured towards girls from overseas. Deep down she was disappointed that perhaps he felt the same. Deciding to tackle the situation head on she spoke. 'Is this your way of asking me if I used to go out with boys?' She scanned his face for any change.

'Am I that obvious?'

Hira nodded.

'I'm sorry.'

Hira shrugged. At least he was up front. 'It doesn't matter, but for the record. I had boys as friends in Uni but no one exclusive. There was a whole group of us. We went to cinemas, restaurants, museums. Life is different over there but my values aren't that much different to yours.' Aaryan sat back feeling bad that she had felt the need to explain.

'I'm sorry. I didn't mean to make you feel bad. I guess I am being insensitive and making assumptions. If I promise not to bring the matter up will you agree not to hold it against me?'

Hira smiled.

'I guess I can agree to that.' The waiter arrived with their food and placed it in front of them. Hira's mouth watered at the mere sight. Placing some food on her plate she tucked in.

'Nice to see you with a healthy appetite, can I ask you a question?' Hira fork stopped midway. She looked at him. 'I just want to know what type of life you led. What you studied? Did in your free time. Music that you listened to? No talk about boyfriends, alright?' She put down her fork and sat back, prepared to impart with parts of her personal life.

'What can I tell you? I attended high school till the age of 18, went on to university and graduated with a degree in landscape architecture. I like most music as long as it has a decent beat. I am not consigned to any one genre; the same with films.'

'That explains your interest in the garden.' He fiddled with his

126

fork. In her mind Hira questioned what other line of questioning he was going to ask.

'Do you have more questions?' she asked him. He shook his head.

'To be totally honest with you, I feel really bad about making assumptions about you.'

'And I said that I would not hold it against you. Let us start afresh. My name is Hira and I have newly arrived in India.' She held out her hand. He smiled, taking her hand.

'How do you do, I am Aaryan Dajani.' The other diners looked on. Hira laughed.

'Can we continue eating? The food is getting cold,' Aaryan called over the waiter.

'Can you reheat this dish? It has gone cold and may we have two more glasses of juice?' The waiter nodded and took the cold food away. Hira scanned the restaurant for Sabina and Amara.

'They haven't come,' she spoke out loud.

'Hmm?' He realised who 'they' were and thought to come clean. 'They've gone to different restaurants. We will meet them at the car in due course. This here, was solely meant for me and you. After all, we have to start somewhere. Don't we?' Hira relaxed. It would be her turn to do some grilling and she would make sure that the questions would be super awkward. She smiled at him sweetly. He would have to answer her questions just as she had done.

It was past midnight when they finally made it home. Yawning, they waited for someone to open the door, but as soon as the door opened they began to wish that they had decided to stay out longer.

'So you decided to take advantage of my silence.' Dadi barred their way. 'I should expect nothing more.' She stood to one side. 'Especially now that the rot has really set in.' She looked pointedly at Hira. 'What was I thinking?' They gathered inside not sure whether to reason with Dadi or to retire to bed. She continued to rant and rave at her granddaughters-in-law, cursing their families, their upbringing, their morals and their lack of respect towards her. Eventually, she made the decision for them. 'What are you standing here for? Get to bed. But be sure to get up before dawn for your chores. You have lapsed today. I will have no more slacking.'

'Dadi why are you shouting so much?' Akilah peered over the bannister sleepily. 'You are disturbing my sleep.' Dadi pointed towards the girls. 'Blame them.' She continued to shout. 'They have been out all evening and are coming home now. Shameless.' For the first time Aiden showed his irritation.

'They were out with us. Why are you being so unreasonable? Husbands and wives go out with each other all the time. We are not doing anything wrong.' Dadi rounded on him.

'Silence!' She shouted. 'This is all your doing?' She accused Hira. 'You are turning my family against me.' Aaryan stepped between the two.

'You are doing this to yourself.' He told her. 'No one behaves in the way you do.' He grabbed Hira by the hand and made his way upstairs. 'Oh and just in case you say we didn't tell you. Dadaji may be coming home tomorrow.' He didn't wait for her answer or her reaction. He had no time for her tantrums.

Hira watched as Aaryan angrily got ready for bed. He sat down and shook his head totally at a loss. His grandmother's attitude had got worse over the years, granted. But in recent days it had got worse. She was reaching the point where one would think that she was becoming unbalanced and the catalyst seemed to be Hira. His anger dissipated a little as he thought of how Hira was feeling. Whatever she did was wrong in the eyes of the old woman. He held out his hand, took hers and made her sit beside him.

'Dadi is going to be gunning for you.' He was almost apologetic. 'I will try my utmost to shield you, but I can't be around all the time. Will you promise me that you will take care?' Hira sighed heavily.

'Aaryan anything I do will wind her up. I don't understand what it is I have done wrong. But between you and me, how long can I live like this? Not just me but Sabina and Amara too. They are treated worse than maids. Why even call us wives?' He studied the palm of her hand.

'Hopefully things will calm down after Akilah's future is decided. I have had a feeling for quite a while that Dadi and Akilah feed off each other. All negative thoughts towards others are manifested threefold when those two are together.'

Hira nodded. Deep down, she was not convinced.

'I think we had better get some sleep, especially if Dadiji is intent on waking us up before dawn.'

Chapter 30

Dada walked through the main doors with a huge smile on his face. His stay in hospital had been extended by a couple more days but eventually he was declared fit to be discharged. He removed his shoes and took his place on the sofa and surveyed his surroundings. Excited chatter reached his ears as Hira, Sabina and Amara became aware of his presence. They rushed out to welcome him home and sat with him for a little while. Dadi, upon hearing the commotion emerged from her room.

'Oh. You are home.' She cast a cursory glance around the room. 'Hira, get off the sofa. You'll dirty the furnishings.' Hira quickly stood up, the little voice in her head told her to bark and pant like a dog, but commonsense willed her to stay silent.

'Soraya. I have just come home from the hospital yet you have a face as if I have a terminal illness or am on my last legs? What is wrong?' Dadi's face softened a little.

'I am just stressed out,' she told him. 'Hafiz will be here later and there is still so much to do. On top of that I was worried that you would not be home in time. It is hard at times carrying this household.' Dada laughed.

'You silly woman.' He chuckled. 'You should have more faith in me. Nothing could keep me in that hospital much longer. And if you are tired of the burden of running the house hand it over to your granddaughters. Together they are more than capable.' Dadi shot him an almost venomous look.

'I shall turn your bed down.' She told him. 'You will need to rest.'

'You do that. I shall be there soon.' He spied Akilah hiding in the background. 'Akilah? Why are you hiding? Will you not come and welcome me?' Akilah moved forward.

'How are you? I am so glad that you are home.' The words were impersonal.

'I was in hospital for practically four days. You did not think of coming to see me once?' he complained albeit in a good natured way.

'I wanted to,' she told him. 'But they would go off without telling me.' Dada nodded knowingly. Some things would never change.

'Well don't you all just stand there? There is work to be done. Hafiz and the family will be here before you know it.' Dadi rallied. 'Aaryan I want you to go and get some provisions. I don't want there to be anything lacking tonight.' She handed over a list. 'Make sure you don't skimp on the quality. Go and don't take all day.' Aaryan pocketed the list. This was Dadi back to some sense of semblance and it seemed to be with Dada's arrival. Dada was somewhat of a calming influence, he deduced.

Dada got up and made his way to the bedroom.

'Is there any chance of a cup of tea and some sweets?' His grandchildren smiled at each other.

Even more when they heard Dadi chide him and hearing him chuckle. Aaryan glanced over at Hira. Maybe it wouldn't be as bad as he feared. With Dada back on the scene Dadi would be fussing over him.

Chapter 31

Aaryan parked the car in the forecourt outside the house and called out to Uday. He opened the boot of the car and started taking out the provisions. Uday arrived to take the bags in, closely followed by Dadi.

'Good you are here. Did you get everything?' She scanned the bags to make sure that he had bought everything. 'Did you get fresh herbs?' She pulled out a bunch of wilted coriander, looked at it disdainfully and then back at him. She waved the greens at him. 'I said fresh.' Aaryan looked at her and shrugged. 'Boys.' She moaned. 'Don't know the difference between fresh and wilted.' Just then the breeze wafted by and carried with it a sweet smell. They sniffed appreciatively. At that moment Hira appeared carrying a bunch of coriander, fresh from the garden.

Lost in thought Hira walked up to where the car was parked.

'Hira.' She heard Dadi call out to her. She looked up and saw her standing with the wilted herbs in her hand, her eyes fixed firmly on what she was holding. She quickly hid the coriander behind her back thinking if the old lady could do that to what she held in her hands, her pride and joy stood no chance. Aaryan watched as she slowly walked up to them. Dadi held out her hand. Warily Hira handed over the herbs. Dadi waved them under Aaryan's nose. 'Fresh. Smell the difference.' She turned to Hira. 'For once you have done something right. These will be perfect for garnishing.' She disappeared into the house.

'*Genius,*' he whispered. 'How did you know that Dadi would complain about the coriander?' Hira looked at him with wide eyed innocence.

'I thought they were weeds.' He did a double take then understood that it was her sense of humour coming through. From inside the old woman's voice carried outside, like the threat of an impending storm.

'Stop dawdling out there. Get in and get ready. The final touches to the food will be needed and I don't want any last minute hitches.'

Everyone waited nervously for their guests to arrive. The

food was cooked to perfection, the house spotless. Anticipation hung in the air. Hira and Sabina made sure that everything was in place. Amara tweaked the napkins into conical shapes and arranged them on the dining table by each setting. Dadi fussed and glared, warning all to be on their best behaviour. She wanted everything pristine and would not have anything to be any less than her expectations.

Polite banter filled the air as Hafiz sat with his family bringing everyone up to speed with the events and advancement in his life. He watched benevolently as the refreshments were offered to him. Next to him sat Riaz. He looked around the place. Hira had served juice and water to everyone. She looked around at the new family and noted the over the top politeness of the guests as they chatted.

***

'Maman. Why don't we get any visitors?' A five year old Hira breathlessly asked as she came home from school. 'Asma came to school and she was telling us about her aunts and uncles who had visited her and her sister because they want her to get married and they stayed all weekend and they brought Asma sweets and clothes and Mariyam's aunties all came to her house when her baby brother was born. Why don't I have any aunts and uncles?' Hira's mother smiled, sat her at the dining table and placed her dinner in front of her.

'Why do you need aunts and uncles when I buy you all the sweets and clothes that you want?' She poured milk for her. 'I have no brothers or sisters. All I have are cousins and they are all the way in India so they can't come visiting like Asma's aunts and uncles.' She stroked Hira's hair. 'You have my friends whom you call aunty and uncle. Isn't that enough? Hira looked back at her with big eyes and a mouthful of milk. She quickly gulped it down.

'But Khalida Aunty just tells me to be quiet and be a good girl all the time. She does not bring me any sweets. She just wants to sit in front of the mirror and look at herself all the time.' She leaned forward. 'And you know maman. I saw one day that she was putting a

133

pretend face on. She put these things on her eyes and then she got her teeth from a glass. She's not a true person.' Laughter filled the kitchen as Hira's mother listened to her daughter's words.

'Don't worry. One day you will know the reason for all this. We will have visitors one day. Lots of them and they will see you when you get married.' Hira's face lit up.

'When maman?'

'When the time will come for you to get married. We will need to see lots of people then. They will come here and ask lots of questions about you and you will give them juice and nibbles.' She had a faraway look in her eyes. Hira pushed back her empty plate.

'Can I go out and play?' she asked, slipping down from her chair and running off before getting an answer.

***

'Hira!' The sound brought her back to the present. She jumped. Dadi glared at her, ordering her with her eyes to top up the guests' glasses and plates.

'Who is she?' Hafiz asked. Dada smiled broadly.

'Hafiz, this is Hira, wife of Aaryan.' Hira offered her salutations to the guests.

The visitors looked surprised.

'Her?' asked Hafiz, the surprise and shock was evident in his voice. Hira looked puzzled and hurt but nonetheless prepared herself for further scrutiny. Hafiz sensed that he had said the wrong thing. 'Don't get me wrong, beta,' he apologised, 'forgive me but you do not look as if you are married.'

Hira looked at Aaryan, puzzled. He looked uncomfortable. True there was no vermillion in her parting. Theirs was not the tradition. Hafiz went on. 'Bhai. There is no jewellery, no mehndi on her hands. We expect a newly married girl to be adorned as a bride, for the next few months at least.' He was a stickler for tradition and adamant that things should be followed and done correctly.

'Hafiz, Hira came over in August,' Dadi cut in.

'So when was the engagement, the walima, the rukhsati?' he grilled her, going through each pre and post wedding ritual. 'How can

134

that be right? All these things are important. It is part and parcel of a marriage. More so for the bride and groom, they have to feel that they are getting married. All this cloak and dagger stuff. It is useless. I look at these two and see no spark. One wonders whether there is a reason for the swiftness.' He stared directly at Hira, who had cottoned on to what was being inferred and she looked at Hafiz in shock and irritation. He continued unabated and looked at Dadi. 'Are you expecting your granddaughter's wedding to be a low key affair too?'

'No,' Dadi replied. 'Akilah's wedding will be done properly.' Hafiz understood well enough.

'Ah, I see. For she is your granddaughter and you did not see fit to accord your grandson the same treatment as the others?' He stated giving Grand Aunt a knowing look. Dadi looked uncomfortable. Hafiz turned to Hira, who by now was standing ominously close, ready to tip the tray of half-finished juice straight into his lap. Dadi would give her hell but some things were worth reacting against, especially when nobody else was going to say anything. Hafiz saw Hira's expression and the warning look from Aunt Zehra arrived too late.

'To hell with it,' Hira thought. She took a deep breath. Forget throwing the juice in his lap accidently on purpose.

'With all due respect I am neither of loose character nor am I sullied. It is not right to make presumptions, especially if you do not have the facts.' She heard a sharp intake of breath and did not dare to look in her grandmother's direction and figured that she would pay for it later.

'I am sorry again beta I have said things out of turn. I do not mean to be rude. I am a forth right person and don't believe in beating about the bush.'

He turned to Dadi.

'You didn't say. When were the rituals completed?' he questioned looking pointedly at Dadi, who literally appeared to squirm. His line of questioning unnerved her. *'Had Zehra said something to him?'*

'We only performed the nikkah,' she muttered omitting the fact that it was over the phone. 'And there is nothing to hide. I wanted Aaryan to get married and Hira was abroad. It seemed to be the best way forward.' Hafiz shook his head sadly.

'You have all the facilities and capabilities to send your eldest grandson and his bride on the biggest journey of their lives and you didn't even accord them that.' Hafiz was scathing by now. Grand Aunt stared at Dadi indifferently. Their relationship had been strained since they had last visited her but Dadi remained unrepentant. Grand Aunt turned to Hafiz.

'Hafiz.' She chastised her cousin. 'Please. No more. Look at the distress you are causing to Hira.' She turned her attention to Hira. She smiled at her. 'I am sorry beta. Hafiz does not know when to stop.' Hira was feeling suffocated by the minute.

'I just need to check on something.' She made an excuse and left leaving both Aaryan and Dadi feeling uncomfortable.

'Are you alright?' Sabina asked. Hira's attention seemed far away. She snapped back to the present.

'I'm fine. Do you need me to do anything?'

'Yes, if you can get the other serving bowl? We will lay things out and then I will go and get Akilah and introduce her to her future husband and in-laws.' Hira silently put the dishes out on the side and grabbed fresh glasses. Sabina darted a quick look in her direction before setting off to bring her sister-in-law for the cattle market that was the presenting of the girl to her prospective in-laws. Hira finished off and braved the family again. Aunt Zehra saw her and motioned to the place next to her for Hira to join her. She perched on the edge. Grand Aunt pulled her to the seat next to her and patted her arm. Tired, silent eyes looked at her, boring into her soul. Grand Aunt shook her head as if to ask her to forget about what was said.

Riaz sat looking expectedly towards the staircase waiting for his future bride to make an appearance. He looked nervous and kept licking his lips. While he was intently staring in the other direction, Sabina appeared from Dadi's room with Akilah. Grand Aunt chuckled as they appeared.

'Hey Majnu. Don't look to the skies for your angel. You will find her on the ground.' She indicted to the corridor as Akilah was led in. Riaz quickly turned round, anticipation showing on his face. Akilah was prompted to offer a greeting to everyone. Hafiz stood and placed his hand on her head, blessing her. Grand Aunt made room next to her and Sabina guided Akilah into the seat. Dressed head to toe in a splendid purple and gold lehenga suit, she looked a different person to the one that tormented them day after day. Riaz smiled broadly. Grand Aunt nodded her head knowingly. She nudged Akilah. 'Well we know one thing works.' She winked. Akilah looked blank but on the other side both Sabina and Hira suppressed a giggle. A glower from Dadi was all that was needed for them to compose themselves and that too with some difficulty. Grand Aunt was a balm to sore nerves.

The family made small talk with Akilah and then for a brief moment she and Riaz sat to one side and chatted. They returned to the fold. Everyone held their breath, wanting them both to find each other compatible but for different reasons.

Eventually they made their way back to the group.

'Well?' Hafiz asked Riaz.

'I'm happy, Grand Uncle,' Riaz replied.

'And Akilah?' Akilah smiled and looked away.

'You can take Akilah's silence for her agreement,' Dadi interjected quickly.

'Excellent.' Hafiz beamed and indicated to his neice. She handed a small jewellery box to Riaz. Dadi did the same with Akilah. The young couple stepped forward and placed rings on each other's fingers, sealing the engagement. Dadi beamed.

'Congratulations,' the family members chorused and offered their good wishes. Grand Aunt blessed the couple.

'We suggest that the wedding takes place at the end of the month. Is that acceptable?'

'That is perfect.' Dadi stood up. 'Now that everything has been finalised let us eat. After that I will show you to your rooms.' She moved towards the dining area and glared at her grand daughters-in-law to hurry and serve the food.

Chapter 32

Three tired young women sat around the small dining table in the kitchen. It was well into the early hours of the morning and they struggled to stay awake. The guests had retired to bed not long before. With a final cup of tea they had been sent to their rooms. Hira sat listlessly stirring her coffee, her hand propped up against her cheek to stop her head from falling.

'Hira? Are you alright?' Sabina touched her arm. 'You have not been yourself all evening.'

'It's been a very long day,' she said wearily. Sabina sensing her unhappiness gave her a hug.

'Drink your coffee and then get yourself upstairs. If anyone needs to rest then it is you. Dadiji has worked you like a mule for the past few days. Go to bed.' Hira pushed away her cup.

'I can't finish it. Sorry.' She got up, swaying slightly. Upon reaching the kitchen door she was met by Grand Aunt. Seeing the weariness in her eyes, Grand Aunt reached up and placed her hand on her head and blessed her.

'Look how tired you are.' She looked sad. 'All of you. That sister of mine is a ruthless woman. Are you going to bed?' Hira nodded. Grand Aunt patted her cheek. 'You do that. We shall meet in the morning.' She looked at Hira as if wanting to say something but instead ushered her out. 'You two vamoose and I don't want to see you down here until much later in the morning. I shall handle breakfast.' She said to Sabina and Amara.

Aaryan was still awake when Hira finally managed to drag herself up the stairs. He got up from the bed to meet her as she walked in.

'I'm sorry,' he apologised.

'Hmm?' Hira could hardly keep her eyes open.

'Sorry that you had to put up with those questions and insinuations.' She could only stifle a yawn and nod. Collecting a towel she headed for the bathroom. 'Of course, he is not wrong.' She turned. 'You have nothing of the adornments that a newly wedded woman would have.'

'Doesn't the weary, tired look say it all?' He looked puzzled at her phrase then smiled an uneasy smile.

'It is something that we will have to rectify,' he whispered. Hira did not hear him. She had already entered the bathroom.

Replacing her tooth brush in its holder, she washed her face then sat down on the stool, rested her head against the cool tiles and closed her eyes.

She awoke in bed the following morning. Confused she looked about her. She definitely didn't make it to bed last night. She must have fallen asleep in the bathroom.

'You're awake.' Aaryan appeared from the bathroom. 'You were so tired. I called out to you and you didn't reply. When I peeped in you were asleep in the corner, behind the vanity.'

'So you brought me here?' He nodded. 'What time is it?' She looked around for the clock and seeing how late she was she scrambled out of bed, rushing to get ready.

'Don't fret,' He told her. 'Breakfast has been arranged.'

'Arranged?'

'Yes. Apparently Grand Aunt has ordered breakfast for us and it will be delivered in half an hour along with waiters.' He pulled a tie out of the wardrobe and put it on. 'Well hurry up. It is the first time we will all sit and eat together.' Hira grabbed a towel, rolled over to the opposite side of the bed and rushed to the bathroom. He stood at the dresser and checked himself in the mirror, suppressing a chuckle as she nearly tripped on the way in.

Dadi looked disdainfully at the platter of fruit which was placed before her at the breakfast table. She glared down the table as she watched the interaction between her grandsons and their wives. Despite her protests Grand Aunt had gone ahead and made arrangements for breakfast. As she, anticipated friction between herself and her sister she placed herself well away and sat among the younger people as they ate and chatted. She smiled as she watched Sabina and Amara with their husbands and viewed how Akilah shyly accepted food that Riaz passed to her. At the same time, she noticed a little awkwardness between Hira and Aaryan but she was pleased that they were better with each other. The last time she had seen them, she was concerned. She smiled to herself. They did make such a lovely couple.

It was late evening by the time the visitors got ready to leave. Hafiz bid everyone goodbye but stopped for some time with Aaryan. They stood on the forecourt and chatted.

'I am sorry that I gave you a grilling. I fear that I upset not only you but Hira as well.' Aaryan looked beyond Hafiz and into the small patch of garden that Hira tended.

'If I said that it is alright, I would be lying. But hopefully, it is something that perhaps we might be able to work through and don't worry about Hira. I am sure that she bears no grudges.'

Hafiz smiled wistfully.

'If my daughter had been alive then she would never have let things happen the way that they have.' Aaryan turned and smiled at his maternal grandfather.

'I believe if both our mothers were alive that things would have been done differently.' Hafiz looked at Hira.

'Do I take it that all is not lost there?' Aaryan shrugged.

'We have been thrown together and the circumstances have been awkward but I think we will get there.' He saw Hira looking in his direction and smiled at her. Puzzled she looked behind her to see if there was someone else that he was smiling at. She then turned, shrugged and gave him another quizzical look. Hafiz smiled benevolently.

'She seems well suited for you.' Aaryan looked at him. 'Spirited, I like her,' said Hafiz and hugged Aaryan. 'You take care of yourself and her. Your Dadi is a force to be reckoned with. From what I see it shows clearly that she has no affinity towards her granddaughters-in-law. Hira is spirited. She will need your support and understanding.'

Aaryan returned the hug and then made room for his brothers to spend a few moments with Hafiz. He stopped and chatted with them for a while before he ordered the driver to start up the car. They bade their goodbyes and watched until the car left the drive and set off down the road.

Dadi stood and mentally gnashed her teeth as everyone headed off to their rooms.

Akilah saw the anger and moved forward to offer her another dose of water onto an already burning oil fire.

'How rude was Hira, Dadi? She spoke to Grandpa Hafiz so

140

badly,' she commiserated. 'Are you going to let her get away with that? Such a nerve!' Her grandfather appeared behind her.

'And what would you do if someone was insinuating that you were of loose morals?' Akilah opened and shut her mouth trying to come up with her defence. His piece said he ambled off in the direction of his room. Akilah glanced at Dadi waiting for her to answer. Instead she pulled her by the arm.

'Where were you the night before last?' she hissed. Akilah feigned ignorance.

'I was here.' Dadi shook her.

'Now you know as well as I do that you are lying. Stop these things.' She glanced around. 'It does not behold an engaged girl to be behaving so.' Akilah smiled an innocent smile.

'Dadi, I am tired and I want to get out of this heavy, olde worlde clothing.' She indicated her heavily embroidered lehenja set. 'I think you should think of a suitable punishement for Hira. I am going to bed.' She walked off leaving Dadi to simmer away in anger.

Chapter 33

Early evening saw Dadi sat at the table, rummaging through the papers which she had gathered. Hira and Amara walked past on their way to the garden. She peered over the rim of her glasses.

'Where do you think you are going?' They stopped in their tracks.

'We were just going out to the garden,' Hira replied. Dadi shook her head.

'No. Come and help me with this.' They sat at the table and looked at Dadi for instructions. Dadi thrust an address book at them. 'I have marked out the names to invite to the wedding. The cards are over there,' she indicated towards the side table. 'I want them all written out in your neatest handwriting. No scrawling. I want each card to be perfect.' Hira picked up the cards and looked at the first one. 'Don't be taking all morning. There is other work to be done. Especially now as Sabina has decided that she is not well.' Dadi walked off grumbling. 'The girls of today. No backbone whatsoever. A little sniffle and they take to their bed.' They watched her retreating figure.

'I should be shocked but I am not,' Hira said to Amara, who in turn grinned.

'You have become desensitised.' She giggled, picking up the first card and began writing.

The cards were neatly stacked in a pile when Akilah happened upon them. On seeing Hira and Amara finishing off the last two she swiped the pile onto the floor.

'Who said that you could handle my cards?' She screeched, sending them flying to the floor.

'Dadiji asked us to write out the invites,' Amara stated timidly. Akilah rounded on her.

'Don't lie. Dadi would never ask you,' Akilah sneered. Hira stood up.

'What? She would ask you? If you don't believe us, you could ask Dadiji. We were just helping out.'

'Sure you were.' She walked up to Hira. 'Oh you are really helpful. Just like you were so helpful in the mall? Shall I tell you something?' She walked up to the two. 'I did not need your help. I

could have got away and no one would be the wiser.'

'Hah. That is why you were snivelling in the security offices and spent the next day with a scowl on your face? We helped you out and all you can do is gripe and be ungrateful about our help.' She looked Akilah square in the eyes. While Amara looked on fearfully, Hira stood her ground. Akilah continued. 'There is not one mall that I have been caught stealing in that could pin anything on me.' She laughed. Hira and Amara exchanged worried looks. 'They wouldn't dare. I could have got away if it wasn't for you. All I had to do is claim that I was molested. But no, you three had to step in and be the responsible sisters-in-law and ruined my chances of getting away with my stash.' Hira and Amara looked uncomfortable.

'You were caught stealing?' Akilah turned round slowly and gulped. Dadi stood in front of her, waiting to hear her answer.

'Dadi. I... I...' she stammered. For the first time Dadi's ire was directed towards her darling granddaughter.

'Well I am waiting for an answer?'

'It was all a misunderstanding,' Akilah said, defending herself. 'A case of mistaken identity.' Dadi stared intently at her.

'Shameless wretch. You are lying too.' Akilah's discomfort grew. They were soon joined by Aaryan, Aiden and Sabina.

'What's .... ?' Sabina started to ask. Hira quickly shook her head, silencing her.

'How long has this been going on?' Dadi demanded. Akilah remained silent. 'Answer me!' Dadi shouted. Akilah jumped. Right on cue the waterworks started. 'Hmm. I knew you could not have done this on your own. I have always said that your friends are a bad influence. Haven't I always said that?' Akilah nodded furiously in between her sniffling, ready to agree to anything. 'Right. From now on until your wedding you are not to leave the house on your own. You will not meet any of your friends. I would rather have you at home than going out and getting into further mischief.' Dadi honed in on Hira, her eyes beginning to blaze. 'How did you help Akilah? Were you helping her to steal too?' She took a step forward. Hira stepped back. 'Not that I expect anything better from you. Your mother was not likely to teach you right from wrong. Was she?' Hira's eyes burnt with anger.

'Dadiji, say what you will about me but leave my mother out

of this. It is not fair to talk about her, especially as she is not here to defend herself.' Dadi puffed up.

'You dare to tell me? Well let me tell you. Your mother was a no good useless woman who ran away at the first sign of trouble. She had no morals and flaunted herself before others. Back stabbing, insolent viper,' she spat. Hira's anger rose with every insult that was thrown at her mother's memory.

'Dadiji,' she raised her voice, stopping the old lady in her tracks. 'I said before, say what you like about me but never say a word against my mother. You never even knew her. What right have you to say such things?' She unconsciously took a step forward. Dadi seemed to back down. Aaryan stepped in, held Hira by the waist and placed some distance between the two. Dadi recovered quickly.

'So if you didn't steal, what did you do?' Amazingly Amara stepped forward. In a faltering voice she narrated the events of that day. Dadi was not convinced.

'What proof do you have?'

'You can contact the mall or the shop,' Hira suggested. Dadi glared.

'Hira, do you still have the chit from the manager?' Sabina reminded her. 'Was it in your bag or mine? I can't remember.' Hira thought for a moment. Dadi folded her arms.

'Well, if you have such a thing. Bring it to me.' Hira turned on her heel and raced to her bedroom.

Madly scrabbling about in the back of her wardrobe she looked for the bag that had her suit and where she remembered she had put the piece of paper. The bag was empty. She thought for a moment and wondered if Akilah had managed to dispose of it at some point. After much searching she placed the bag back into the cupboard and gave up looking. Instead resigning herself to the fact that Dadi would call her a liar and probably bad mouth her mother too. That was worse. Just as she was about to close the wardrobe door, she spied something at the very back. Picking it up, she saw with some relief that it was the same handwritten paper that the store manager had given her. Grabbing it she headed back to the family.

Handing it over, she stood in silence as Dadi read it. Finally she looked at Hira. Without looking away she tore the paper into small pieces and let it fall to the floor.

'No one will say a word about this,' she stated. 'It did not happen.' Hira looked on aghast.

'*Did Dadi actually say that*?' She looked to Sabina and then at Aaryan who wore a look of confusion.

'No malls, visits to the city, or even shopping in the local town.' She waggled her finger at Akilah. 'You are to stay at home. No more time wasting. You will spend the remaining days helping out at home.' Akilah opened her mouth to protest but the look on Dadi's face silenced her. Instead she sulked silently. 'And as for you three.' Dadi turned on them. 'How dare you take such a step and not say anything? You literally encouraged Akilah to do wrong. I shall decide on a fitting punishment for you three later. And you.' She waggled a finger at Hira. 'Let it be the last time that you raise your voice to me. I will not have you disrespecting me for the sake of your mother.' She faced up to Akilah. 'For many years you have only experienced my affection. Now you will see what my anger is like.' She walked away with Akilah hot on her heels.

'Dadi I was misled. I didn't mean to do what I did and I didn't steal from all those malls. I was just boasting.' Dadi glared and without saying a word stomped off. This was a new experience for Akilah, she didn't like it and followed Dadi in the hope of placating her. She needed Dadi to be on her side. How else was she going to ensure that she had an easy time at home?

'You really shouldn't shield Akilah.' Aaryan looked at the three.

'We thought we were doing the best thing,' Hira answered. 'We didn't want Dadiji and Dadaji to face having to come up to the mall or the police station.'

'You thought about that?' He sounded incredulous. Hira glared at him. Sabina tapped him on the shoulder playfully.

'Don't tease,' she chided him. He looked at Hira with serious eyes.

'You really should have told one of us,' he told her. 'What if it had all gone wrong? All of you would have got into trouble. As it is Dadi is not going to let this go.'

'We honestly thought it was for the best.' Sabina reiterated Hira's words. 'As it is Hira wanted to say something but we stopped her. Don't be too hard on her.' He understood and looked at Hira

'What is there to be hard about? I am not a complete idiot. Not a word,' he warned her, seeing the mischievous glint in her eyes. 'I can withstand a lot of things but I will not be made fun of.' The first look was replaced by a different one. Hira feigned innocence much to the amusement of Sabina and Amara. Even Aaryan could not help himself. Throwing his hands up in the air he conceded defeat. 'I think I am going to get away from here while I still can.' He laughed. 'I need to catch up with some work. Call me when dinner is ready, please?' Hira nodded and gave him a grateful smile for understanding their predicament. He acknowledged her and went to the study.

Chapter 34

Dadi watched as Hira moved around her room putting away her newly washed and ironed clothes. No matter how much she had piled extra work on her Hira still carried it out without much complaint. Dadi hadn't expected that. Hira was her own person but she still abided by the rules laid down for her. Each time she had reprimanded or punished her Hira had just looked at her, listened and then carried on with some other work. She didn't seem to hold it against her. It was unnerving and it was fast becoming clear that she was losing the battle of wills against her. She needed to decide on a new tack. She thought for a while and then executed her plan.

'You loved your mother very much, didn't you?' Hira was thrown by the question. She put away the final item and faced Dadi. Wary of whether Dadi was going to use this against her she nodded. 'Why?'

'Because she was my mother, she gave birth to me and looked after me single handedly. It was not an emotion I had any control over. She was just that. My mother.' She re-arranged some of the items on the dresser. Dadi stared at her closely.

'What of your father?' Hira became uncomfortable at the line of questioning, absolutely sure that it would be used against her at some time. 'Were you born out of wedlock?' This question threw her and she was not absolutely sure why Dadi would ask. All the same, almost as if there was a power within Dadi to extract this information Hira found herself answering.

'My father passed away when I was three. Mum worked hard to make sure that I did not miss his presence. I was still too young to register many memories of him. Mum said that he loved us both very much.'

'What happened to him?'

'Mum said that he was attacked when he was coming home from getting some fish and chips. He was at the bottom of our street when couple of youths battered him to death. According to the police he did not stand a chance. There were six of them.' Dadi's eyes narrowed sceptical that Hira could ever have a father. She did not hold much faith that Ishrat, Hira's mother would have followed the ways and customs of her family. As far as Dadi was concerned her daughter had turned her back on her family ancestry and traditions.

'How do you know? You said that you were three when he died? Is this more lies made up by your mother?' Hira's heart did not know how much more pain it could take. Dadi looked pleased when she saw the hurt in Hira's eyes.

'Mum still kept the newspaper clippings. Why are you so intent on insulting my mother? You hardly knew her.' Dadi raised herself up to her full height.

'Oh I knew her alright. Acting innocent and denying she did any wrong. She was still singing the same old tune when she came to see me. We are blood. Let bygones be bygones. She whined on for hours. Thankfully I was alone that time. At least my family was saved from seeing her sorry carcass.' Hira looked shocked. Her mother had never mentioned that she had even met Dadi. 'She stood there, large as life. Making out that she had done no wrong ever, trying to reason with me. She even tried to make me believe her lies.' Dadi had a wild look in her eyes and was practically frothing at the mouth as she told her in minute detail of Hira's mother's visit to see her. Hira zoned out momentarily. 'She would not leave. Stubborn as always, in the end I had to literally push her out of the room. She fell right where you are standing. I thought that she was not going to get up but after a while she did. Without saying another word she left.' The glint in Dadi's eyes looked even more menacing as she imparted with this knowledge.

Hira's mind raced. Her mother had come to see this witch? Only god, Dadi and her mother knew for what reason. Slowly some pieces of her mother's last moments in India came to the fore. The fall had been fatal. Not being able to hear anything more Hira rushed out of the room with tears stinging her eyes. Dadi watched her go with a cold smile. She had been thinking of an apt punishment for Hira because of the events at the mall but this was way better and it gave her the desired reaction she had required for some time. She was closer to breaking Hira.

Dada stood outside the bedroom door. He shook with rage at what he had heard. Part of him had wanted to call Hira back as she had rushed out. But she had not noticed him in her haste and had run off along the corridor to seek solace. With his head hanging in shame he slowly walked away. Right now he did not want to face Dadi or anyone else for that matter.

Hira rushed into the bedroom, stopped as Aaryan looked up from his work, she dived into the bathroom and locked herself in. Aaryan put down his laptop and rushed to the bathroom. He knocked on the door.

'Hira? Are you alright?' There was no answer. He put his ear to the door only to hear the sound of running water. He stepped back. 'Hira. Open the door.' The sound stopped. The door opened a little and he saw Hira's tear stained face. 'What happened?' He reached forward and pulled Hira out. She shook her head unwilling to tell him. 'Tell me?' he whispered. He looked at her with such tenderness and understanding that Hira could not help but move towards him. He enveloped her in a hug and she slowly felt herself unravelling. She wanted to tell him of the conversation with Dadi. Instead, she hugged him tighter. 'Has Dadi said something to you?' Her silence confirmed that she had, he knew that it must have been personal and cut to the quick. He was concerned. Hira had never before taken any of Dadi's words to heart.

'I'm okay,' she told him. 'Just a little upset that is all. Can I borrow your laptop for a moment?' He looked at her. 'Only if you have finished with it,' she added. He smiled and turned it towards her.

'Be my guest. I'm going to shower.' He got up. 'Just shut it down when you have finished.'

He found her fast asleep. The laptop was still on. Gently he removed it from her grasp, touched the mouse pad in order to run through the sequence to shut it down. He looked at the page that Hira had browsed.

'*Why did Hira want to know about blood clots leading to death*?' He thought, then shut down the laptop, switched off the light and got into bed.

Dadi flounced about at breakfast the following morning. Upon seeing Hira's face she smiled even more. Today was going to be a much better day than of late. She sipped her tea contentedly and kept glancing at Hira. Satisfied with herself for once. Even the angry look and cold attitude from Dada did not deter her. Anxiously she waited for Akilah so that she could tell her of her little conquest.

Akilah still hadn't appeared by the time breakfast was eaten. Dadi, unable to wait any longer headed up the staircase and to her room. After a few minutes Dadi was heard shouting for her. Worried everyone rushed to Akilah's room expecting to find Akilah in some sort of mishap.

Dadi emerged from the ensuite looking flustered, even more so when she bumped into Aiden and saw everyone else. Quickly she tried to cover up Akilah's disappearance but too late. Her granddaugter's absence was noticed.

'Where is Akilah?' Dada levelled his question at Dadi.

'She is around here somewhere.' Dadi lied.

'Then why isn't she answering when you called her?' Dada looked directly at Dadi.

'She might have slept elsewhere.' Dadi wasn't going to back down in protecting Akilah.

'She is not in the bathroom and her bed has not been slept in.' Aaryan surveyed the surroundings. 'It can only mean two things. One that she has run away ...'

'Nonsense!' Retorted Dadi. 'She was going to be married shortly.' Aaryan ignored her statement.

'Or two? She has been abducted!' Sabina gasped.

'If she has been abducted then we should call the police.' Dada took out his phone.

'Let us not be hasty.' Dadi stopped him. 'After all we don't know for sure that she has been abducted.' Just at that moment there was a rustling at the window and Akilah fell into the room at Dadi's feet.

Only just aware that she had an audience she quickly got to her feet and swayed slightly.

'Where have you been?' Dada demanded. Akilah hung her head and cast a sideways glance at Dadi. 'Here we were thinking all sorts. I asked? Where have you been?' This only earned him a smile and a hiccup. Dadi moved forward to shield her.

'Don't Soraya.' Dada's anger was culpable. He pointed at Dadi. 'Did you know what she was up to?' Akilah laughed. Dadi tried to hush her up.

'Dadi knew.' She sat down on her bed. 'She knew all the time.' She sang then passed out. Dada exploded at Dadi.

'Soraya! How many times did I tell you not to indulge her in all this? Why can't you see that you are damaging her future by turning a blind eye to her antics? I warned you that it will not bode well.' He turned to Akilah. 'If you have any hope of marrying then I suggest that you change yourself and do it now. I do not intend to have our name dragged through the mud because of you. Sort her out.' He ordered and stormed out.

'You heard your grandfather,' Dadi said in a low voice.
'Hira can you help me with my shirt. It is missing a button.' Aaryan dragged Hira away. Aiden and Alman also made their excuses and engaged their wives in other jobs. With an angry sigh Dadi decided to leave Akilah to sleep off her hangover. She would deal with her later.

Noticing Hira on her own Dadi moved in for some more blood. She knew she had made her first cut with the barbs yesterday.
'So what else did your mother have to discuss about me?' She sneered. Hira put away the last of the plates she had finished drying.
'Nothing,' she told her. 'Mum didn't say a word when she came back.' She was not going to tell her that she couldn't. Her mother had lost the ability to speak when she returned. She picked up the damp teatowel to take to the utility room. 'She didn't say anything but I will.' She took a step forward. 'Mum died of a bleed to the brain caused by a blood clot. The doctors said that the clot may have been caused by a fall. You admitted that you had pushed her making her fall. There is nothing else in my eyes. You killed my mother. You have my mother's blood on your hands.' Hira looked directly at her. Dadi saw no fear in Hira's eyes, instead she saw contempt. Dadi began to speak but for once she could not reply. She had not expected Hira to stand there calmly and blame her for her mother's death. Momentarily silenced, it was all she could do but watch Hira walk out.

Some time later she pulled herself together. Hira would at some point reveal the conversation that she had had with her in her room. In order to save herself she would need to paint Hira as a liar and an attention seeking, unstable girl. She formulated a plan in her mind. She could not afford for Hira to tell anyone but if she did, she would be ready with a counter attack. Dada was already distancing himself from her. If he knew about this then she was sure that he would surely disown her. She shook her head. There was no way that she was going to let Hira get in the way of her comfort and security.

Chapter 35

It was, for once, a quiet evening at home. Hira walked back and forth in the kitchen collecting provisions for the evening meal. Aaryan and his brothers had been called away to the storage facility in Bhuj for the past week and a half. Sabina and Amara had been sent to the city to collect a number of items and only Hira was left for Dadi to trouble beyond the point of exhaustion. The wedding was almost upon them and the daily frenzy was building to a climax. Dadi had left no stone unturned in the arrangements and readily delegated all the chores to the point where everyone, apart from Akilah, did not know whether they were coming or going. In her own little world, she was on autopilot as she started cooking. A sound at the kitchen door indicated that she was not alone. Dadi pushed Akilah into the room.

Hira stood in the kitchen and stared incredulously. She could not believe that she had heard right

'Don't look like that,' Dadi barked. 'I want Akilah to learn how to make a few basic things. She should leave here knowing how to make the essentials at least.' Akilah stood and pouted. 'You will show her how to make a simple curry, pakora and chapatti.' Hira looked from one to the other.

'In one day?'

'Just show her.' She waved her hand dismissively. 'Make sure you pay attention,' she warned Akilah. 'I don't want any comeback from your in-laws after marriage.' Akilah shrugged.

'What cooking? They have servants there and I shan't be eating there very often.'

'Brat,' Hira coughed and earned herself a glare from both women.

'Behave yourself,' Dadi warned her. 'Your sister-in-law has only limited days left in this house. She should not be subjected to any irritations.'

'Dadi if that is the case, why not forget about cooking?' she cooed. Dadi looked at her sternly before heading back to her room.

Akilah crossed her arms and leant against the workstation.

'So Madam Hira what dish are you going to teach me?' Hira looked at the hob. 'Don't show me how. Just make it and tell me what you did and how you did it.' She surveyed her recently manicured nails and smiled. 'Look at you. All three of you doing all this work and you won't even get a chance to be at the wedding.' She narrowed her eyes. 'You do know that I don't want you at the wedding.'

'So I heard,' Hira responded and continued cooking.

'Aren't you upset?' Akilah asked sweetly. Hira shrugged.

'Your wedding, your choice.'

'My friends will all be here. Won't you feel left out?' she asked sweetly. Hira stared at her. The saccharin sweet smile on Akilah's face alerted her to her ploy. She chose not to rise to the taunts and continued cooking.

'As you can see once the onions are transparent you add the spices.' She picked up the canisters and noticed Akilah's disinterested look but continued. Dadi had given her a task and she was going to see it through. 'Do you want to mix the ingredients and gram flour to make the pakoras? The oil will need to be heated to the right temperature.' Akilah looked bored.

'Look. Just do what you have to do. Don't involve me.'

'Are you paying attention Akilah?' Dadi appeared at the door. Akilah quickly picked up a spoon and started stirring furiously.

'Yes Dadi.' She answered sweetly. 'I am taking everything in.' As soon as Dadi walked away she stopped. 'Cooking is so boring.

Chapter 36

Aaryan placed the car into fifth gear and cruised down the Ambala Chandigarh Expressway and smiled. He was looking forward to being home and relished the thought of being able to spend the night in his own bed. He glanced at the bags on the passenger seat and mentally patted himself on the back. He was sure that Hira would appreciate the gesture and had taken great pains to choose wisely. He cast his mind back to the text conversations they had late at night and was thankful that Hafiz had advised him to get Hira's phone switched over to an Indian provider. He looked at his reflection in the rear view mirror and smiled. Then chided himself for looking like a prize fool. But he was happy. He hadn't looked forward to getting home in a long while.

The sound of Akilah's voice, whining, carried from the kitchen as he stepped over the threshold. He sighed deeply.

'Another one of her tantrums,' he muttered and headed towards the sound. 'A few more days,' he consoled himself, 'a few more days.' Silently he walked to the kitchen then felt his blood run cold. In slow motion he watched, horrified, as Akilah picked up the wok from the burner and threw the contents at Hira.

'Hira!' His shout was almost drowned out by her screams as the hot liquid hit her back. He was at her side within seconds taking care not to slip on the remainder of oil on the floor. He laid her on the floor and ran the tap, constantly pouring water over her to ease the burn. Picking up the knife he cut away her soaked dress and lifted the flaps away from her back, making sure that it was not sticking to her. The skin was already looking very red and angry. He continued to pour tepid water over her. The floor was awash with water and oil but that was not his concern right now. His mind raced as to the pain that she must be feeling as she writhed helplessly and tried his best to soothe her.

Akilah melded into the background and slowly inched away, running as soon as she reached the door.

'What in god's name is going on in here?' Dadi demanded,

appearing at the doorway. 'And what is all this mess.' She saw Hira on the floor and started to rant. 'Can't this child ever do anything right? Every chance she gets, she makes a complete mess and then has the audacity to lock horns with me. Her mother spoilt her for too long.' Aaryan glared at his grandmother. 'Who is going to clean this mess?' Aaryan reached for his phone and dialled. Before it connected he heard Aiden and Alman in the hallway.

'Aiden, Alman.' He called out. His brothers appeared at the door with Sabina and Amara a little way behind them. Frantically he indicated to them to cover the doorway so that no one would see. 'Can one of you get me a clean sheet?' He shouted.

'I'll get one,' Sabina offered, going to the nearest cupboard wondering why he wanted the sheet. Amara took the recently bought provisions to the stockroom. Neither had come close to the kitchen and were oblivious to what had happened. Hira by now was beginning to shake with shock. As soon as they were out of earshot he spoke again.

'Aiden, I'll need you to drive us to the hospital.' He nodded.

'I'll get the car started.' Sabina appeared with the sheet.

'What did you want the sheet... ?' she asked then saw Hira on the floor. 'Oh my god. What happened? How badly is she hurt?' Tears flowed as she tried to calm herself.

'Just a stupid little accident,' replied Dadi. 'Clean it up quickly.'

'Later,' Aaryan ordered. 'Nobody is going to clean just yet. Get me that plastic film you put over food,' he told Sabina. She grabbed the roll and handed it to him. He discarded a metre or so and then placed a length of it on Hira's back. Finally he took the sheet from Sabina and placed it over Hira.

'The car is ready,' Aiden came back and informed. Carefully, Aaryan handled Hira, taking his brother's help and exited the kitchen gingerly.

'Alman, you stay here and handle things. Look after Sabina and Amara.'

'I am coming with you.' Sabina had decided and dared Aaryan to say otherwise. He mulled things over for a split second before agreeing.

'OK. Come, Alman, keep an eye on things.'

156

Hira was taken to hospital by car. Aiden had chosen the people carrier, dropped the rear seats to a horizontal position and Hira was placed on her front and her burn was continuously cooled. Amara had chanced upon them as they were leaving. Not being able to accompany them to the hospital, she had grabbed some muslin material from the store room, a small tub, ice from the freezer and handed it to Sabina. Teary eyed she begged them to keep her up to speed.

The doctor stared at them accusingly as he confronted them after Hira's initial examination.

'Your wife has second degree burns to her shoulder and upper back. We have set up a drip to reinstate lost fluids, given her some painkillers and attending to the burn. Chances are that it will blister in a day or two and should that burst there is a risk of infection. How did this happen?'

'It was an accident,' Aaryan muttered.

'The number of times I have heard that excuse.' The doctor bit back. 'Does it make you feel big doing that to a woman?'

It didn't take long for Aaryan to realise what the doctor was saying. As the words sank in, anger bubbled within him. Without a second thought he grabbed the doctor by the collar and shook him.

'What are you implying?' he said through gritted teeth. 'How dare you make assumptions like that?' Aiden quickly extracted the doctor from Aaryan's grip and turned to the doctor.

'It was an accident,' he affirmed. 'There is no question about it. Would we have brought her in if that was the case?'

'I want to take Hira home,' Aaryan demanded. The doctor was hesitant.

'We would like to keep your wife in for a few days at least.' He saw the look on Aaryan's face. 'If infection sets in we are well placed to treat it here,' he reasoned.

'That may be so,' Aaryan replied. 'But I want her home. Even if I need to hire a nurse to keep an eye on her I shall do that. Just complete the discharge papers. We'll take care of her at home.' The doctor took note of Hira's reports and made some notes.

'Her vital parameters are still a little unstable. Until then we cannot discharge her.' Reluctantly Aaryan agreed. He sat down dejectedly in the chair opposite, ran his hands through his hair and tried desperately to rid his mind from the sound of Hira's screams. He looked as if he was about to cry. Sabina sat with him.

'This is a nightmare.' He turned to her.

'She's in good hands,' she reassured him.

'I'll get us some coffee.' Aiden offered before walking off to find a working vending machine.

At home, Dada got to the bottom of what had happened. Akilah stood before him.

'Did you even think of what you were doing or the damage that your actions would have caused?' Akilah shrugged.

'She had it coming to her?' she muttered.

'What!' Dada roared his face red with anger. Akilah balked. She had never seen Dada in this avatar and she looked at Dadi desperately.

Dadi glared.

'Come with me now,' she grabbed Akilah and dragged her away.

Alman took Dada to one side and sat him down. The old man breathed heavily. Amara handed him a glass of water.

'I have been a fool,' he said sadly. 'I am just as much to blame for what has happened. I gave your grandmother free reign and now I have to see this day.' Amara soothed him.

'Dadaji don't talk like that,' She said tearfully. 'You should go to sleep. I shall wake you when Aaryan comes back. Dada shook his head.

'I will not sleep. No, I shall wait here with you.'

They reached home in the early hours of the morning. At his insistence the doctor had allowed Aaryan to bring Hira home. He did not stop. His main purpose was to get Hira to the bedroom and settled. Aiden fielded questions from everyone. The glaring absence of Akilah and Dadi could not be dismissed. Anger welled in each one present. Words were unsaid but the silence spoke volumes. The total disregard disgusted each one. Dada sat resignedly in the chair. The pain in his eyes could not be masked. Aaryan stopped long enough to reassure him.

'I suggest that we all get some sleep. It is late. Go to bed Dadaji. I will speak to you in the morning.'

'The kitchen.' Sabina remembered. 'It needs to be cleaned.' Dada shook his head.

'No need. Hiralal and Uday dealt with it. They called in their wives and daughters.' He shuffled away, stopped and turned. 'I have hired some help. They will help with breakfast. Goodnight.'

Sabina helped Aaryan to take Hira to the bedroom and laid her on her side so that she faced him and her injuries would not be compromised during the night. Together they made her comfortable and arranged the bedding so that she did not roll over during the night and fall out. Sabina placed Hira's medical file on the bedside table along with the medication. Amara arrived with a jug of water. Aaryan took it from her.

'Thank you. It is getting late. Go to bed. I will handle things from here.' Both girls looked towards Hira.

'If you are sure?' Amara asked. He nodded and saw them to the door.

'Go and rest.'

He was washing his hands when he heard Hira stir. Quickly drying his hands he was by her side. The painkillers hadn't taken the edge off her pain and she whimpered. He pulled up the stool and sat with her, felt her wince as the pain came and went in waves and heard her cry. Not just cry but softly call out.

'Mum,' she whimpered. 'Make the pain go away,' she wept and it tugged at his heart. He put his hand out and brushed a strand of hair away from her temple.

'Shhh,' he soothed. 'The pain will go soon. Sleep.' He stroked her forehead gently so as not to add to her pain. Still the tears fell. He got into bed with her and placed her so that she lay close to him resting her head on his chest. He soothed her like one would console a small child, making soothing sounds. Eventually she fell into a fitful sleep.

He shook his head almost trying to clear the cobwebs and the image that had been left on his mind. How different he had planned for his homecoming to be.

Chapter 37

It was late when he eventually woke up late by Dadi's standards anyway. He figured that by the incessant banging on his bedroom door. Dadi stood with her fist in the air ready to start rapping again. They faced off in silence. Eventually Dadi spoke.

'Are you both intending to sleep all morning? Tell Hira to get up. Breakfast needs to be made.' He turned at looked at Hira then back at Dadi.

'Hira has to rest. She won't be making breakfast.'

'Rest,' scoffed Dadi. 'A little burn and you would think that she had suffered major trauma.' His stomach turned. He had tolerated his grandmother for how she had treated and dictated to him but she had no compassion at all. Part of him wanted to drag her by the arm, take her to Hira and show her the extent of the injury. But he doubted if that would even make a difference to her. She had no heart whatsoever.

'Say what you will Dadi. But I will not have Hira stressed. She needs to rest.' Dadi opened her mouth to say something else but seeing the determination on his face, she backed off. With a last look on Hira's sleeping form she turned quickly and exited the room.

There was silence as Dadi took her place at the table. Dada continued to read his paper. Aiden and Alman had yet to arrive. Undeterred, she turned her plate over and waited for breakfast to be served. Breakfast was brought out.

'Who are you?' Dadi demanded, grabbing the wrist of the strange girl dishing out her food. Dada put down his paper.

'She is here to work,' he replied. 'Let her do her job. I have engaged help from now on.'

'Humph.' She looked up as two of her grandsons joined them and indicated to the help to serve them. 'Where are your wives?' she questioned ready to vent elsewhere.

'There,' Aiden indicated in the direction of the kitchen as Sabina and Amara brought out the remainder of the breakfast, dished up and upon Dada's instructions took their seats. Dadi simmered with rage as they breakfasted together. She cast angry glances towards the landing. Akilah had yet to come down.

Aaryan checked on Hira and then decided to get ready. While he was shaving he heard the bedroom door open.

'*Surely Hira would not be attempting to go down?*' he asked himself and moved to the bathroom door. He spied Akilah enter, move towards the bed and stand quietly, watching. Something made him stay back. He watched closely, ready to spring into action if she tried anything.

Hira opened her eyes and almost shut them again due to the pain before opening them. It was then that she saw Akilah standing there. She lifted her head and watched silently.

'Listen. What happened in the kitchen yesterday was your fault. Don't put any of the blame on me. I did not do anything. You won't say anything to anyone?' The last part was more of a request than a statement. Hira closed her eyes and sank her cheek against the pillow making Akilah twitchy. 'You won't say anything?'

'Why would she say anything?' Akilah whirled round. Aaryan appeared from the bathroom, wiping the remains of shaving cream from his face. 'If there is anyone to say anything, it will be me. After all, I am witness to what you did.' Akilah looked at Hira then to him.

'You would put her above me? Your own sister?' She darted a look at Hira. He stepped towards her, making her back up against the foot of the bed.

'Even my own sister.' He shook his head. 'What you did yesterday is unforgivable.'

'I was provoked.'

'Liar. I heard everything, Akilah and I know full well who the guilty party is in this.' She stood against him in outright defiance. Mentally, he decided that she was not in the least bothered by what had happened. The sooner she joined her new family the better. Perhaps they would have better luck in making her a human being.

There was a gentle tap on the door and Sabina entered armed with a tray of food. She saw the stand-off between brother and sister and was about to walk away.

'Don't go Sabina. Akilah was just leaving.' Aaryan looked pointedly at his sister, who in turn pouted and flounced off. He stared after her.

'Let me guess. She was absolving herself?' Aaryan nodded silently. She placed the tray on the coffee table. 'I have brought you some breakfast and some porridge for Hira. It is still hot so you eat first, by then the porridge will be just right.' She swayed slightly as she stood up.

'Are you alright?' He took her by the arm and steadied her. She nodded.

'When you are finished give me a call. I will sit with Hira. Dadaji wants to talk to you all. A family conference, I believe?' She looked at Hira. 'How did she sleep during the night?'

'Fitfully,' he replied. 'She cried and called for her mother.' His features looked sad as he glanced towards Hira. 'I really felt for her.' He turned back to her and she saw raw emotion in his eyes.

'It is the first time in years that I missed Mum.' She placed her hand on his arm.

'It is only normal for a hurt child to call for their mother. No matter what age. Give me a shout when you have eaten. If you want, I will feed Hira. You take a break.' He nodded.

Chapter 38

'Where were you last night?' Dadi accosted Dada as he picked up his effects from the bedside table.' He looked at her indifferently.

'In the guest room,' he finally spoke.' Dadi blustered.

'Why would you sleep there?' What is the point?' Stop behaving like a child and move your things back.' she demanded. 'He ignored her demands and continued with his task. 'Eventually, she stood in his way, blocking his exit.

'Let me go Soraya,' he stated gruffly.'

'We have had differences before,' she said. 'This will blow over. 'Now put your things back. 'He shook his head.

'Not this time Soraya.'

'Not this time?' The penny dropped.'You will distance yourself from me because of that wretch,' she spat. 'Since she came here she has questioned me, turned Aaryan against me, emboldened Sabina and Amara and victimised Akilah.'

Dada just looked at her with sad eyes.'Don't side with her.'

'I think I know who is being victimised here, Soraya.' I have not exactly been walking round with my eyes closed. 'I told you time and time again.'Change yourself.'Don't treat the girls as you do but I see that there is something in you that is so bitter.'What have they done that warrants being treated like they are nothing?' He sighed heavily as if all was lost. 'I only wish that I had done something earlier.'At least Hira would have been spared the pain she is feeling.'

'Oh, and your heart bleeds only for Hira?' She is very important to you.'

Dada moved her aside.

'I don't know what enmity you have with Hira. She does not deserve this. Nor anyone else for that matter.' He thought for a while. 'I don't think that this wedding should go ahead as planned.'

Dadi was stunned into silence. 'Not for one moment did she think that he would ever confront her in the way he did now and on top of that his decision on Akilah's wedding.' She had to act before he went ahead and postponed the wedding.' All her planning to get Akilah married into a family where she would not be inconvenienced would go to pot if she did not act quickly.' She went off to find Akilah and formulate a fool- proof plan.

'If her husband was adamant to delay the wedding then she was adamant that the wedding would go ahead.'

Chapter 39

Hira woke feeling a cool hand on her forehead. She opened her eyes and focused on the worried features of Aaryan. She tried to get up and ending up wincing instead. Aaryan leaned towards the side table and picked up a glass of water, handed it to her along with the painkillers.

'Take it easy,' he told her, 'there is no rush. Take your time.'

'The wedding,' she croaked before sipping some more water.

'Over and done with,' he said with relief.

'Over? How long...' He took the glass from her.

'Little over a week ago, you were out for three days initially.'

Hira was wide eyed.

'We asked the doctor to sedate you while the wedding was underway. Under the circumstances it was for the best. There was too much noise going on and it made you uncomfortable. After that you slept a lot of the time.' He looked at her intently. 'It was really hard to see you in distress. But the doctor reckoned it was the best way. Anyway, while you were out, you had a steady stream of visitors. Grand Aunt was really worried for you. She spent a few hours at your bedside. Shooed me out and sat with you. In the end we had to send her home. She didn't want to leave. The only reason she left was if I promised to send her updates every day.' He stood up. 'Can I get you anything?'

Hira shook her head and closed her eyes momentarily. She looked at him. 'I can feel the pain but how bad is it?'

Aaryan sat on the bed. 'You have second degree burns to the upper quarter of your back up to your left shoulder. The nurse has been coming every day to check, change the dressing and tend to your needs. So far there has been no infection but the burn is still wet.'

'Will I need skin grafts?' He shrugged.

'The doctor said to wait and see how you heal. Grand Aunt has been using aloe on your back each time the nurse left.' He chuckled. 'The run ins she had with her.'

Hira smiled, envisaging the kindly old lady standing firm against the nurse.

'I wish I had known she was here.' He stood up and smiled.

'Don't worry. She will be here as soon as she hears and there is a driver around to bring her. I'll let Sabina and Amara know that you are awake. They have been practically camped outside the door.'

Within minutes of his leaving the room Sabina and Amara rushed in.

'Hira. You worried us so much. We were so scared for you. How is it?'

'Hurts,' Hira replied weakly, trying to sit up. Amara eased her back.

'Don't sit up on our account.' Hira looked at the relieved faces of her sisters-in-law. Her brow furrowed.

'Aaryan said that the wedding has happened already. How was it?'

'Not bad as weddings go. Guests came, they sang, danced, ate and they went,' Sabina answered. 'Riaz looked so happy and Grand Aunt even danced. It was so good to watch her among the young girls. I hope Akilah realises just how lucky she is. Riaz seemed smitten by her. Maybe he could bring about a change in her.' Sabina patted her leg. 'Never mind that, do you know that Aaryan has not left you alone since the accident? Every time we stopped by to see you he was here.'

'And he even sent us out shopping for you,' Amara cut in. Hira was curious.

'Shopping?' she asked.

'Yes.' Amara walked over to the wardrobe and brought out a shopping bag. She placed it on the bed and took out the contents.

'What are these?' Hira asked weakly.

'Well until your burn heals Aaryan decided that you can't wear the coarse dresses you had so he asked us to go out and get some which are softer for you.' She picked up one of the outfits and showed it to her. 'We got some beautiful colours for you.' She sat down again. Hira looked a little apprehensive.

'New outfits? I can just see Dadi's face.' Sabina looked intently at Hira. Even at the worst of times Hira had accorded respect given to an elder. Now she had even dropped the ji. '*This was a worrying development,*' Sabina thought and hoped that it would not escalate more sour relations between Dadi and Hira.

'Dadi is not here.' Aaryan appeared in the doorway with a bowl of rice pudding taking a spoonful and savouring the sweet taste of it. 'After the wedding, Dadi decided to stay with Akilah for a few days. No doubt she will be back before too long. She can't keep away from here.' Hira looked longingly towards the bathroom. Sabina was quick to see.

'What's up Hira?'

'Shower,' Hira whispered longingly.

'Not yet.' Aaryan waggled the spoon at her. 'After a day or so we will chance putting you under the shower. Until then it is sponge baths for you. Do you want some?' He held the bowl to her. She poked out her tongue at him.

'Spoilsport, no you eat. You seem to be enjoying what you have so far.' He took another spoonful.

'I will get you some more.'

'Later,' Hira added. Sabina took her cue. She grabbed Amara by the hand.

'Let's go Amara. Let's put dinner together. Do you fancy anything, Hira?'

'Mmm, spicy roast chicken legs, with boiled vegetables and creamed potatoes.' Her eyes were closed but there was a faint smile on her face.

***

'Hira. Get back to bed. You are still are feverish. In a few days' time the spots will come out and then you will be moaning that they are itching.' Her mother fussed, feeling her forehead and propelling her back towards the bedroom. She did a childish about turn and re-entered the kitchen.

'But maman. I am hungry.' She whined. Again her mother tried to get her to bed.

'I will bring you some soup.' Hira pouted.

'Don't want soup.' She sulked, arms crossed. Hira's mother smiled and wrapped her in her arms.

'So you don't want soup. What do you want?'

'I want mashed potatoes and chicken.'

'With veg?'

'No veg.' Again the pout.

'Just a little. I will have some too. Okay?' Hira nodded and

smiled, throwing her arms around her mother.
'You are the bestest mother in the whole world.' She told her.

***

To make Hira a little more comfortable Aaryan took the decision that if it was agreeable with everybody else then for once they will eat together in the bedroom. With Aiden and Alman's help he set up a makeshift table and brought together enough chairs for them all to sit comfortably.

Aiden sat and licked his fingers, noisily, enjoying the taste of the spicy chicken that he had just eaten.

'That was perfect,' he complimented.

'Wasn't it just.' Sabina smiled and offered him another piece. She then leant over towards the bed and offered Hira another piece. Hira declined.

'I am full.' She looked about her. 'Where is Dadaji?' she asked. 'Has he gone with Dadi too?' Aaryan shook his head.

'No, Dadaji took the opportunity to go to Lucknow to see Grandpa Hafiz. He and Dadi have not been getting on too well. He will stay there for a few days. He looked in on you before he went and asked us to keep him up to speed with your recovery.'

'Speaking of which, has anyone called Dadaji?' Amara asked. Four confused and shocked people scrabbled for their phones.

'We forgot.' Aiden answered sheepishly. Aaryan dialled Dada's cellphone.

'Hello. Dadaji? Yes it is Aaryan.' In response to the old man's questions he held the phone slightly away from his ear. Sabina motioned to him to put it on speaker. 'Yes Dadaji. Hira is awake. Yes she is speaking. We have just had dinner. Yes Hira too.' Dada's voice came through loud and clear.

'Hira beta. You don't know how happy I am to hear that you are conscious. Now you look after yourself. I am going to be with Hafiz for tonight but when I come back I expect to see you up and about like before.' Hira mustered up the strength to answer him strongly.

'Rest assured Dadaji. I will be ready to greet you on your return.' She replied then wiped the sheen of sweat that had gathered on her upper lip.

'See you tomorrow.' Aaryan told him and cut the call. 'I think that you have had enough excitement for today.' Hira didn't protest. Although she was happy to be amongst them all, it had tired her out. The others took their cue and removed the dinner plates. The chairs went back to their original places.

He pulled back the bed sheets.

'Come on.' Hira looked at him puzzled. 'Bathroom. You kept looking this way so I figured that is what you want.' He said by way of an explanation. Hira got unsteadily to her feet. Gingerly he held her and led her to the bathroom.

'I can take it from here,' she told him.

'What happens if you fall?'

'I will be careful,' Hira replied.

'I'll get Sabina or Amara to help you.' Hira furiously shook her head.

'Please. No.' she pleaded, embarrassed. If there was any way that she was going to hold on to her dignity then she would do all she could.

'What if I don't lock the bathroom door?' she bargained with him. 'I will be careful.' She sensed relief and discomfort in his features.

'If you are sure?'

She nodded.

'I promise that if I get into any difficulties I will call you.'

He grudgingly let her go.

'Leave the door unlocked. If you don't call me in five minutes then I shall come in,' he warned her. She nodded and gingerly entered the bathroom.

Time and time again he looked at his watch and then at the bathroom door. Finally, his fretting got the better of him and he marched to the door. Before Aaryan could reach her he heard her call. Sighing with relief he entered expecting to see her lying on the floor and got ready to chastise himself. As it was she was at the vanity holding on for dear life. In two strides he was with her and supported her while he kicked the bathroom stool out from behind the vanity and placed her on it.

'I should not have let you come in alone,' he scolded her gruffly. 'You need help.'

'I never let my mother assist me ever and you think I would let you?' She tried to make light of the situation. 'Can I have my toothbrush? Please.' She smiled at him. He got her toothbrush ready and handed it to her.

'Just don't give me any grey hairs okay? I think I have had enough drama from you over the past few weeks.'

'Huh.' She scoffed. 'You call this drama?' And gave him a wide eyed look. Even in her weakened state she managed to lift his mood.

'Brush.' He pointed to the sink then supported her until she finished and wiped her face. 'This would be the perfect time to decipher you.' He laughed. 'At least you can't run off or get called away.'

'Decipher?' She asked.

'Yes. I want to find out more about you. Those text messages weren't enough. I want to know more about you and I want you to know about me too.' He looked in the mirror at her and they locked eyes for a moment. 'But we have ample time for that. For now concentrate on getting better.' She turned to him unsteadily.

'Have I said thank you?' He looked surprised.

'Do you have to?'

'It is only polite. Thank you.' He shrugged.

'You are welcome. Come on. Back to bed. You can rest and I need to catch up with some work.' He led her out and helped her into bed then switched the television on and handed her the remote.

'Not too loud,' he warned her. 'I need to finish off a few things.' Flicking through the channels she opted for a serious looking programme. Aaryan brought out his laptop to do some work. When he looked up half an hour later she was fast asleep. Carefully he removed the remote, switched the television off and settled down to sleep too.

Chapter 40

A loud crash woke him up with a start. He glanced around the room to make sure that everything was in its place and then he looked at Hira to make sure that she was alright. Her side of the bed was empty. With a dozen thoughts running through his mind he shot out of bed. The light was on in the bathroom. He knocked on the door and entered immediately.

'Hira? Are you alright? What are you doing?' Hira stood before him with a sheepish look on her face.

'Sorry,' she said. 'The shampoo bottle fell.' He glared at her.

'A shampoo bottle makes that much noise?'

'If you drop it, it does.'

'Funny,' he commented. 'What are you doing? I did say that you would be able to shower in a few days,' Hira held the towel tighter around her and shuddered in pain as it rubbed against her burn, '... and that too on your own. You could have told me or asked Sabina or Amara to help you? What if you had fainted?' Hira looked at him shamefaced.

'It has been days,' Hira complained. 'I couldn't bear another day without showering. I didn't think of that.' She said as his last question sunk in. 'I only wanted to wash but didn't want to put anyone out.' Droplets of water ran from her hair wetting her shoulders, mesmerising him for a few seconds. Despite herself she started to shiver. He was quick to notice this. Sighing in exasperation and concern he stepped forward, lifted her up and took her back to the bedroom.

Placing her on the bed he wrapped her up and proceeded to rub her hands to try and warm her up.

'Look at you,' he chastised her. 'Stupid. Why did you not wait? Now I don't know if you are just very cold or going into shock.'

'Who are you calling stupid?' she retorted, 'the hot water hurt my burn so I turned down the temperature a little.'

'I rest my case.' Still she shivered. The shivering became violent. He gave up on rubbing her hands and arms to improve her circulation and decided on the next best thing. Wrapping them both up in blankets he used his body heat to bring her temperature back up.

Gently he held her close to him as her shivering slowly subsided. Relieved that she was not in shock he closed his eyes.

'I'm sorry.' His eyes opened to find her looking directly at him. 'I didn't think that I would get this bad. I have made you cold too. Sorry.' He moved closer to her, if that was possible, to assure her that it was alright. Her shivering continued. He wrapped the blanket around them even tighter. Being swaddled in the bedsheet her temperature regulated. Hira snuggled up against him and shut her eyes.

An hour later Aaryan woke with a start. He had dozed off just as Hira had done. Gently he got out of bed so as not to disturb her. He needed to get ready and Hira's burn would need to be dressed. Silently he hoped that he hadn't inadvertently made it worse.

He emerged from the bathroom washed and dressed, armed with fresh dressings the special aloe burn cream Grand Aunt had left.

'Now you make sure that you apply this on Hira, daily. Don't skimp. Because if you do. I will know. I have spies everywhere,' she had warned him, holding his hand in her vice like grip and whispering in his ear. 'You take care of my girl. She now has me on her side. Don't think that she is alone.'

'Hira,' he spoke gently. 'Hira I need to put on a fresh dressing.' He lifted the blanket. She stirred and he helped her onto her front so that he could dress the burn. As he cleaned and applied the aloe she flinched, which in turn make him flinch too. Eventually the job was done. He stepped back, removed the gloves and wiped his brow. Second to the initial burn this had to be the hardest thing he had to deal with.

'I'll get you your pyjamas.' He moved towards the wardrobe.

'Aaryan.' She called to him. 'Is there any way that I can come down to breakfast too?' Brown eyes implored him.

Are you sure you want to go down for breakfast?' Hira nodded.

'The sooner I get back to a bit of normality the quicker I will get better and it has been a good two weeks since. I think I can cope.'

'I get you,' he said, agreeing with her. 'But the moment you feel any discomfort you tell me. Alright?' She nodded. He looked in

172

the wardrobe. 'Do you have a preference on colour?' He scanned the recently bought clothes.

'Blue?' He nodded and pulled out an outfit and handed it over. 'Shall I help you?'

'I should be fine.'

He nodded and moved to the dresser. Through the mirror he watched as she dressed. Struggling a little as she found putting the dress over her head somewhat difficult he weighed up whether he should help her or not. As he moved she finally got the dress on and smoothed it down. A quick comb through her hair and at last she was ready.

'Remember what I said earlier? The first sign of discomfort and you are back up here.'

Sabina and Amara beamed as they spied Hira and Aaryan descending the stairs. Both placed the food on the dining table and rushed forward.

'Hira. We were going to bring breakfast to you. Are you sure that you are well enough to be down here?' Amara gushed.

'Of course she is well enough,' Aaryan puffed. 'She has been cared for by the best.' Aiden came up behind him.

'More likely, that she had to get better quickly to get away from your care,' He teased and took his place.

'I am very hurt,' Aaryan huffed. 'What do you say?' He turned to Hira.

'I'm hungry.' She replied diplomatically, taking her seat. 'Can we eat?'

'Tactical, Hira does not want to upset anyone. But she is not wrong. We are all hungry.' He took his place and reached for the food. Sabina looked at Amara and then at the helper.

'I guess we are hungry.' She laughed. 'Tuck in. We can catch up later.'

Three sets of mobiles rang. Aaryan was the first to answer his. They watched as he listened.

'Dayal. Don't fret. Keep them busy. We will be there as soon as we can.' He cut the call. 'The team from Bhuj are at the offices.' He looked at Hira. 'I have to go. Will you be alright?'

Hira nodded.

'I will be fine.'

'No stupid stuff?'

'Not at all. Besides down here what trouble can I get up to?' she asked him sweetly. He stood up.

'With you? Anything is possible,' he teased, much to the merriment of his brothers and sisters-in- law.

'Don't worry. While Hira is with us she will be fine. We will look after her.'

'I will be back as soon as I can.'

Sabina smiled benevolently.

'Aaryan there is really no need. We are here,' she indicated at Amara. 'As I said, we will take care of her.'

Aaryan agreed reluctantly.

'If there is anything you will call me.' It was more of an order. Sabina nodded. With a glance towards Hira to make sure that she was going to be fine he went off to get ready.

Chapter 41

Hira was napping on the sofa in the early evening, when there was a commotion at the main door.

'Is there anybody here? An old lady needs a little help.' Hira looked up and smiled. Grand Aunt Zehra stood at the door laden with flowers and bags of shopping. All of them in danger of slipping from her grasp. Before she had a chance to get up the help appeared, greeted Grand Aunt Zehra and relieved her of the bags of shopping.

'Grand Aunt Zehra.' Hira got up and slowly made her way to her, 'It is so lovely to see you. Come in.' She turned to the help, Kavita. 'Can you let Sabina and Amara know that Grand Aunt is here.' The help nodded.

'My child.' Grand Aunt reached up and touched her cheek lovingly. 'How happy I am to see you up.' Tears filled the old lady's eyes. 'When I heard what had happened I could not help myself. I had to come and see you but you were asleep the whole time. These are for you.' She handed over the bouquet of flowers.

Behind them a driver appeared with a number of large cushions, comforter and a pair of slippers.

'Place the cushions over there?' She told the man indicating to the sofa where Hira had sat '... put the comforter with them. I shall sit there.' She smiled at Hira. 'What can you do? When you get to my age you have to take your comforts with you where possible.' Hira led her to the sofa. When Grand Aunt was finally comfortable she finally concentrated on Hira.

'Grand Aunt? What was the need to bring all these cushions? You know that we would have a bed ready for you if you got weary.'

'I know. But going to bed would mean that I would not be able to be with you. How are you? Aaryan told me that you didn't want to stay in bed.'

'Oh Grand Aunt, it just got a bit too much. Being in bed and not doing anything and then seeing the same walls day in day out. I wanted a change of scenery.' Grand Aunt leant forward with a mischievous glint.

'I take it that, that grandson of mine didn't attempt anything to take your mind off the boredom.' Hira looked at her with big innocent eyes. Grand Aunt nudged her gently. 'That look won't wash with me.' She laughed. 'I invented it. Alright, but he did look after you well? Yes?'

'Yes Grand Aunt. He did. Can I get you some tea? Juice? Food?' Gingerly she moved forward. Grand Aunt held her back.

'All in good time, all in good time. But I will help myself. You don't worry. I came here to see how you were. Not to make you run around after me. Now you sit down and stay with me.'

Hira gingerly leant back and closed her eyes. Grand Aunt studied her features. She reached out and moved away a strand of hair from her forehead.

'You have some of your mother's qualities,' she whispered. Hira opened her eyes in surprise.

'You knew my mother? How?' Grand Aunt Zehra looked at her with sad eyes.

'Her grandfather lived in the same area as us. She used to come and visit him. When she was a baby she played in my lap. Then in subsequent years she visited me often. The day she left for the UK was the saddest time. She was still a young girl. I didn't see her for a long time after that and thought that she had forgotten me. That is until May just gone. When I saw you that day at the house I wasn't sure you were her daughter until I asked Appa.' Hira watched her intently.

'What was the relationship between you? Mum never said a lot about family back home. She was always sketchy. I only knew about Dadi's existence because Mum spoke a little about her but nothing else.' She sat up straight. 'You met mum when she visited. How was she? When she came home she was different. What happened while she was out here?'

Grand Aunt patted her arm to pacify her. Her mind thought things over. *'Would Grand Aunt know what had transpired between Dadi and her mother? Maybe she would be able to shed some more light on the events? Why had her mother come to see Dadi and for what reason.'* She thought.

'So many questions? I saw your mother as my niece. Not through blood, but I adored her like she was my own. When she came she only visited me briefly for a couple of hours then came to see Appa. Straight afterwards she left to go back to the UK. Didn't meet with anyone she just left.' Hira looked sad and looked away. It appeared Grand Aunt was in the dark too.

'When she came back she was different, quiet.' Hira

continued. 'Moody. She wouldn't talk to me properly and kept crying. After a week or so she became sick. One day she collapsed. They said at the hospital that she suffered from a bleed on the brain. She had a blood clot which they thought might have been caused by a fall. She never came back after that.' Hira cried, letting the tears fall unabashed. 'I sat at her bedside for so many days and nights. I would tell her about Uni, my studies. I even talked about old times just to get a reaction. I never dreamt that she would not be coming home. I was with her most of the time. But when she breathed her last I wasn't there. I wasn't there. She left me all alone and then I came here and couldn't understand why this had happened, why I had to agree to all this.' For the first time since Hira's arrival to India she cried in public. Already feeling delicate, finding a kindly soul in this elderly lady tipped her over the edge and she let her guard down. Grand Aunt tried to soothe her but she had tears in her own eyes too. She hugged Hira and together they cried.

Sabina and Amara had just come in from the garden when they heard crying. They rushed to where Hira sat, fearing the worst. Grand Aunt wiped away Hira's tears.

'Hira. Have patience. The pain won't go away but it will ease. But my child you have kept all this to yourself. I want you to remember the good times with your mother and know that we are all here to help you.' She looked up and saw Sabina and Amara. She put her arm out and beckoned them to her. The huddled together, joining in Hira's sadness and comforting her while she still wept uncontrollably. 'You have found two sisters here who love you. Two brothers who have welcomed you, a husband who is beginning to care for you as each day goes by. On top of that you have me and my family. Never consider that you are alone. You have us.'

It took a good while for the crying to subside. Eventually it was reduced to sniffles. Grand Aunt looked up and spied Kavita hovering nearby. Silently she indicated to her to make a pot of milky tea. Kavita nodded and disappeared to make the brew. When she brought out the tea everyone had composed themselves and freshened up. They led both of them to the table and helped themselves to a cup to soothe their minds, puffy eyes and a balm to their minds.

'Hira. Why don't you sleep for a while? You look done in. If you want I can set up a bed for you in the guest room?' Hira shook her head.

'I will be fine,' she said. 'I can snooze on the sofa if need be.' She got up and went over to the sofa.

'Hira. Listen to them. I will come and sit with you,' Grand Aunt declared. 'I just need my comforter, a few more pillows, tv with some good programmes and ice cream. Lots of ice cream.' Amara smiled.

'We will send out the driver to get some ice cream. What flavours would you like?'

'No need.' Grand Aunt looked pleased with herself. 'It is all taken care of. I handed your maid a couple of shopping bags. I bought ice cream, samosas, pakoras, more snacks and dinner for tonight. There is no need to do any cooking.'

'You are spoiling us,' Sabina told her. 'We will get used to it.' Grand Aunt made a face.

'Unlike my sister I believe that you can achieve more with kind words and kind actions. I have seen the way she behaves towards you and it is wrong.'

Amara looked over at Hira and noticed her asleep. Quietly she got up, collected a blanket and covered Hira with it.

'She practically cried herself to sleep,' she said sadly as she sat back down.

'She will have many more days,' Grand Aunt said sadly. 'She will remember the days she spent at her mother's bedside and seems to blame herself for not being there when she finally went. It is a lot to deal with. But she has you all and I am sure that you will support her as you have always done.'

'It is hard not to,' Sabina told her. 'Hira is so easy to get on with. She gelled with us from the start.'

'You three are so much like my daughters-in-law.' Grand Aunt patted her arm. 'You all rub along nicely. I have been fortunate. Pity Appa can't see that. It will be her downfall one day.'

At the mention of Dadi both Sabina and Amara looked uncomfortable. To break the impasse Sabina stood up.

'I'll just go and lay out some of the snacks. Can I get you anything?' Grand Aunt smiled and shook her head.

'I think I will take a leaf out of Hira's book and have a little snooze.' With a little effort she got to her feet, grabbed her comforter and settled down.

'I'll get the television wheeled out for you in case you want to watch.' Amara headed off to the study. As she returned she found Grand Aunt asleep and snoring gently. With a smile she left the television and tiptoed away.

Aaryan entered the bedroom and placed his case on the table. He had stayed at the office longer than he had anticipated but it was all productive. He felt a huge sense of achievement. In the dim light he saw Hira sleeping and crept up to her. Gently he placed the back of his hand on her forehead then her cheek and frowned. He sat on the edge of the bed.

'Still feverish. It was too soon to have left the bedroom. Next time I will go with my gut instincts no matter how hard you try and bargain.' He stroked her hair affectionately, leaning closer he placed a light kiss on her temple.

'Aahhh. That's what I like to see, so touching,' Aaryan started.

'What?!' In his surprise he slipped off the edge of the bed scrambling on the marble floor in his socks. At last he composed himself. 'Who?' He switched on the bedside lamps and came face to face with Grand Aunt. She grinned at him.

'Don't be alarmed. It is only me.' Aaryan let out a sigh.

'You startled me.'

'I can see that,' she laughed. 'It was so funny to see a normally composed Aaryan react the way you did. But that was so touching and cute. I just had to say something before you got any further.' She winked at him. He laughed a little uneasily.

'How are you?' He walked to her and accepted her blessings. 'But it is naughty of you to hide away,' he joked.

'I didn't hide away.' She told him. 'You just didn't see me sat here... and I did speak out.' Aaryan looked at Grand Aunt and then to Hira. He saw shades of the same personality just then.

'I guess I should be thankful for that?' He ran his fingers through his hair. A trifle embarrassed. Grand Aunt hugged him.

'I felt a certain peace in my heart when I saw that scene.' She whispered. 'I was so worried, for you as well as Hira.' Aaryan returned her hug.

'You don't worry, Grand Aunt. Hira and I are fine and I am

sure that we will be extremely happy one day.' He straightened and looked at Hira.

'I am sure you both will be.' She moved towards the door. 'Now that you are here can you see me home? I had wanted to stay overnight but my back is beginning to play up.' Aaryan's heart went out to Grand Aunt. She had probably sat at Hira's bedside all evening.

'As if you have to ask?' Gently he held Grand Aunt by the arm and led her away, ensuring that she was not harried.

'You are a good boy.' She reached up and placed her hand on his head. 'I pray that you will always find happiness.' She blessed him.

A thought came to his mind.

'Aunt, can I ask you something?' She reached up and placed a hand on his shoulder.

'Of course.' He asked her to sit with him and told her of his plan. When he had finished Grand Aunt beamed. 'What a wonderful idea. I'm on board.' Aaryan sat back, pleased with himself.

On the drive to Grand Aunt's place he fielded all her questions about Hira's care, use of aloe gel for the burns and his patience towards his patient after which they discussed plans. Grand Aunt advised him that it would be worthless keeping things from Hira. That it would be best to make all the arrangements and then let her into his plans. However she was happy to keep Hira in the dark for as long as she could. He weighed everything up and agreed with her.

'And Hira can stay with me until then. Things will have to be done right. I will come back and take her with me. We can try and keep as much as possible in keeping it as a surprise. When did you want to set things in motion?'

'I want Hira to recover fully. We could give it another three weeks or so maybe a few more months is even better. By then she should be a lot better.' Grand Aunt rubbed her hands happily. 'This is going to be so exciting. I shall come to your house the week beforehand and take Hira with me. Let us do things properly.' She yawned loudly, making him laugh at her. 'Sorry. I guess it is way past my bedtime.' He laughed.

'I thought old people didn't need much sleep.' Grand Aunt feigned anger.

'I am not old. I am just cured longer than most. Come in for some tea?' He shook his head.

'I thought you were tired? Besides I should get back. I might be needed. You know with both Dada and Dadi out of the house.' Grand Aunt agreed. A manservant arrived to escort Grand Aunt into the house.

'Drive carefully.' He nodded and set off.

Chapter 42

Aaryan had checked all the rooms in the house but he could not find Hira. Everyone had retired to their rooms after dinner but she was nowhere to be seen. He even checked the storeroom. In the end a little voice told him to try the garden. Putting on his chappals he ventured outside to look for her.

She was there pottering among the flower beds which now held a blaze of colour and the sweet fragrance was nothing like he had smelt before. She had created a little piece of paradise in that part of the garden. Hira looked up and smiled at him.

'It had become quite wild,' she told him. He noticed how relaxed she looked. Thankfully as the weeks had progressed her recovery became easier. Now the pain was all but gone. There was scarring but not as bad as it could have been. He was grateful to Grand Aunt for all her good advice during the worst of the days.

'You must have been working here for some time,' he noted and sat on the bench which encircled the tree. 'You got the fountain working as well.' Hira looked at it and chuckled, remembering how the last time it had sprung into life then fizzled out.

'Yeah. It just needed a new connector and it is as good as new.' Aaryan sat back, closed his eyes and breathed deeply. The sounds and the smells that assailed his senses transported him to another plane. When he eventually opened his eyes Hira was watching him intently.

'You know Dadaji was sitting there exactly the same as you.' Aaryan wasn't surprised.

'It is very relaxing here. What are you doing with that?' He pointed to the makings of a canopy above him. She jumped onto the bench and reached up.

'This?' She pruned away some twigs which were in the way. 'I want to make a canopy. So it is comfortable to sit here when it is very sunny. The only thing I can't work out is how to create a lip so that if there is any creature up there that is likely to drop, it won't land on you.' She stretched higher to cut away some more but they were just out of reach.

'Wait.' He told her and stood on the bench. He bent down encircled her in his arms and lifted her up. Quickly she cleared around the branches. When she was done she looked down at him. He was

182

holding her closely to him, tight and he had an odd, vacant look on his face.

'You can let me down now.' She whispered.

'Hmm?' He snapped out of his reverie and slowly lowered her, holding her so close that not even air could come between them. To steady herself Hira placed her hands on his shoulders. She now stood there rooted to the spot as she stared deep into his eyes and felt herself returning his look of awe and affection. Still standing close he cupped her face, caressed her cheek and the corner of her lips. Feeling emboldened he leant forward and kissed her on the forehead, the cheek, corner of her mouth before placing a lingering kiss on her lips.

First he felt her hesitate then she relaxed, became more comfortable with the kiss and found her kissing him also. Aaryan felt an immense amount of happiness and relief. How easily she could have rejected him especially after his initial behaviour. He drew back and looked at her. She had twigs in her hair, was devoid of any make up, wearing old jeans and a t-shirt. He didn't want to be anywhere else or with anyone else. Both were totally lost in the moment that they did not notice that the rain that had been promised had finally arrived.

The sound of a throat being cleared made them jump. Hira nearly lost her balance and almost fell off the bench but was caught by Aaryan in time.

'When you love birds can spare a moment.' Dada stood before them, sheltering under a black umbrella, his kindly eyes settling on them and he smiled benevolently. He looked up towards the sky. 'As you haven't noticed the weather has broken. Best hurry. You don't want to catch a cold.' He turned and made his way back.

Hira jumped down and collected the tools. With a last glance towards her garden she looked towards Aaryan and smiled. He took her hand in his. In no obvious hurry they went indoors.

Hira stood by the window and dried her hair. Summer rain had always held a certain power over her. In India it was no different. She listened to the sound of the rain as it fell on the glass and closed her eyes. Aaryan sidled up behind her.

'Where are you?' He was bemused by the look on her face. She opened her eyes and turned to him.

'There is nothing quite like this, is there?' He sensed her love of the rain.

'I suppose not.' He took the towel from her and helped dry her hair. She laughed and took the towel from him.

'Hey Mister, before you start drying my hair perhaps you should have a look at yourself.'

'What? And what is wrong with me?' Hira looked him up and down. He was in dry clothes but his hair was still dripping wet. Much as hers dripped, but she was not going to admit to it.

'I think you need to learn how to dry yourself properly before you start to help others.' She giggled. He looked affronted.

'Is that so?' He asked, taking the towel from her and twirling it, getting ready to flick it at her. Hira backed up. She was aware of the towel torture from her school days. Even the girls used to indulge in the practice. She gave him a cheeky look.

'Of course it is.' Aaryan pretended to get ready to flick the towel at her but threw it instead as she ran, laughing and running around the bed to seek sanctuary in the bathroom where she could lock herself away. However she did not bank on Aaryan second guessing her. He reached the bathroom door before she did and grabbed her round the waist, lifted her up and swung her around. The towel landed on the floor and tangled in his feet, tripping him up and they landed on the bed. The giggling gave way to nervous silence as they looked intently at each other, both realising where they would be heading from this point. Aaryan had enjoyed the kiss earlier. As he looked into Hira's eyes he saw the same emotion in hers. He brought his lips down on hers. She reached up and ran her fingers through his wet hair and drank in the kiss …

***

Dadi sulked as she moved around her room. Since Dada had chosen to sleep elsewhere she was finding that she missed him. He had always indulged her, gave into her every whim and she did pretty much what she liked. This episode was temporary too she reasoned. After a while he will come back. But she was not going to make it easy for him. She smiled coquettishly to herself. He would have some major making up to do. That thought gave her a little spring in her step. Gathering her white dupatta, she wrapped it tightly around her head and went off in search of him.

Dada was lying on the bed. His eyes closed. She knew that he wasn't sleeping. Even as she sat on the bed he did not stir.

'Listen Ji,' she started demurely, taking his hand in hers. 'I know that I have disappointed you but how long can you be angry with me?' She massaged his hand. 'Come now.' She began placating him. 'Throw aside your anger. Come back to your bed. You know that I don't like it when you are angry with me. I will make you your favourite dish, rice pudding with almonds, pistachios and saffron. You will like that won't you?' Dada opened his eyes.

'If only I can believe that you are sincere in your words Soraya.' She looked at him. He removed his hand and sat up. 'But I have seen and heard enough these past few months, this year even. I asked you to change, to mend your ways but time and time again you disappoint me. How am I supposed to feel?'

'But I am not always at fault. The girls know nothing about household things. If I do not keep them in line who will? Under their care you would even get a decent meal twice a day.'

'These girls know more about household work than your very own granddaughter, Soraya. Together they have looked after not only me but you as well. All three of them and yet you mistreat them. Are you that jealous of them?' He looked at her long and hard. 'What were you thinking of when you indulged Akilah?' Dadi began to knead and massage his legs, not wanting to look him in the eye. 'You do realise that Akilah has been causing trouble at her in-laws?' Dadi quickly looked at him. 'Yes,' he told her. 'But unlike here, there are people there who will not stand for her tantrums. Because of you and the way you have always indulged her she is having trouble settling in.' Dadi nodded her head silently, making a mental note to call Akilah and give her a pep talk. Dada turned on his side ready to sleep.

'Are you still going to sleep in here?' Dadi was sure that she would be able to melt his anger a little.

'Soraya I am not going to decide just yet. For now I am observing and to be honest what I am seeing, I am not liking,' he yawned. 'I think it is best if you go to your room. I need to sleep. I am going to visit Ashraf tomorrow and will be away for a day or two,' he told her. Dadi got up. It was the first time she admitted defeat.

Previously she would have dogged him until he gave in. Sadly she walked out and entered her room. She was thankful, at least, that Dada's room was across the corridor. He hadn't distanced himself from her completely. She still had time to work on him and bring him round.

Chapter 43

Dadi watched closely at the interaction between Hira and Aaryan. There was definitely a change in them. Not for the better in her eyes. She saw the little half smiles, the secret meeting of hands accidently on purpose and Hira's blush. The signs gnawed at her until she could not take any more. The food she was eating became like cardboard and unpalatable. The happier Hira looked the angrier and the more jealous Dadi became.

Dadi cornered Hira as she cleared up in the study. Taking great pains to ensure that they were alone she made her move.

'What do you think you are playing at?' she hissed. Hira stopped what she was doing.

'I am not playing at anything.' She stood firm. 'What are you talking about?' Dadi took a few steps towards her. Mindful of the conversation regarding her mother's demise Hira made sure that there was enough distance between them. She didn't trust the woman as far as she could throw her.

'Playing happy families is what you are doing. I have seen those looks between you and my grandson. Do you think I am blind? You crossed the line that separated you from a girl to a woman. Don't think that I haven't noticed.' Hira looked at Dadi opened mouthed.

'Was this woman for real?' she thought.

'Isn't that what you expect married people to do? Those who have a deep affection for each other?'

'Silence!' Dadi screamed. 'Don't tell me what to expect and what not to. How dare you. You were not even here as a permanent fixture and now you have flaunted yourself in front of my grandson. I will not allow your shadow to even grace this house from now. You inherited the unsavouray traits from your mother. She was tainted and so are you!' Despite herself Hira allowed her anger to get the better of her.

'What do you mean tainted? If she was tainted then what are you?' Dadi gasped, feeling the air leave her lungs. 'You admitted to me that when my mother came to see you, you argued with her and pushed her. She was not tainted enough for you to kill her!' Dadi gasped. Hira would be her undoing. 'Why did you hate her so much and why do you hate me? I have done nothing to you. In fact before I came here I hardly knew you. What gives you the right to treat me like muck?' They faced off each other before Hira made the first move and pushed past the old lady.

'I have the right because your mother was my daughter,' Dadi spoke in a low voice. Hira turned around in shock.

'What?' Aaryan stood in the doorway, the shock on Hira's face mirrored in his. 'What did you say?'

Dadi seemed to shrink a little.

'Hira's mother was my daughter. Hira is my own granddaughter,' she eventually said.

Aaryan and Hira looked at each other. Both appalled at the revelation

'This is some kind of sick joke.' Aaryan turned to Dadi. 'You are just saying this to spite Hira.' Dadi shook her head.

'It is the truth. I disowned Hira's mother as a small child.' They scanned Dadi's features. She stood, unflinching, unremorseful and most of all unkind.

Hira could not bear to hear anymore. She pushed past Aaryan and ran to the bedroom.

'Hira. Wait.' Aaryan called after her. He stopped long enough to glare at Dadi. 'Are you only happy when you ruin things? What type of a woman are you? Is it true what Hira said?' He didn't wait for her to answer. 'You are just sick.' He left Dadi rooted to the spot.

Hira locked the door before Aaryan reached and started banging on the door.

'Hira. Open the door. Please open the door.' Hira turned her back to the door and tried to compose herself. But it was all in vain. Her eyes rested upon the bed and she saw in flashback the scene from the night before. Feeling sick to her stomach, she slid down the length of the door. Weeping silently, she wept for her mother, herself but most of all for the relationship with her husband that could no longer be.

On the other side of the door Aaryan was in no better shape. After trying to console Hira he too succumbed to the feeling of helplessness and loss.

'There was no coming back from this.' He thought and slid to the floor. 'Hira.' He uttered her name helplessly.

Sabina and Amara had heard the shouting and came running in time to see Hira run up the stairs. They tried to follow but were thrown when Aaryan rushed out of the study and chased after Hira. They stood open mouthed, looking towards the direction of the bedroom, scared as to the turn of events and worried as how to smooth things over.

Dadi came out of her study using her scarf to wipe the perspiration from her face.
'Don't stand there and gawp. Get on with your work,' she ordered. Quietly Sabina and Amara complied. Without a look back Dadi walked past them and retired to her room. 'I will not be eating tonight. I am not hungry.'

The atmosphere in the house screamed that there was something amiss. Hira had not emerged from her room for two days. Aaryan moved into one of the spare rooms yet he had lost the will to function normally. He sat for hours on end staring into space. Work did not interest him; play was a pass time that was lost for him. Even Aiden and Alman could not lift his mood at all. They were fast becoming at a loss as to what more they could do.

Sabina juggled the tray in her hand and knocked on the door.
'Hira. It is me. Open the door. I have brought you some soup.'
'I don't want it.' A sad Hira replied from behind the closed door. 'Take it away. I am not hungry.'
'Hira you have to eat,' she called out softly to her. 'Won't you heed the request of your sister and at least have a little.' She thought that again Hira would send her away. 'Please if you don't eat you will get sick.' Tears coursed down her cheeks. The sound of the door being unlocked gave her hope.

Hira opened the door and stood to one side looking forlorn and with eyes downcast. Sabina entered, placed the tray on the table and looked around the room. It was a mess. Hira in a rage had emptied the wardrobe. Throwing her clothing on the floor, mingled with them was the small amount of make she had brought with her.

'*The room can be sorted later,*' Sabina thought, but for now Hira was hurting. She would try all that she could to bring back the Hira of the past week. She manoeuvred her by holding her shoulders and led her to the table. 'Hira, please have some soup. You haven't eaten properly for days just a little bit here and there.' She picked up the spoon and put it in her hand.

Hira attempted a few spoonfuls before she pushed the bowl away.

'No more,' she whispered. Sabina stroked her hair.

'What has happened Hira? What has gone wrong? You and Aaryan seemed so happy.' Tears welled in Hira's eyes.

'It has all gone wrong,' she wept. 'Everything has gone wrong.' With a desolate look in her eyes she grabbed Sabina by the hands. 'Sabby, help me get back to the UK. I can't stand being here. Get me my passport. Please?' Sabina looked helplessly at her. This was something that was out of her reach. Instead, she held her until the tears stopped. Somehow there were no words that seemed to offer any solace.

Aaryan sat in the armchair in the guestroom and looked into space. He racked his brain to try and make sense of what had happened but he was at a complete loss. For a long time he stared at the white handset which was by the side of the bed.

In one quick movement he lurched forward, picked up the handset, dialled and waited for the call to connect.

Chapter 44

Hira watched as Grand Aunt pottered around the bedroom packing a bag. 'What are you doing?' Hira raised herself on her elbow and looked quizzically.

'You are coming to stay with me for a few days.' Grand Aunt told her picking things out from the wardrobe and dropping them in the bag. 'Look at the state of you?' she sympathised. 'Get ready. We will go as soon as possible.' Hira looked on. She tried to protest. 'No excuses. I will not entertain them.' She zipped up the bag. 'A few days at my place and I will soon have you forgetting all your troubles.' Hira looked at her with a mournful expression.

'I don't think that there is anything that can do that Grand Aunt.' Grand Aunt sat next to her and stroked her hair.

'Not Grand Aunt. From now on you will call me Grandma. A few days away from here will help. Now come on. Get ready. We will stop off and have breakfast somewhere nice. Come on.' She coaxed. Hira thought for a while. In the end she got up. 'That's my girl. I promise you that I will have you smiling within days.'

Washed, brushed and ready Hira stood at the foot of the bed and watched while Grand Aunt lay with her eyes closed, mouth open and snoring gently. Hira smiled a weak smile. This old lady was doing so much for her.

Grand Aunt opened her eyes, looked about her and smiled.

'Did I fall asleep?' Hira nodded. 'I have a habit of falling asleep wherever I lay my head.' She told her. Ready?' Hira nodded and picked up the holdall. 'Good let's go.'

In the shadows Aaryan watched silently as they left the house. Dadi walked up to him and touched his arm.

'Maybe it is for the best.' She told him. Aaryan shrugged her off.

'Don't tell me what is for the best when you have watched me open my heart and then looked on happily as you destroyed everything,' he told her and stomped off. She did not bother to conceal the smirk as she watched him go.

Dada walked outside towards Hira's garden. For days he had sung Hira's praises to Hafiz and today he had persuaded him to visit. His eyes focused on a sorry figure in the garden sitting under the tree.

He shot Hafiz a puzzled look and walked towards the man. Drawing close he gasped with shock.

'Aaryan what are you doing here? What has happened to you?' Aaryan sat before him with unkempt hair, days old stubble and sunken eyes. Normally a resilient and grounded man, today someone else sat before him, broken and a shadow of what he had been. He looked ready to pass out. Hafiz rushed forward and propped Aaryan up. Aaryan leant against his grandfather.

'Aaryan beta, what is wrong? Tell me? Tell your Grandpa Hafiz,' he coaxed and cajoled his grandson trying to get to the bottom of things.

'Things have got worse. There is no way back.' Both grandfathers looked on concerned, fearing the worst.

'How bad can they be?' Grandpa Hafiz tried to put on a brave face. Seeing his grandson in this state, for the first time in his life he felt close to tears himself. Such was Aaryan's plight. He exchanged worried glances with Dada.

Finally Aaryan's resolve broke and he broke down in Grandpa Hafiz's arms, narrating the events that had led him to the state where he was now. Both grandfathers listened, shock and anger reflecting on their faces. Eventually Dada couldn't hear any more. He shook Aaryan by the shoulder.

'You have allowed yourself to get into such a state.' Dada looked into Aaryan's eyes. 'Now listen to what I have to say. You will be strong and you will see this through. We are here for you.' He looked darkly towards the house. 'As for your grandmother, this is the last straw.' He stomped towards the house, his anger growing with each step.

Hafiz turned to Aaryan. He wiped the tears from his face.

'Dry your tears,' he told him. 'You can't accept defeat. You are my grandson,' Grandpa Hafiz comforted Aaryan. 'Things are not as dark as they seem.'

Chapter 45

It was the dead of night. Hira's sleeping patterns returned to what they were when she arrived in India.

'At least Aaryan is not here to give me a hard time for disturbing his sleep,' she thought bitterly.

Taking full advantage of that fact she snapped on the bedside light, taking the opportunity to survey the room. Her eyes settled on her holdall. She got up, picked it up and emptied the contents on to the bed. Her clothing had been taken out and hung up for her but there were a few things still left in behind. The first thing she picked up was a photo of herself with Amara and Sabina. Taken in somewhat happier days, when Aiden had surprised them. She smiled remembering how the three had told him off for creeping up on them. She placed the photograph on the bedside table and picked up the next one, before dropping it as if it was aflame. Aaryan smiled out at her. She turned the photo over. Before her vision blurred with more tears they alighted on a burgundy red document peeking out of the brown package that Aaryan had given her months ago. She scooped it up and quickly rifled through. It was her passport. But how? She was sure that Dadi had taken it. She shrugged. Either way it was back in her hands and her ticket back to the UK. For a moment her heart soared. In the morning she would ask Grand Aunt if she would lend her some money to buy a plane ticket. She would pay it back.

Placing the passport safely in the side pocket of the holdall her eyes settled on the papers that were with the passport. A feeling of guilt came over her. She had not even bothered to read them since they arrived. *'Oh well,'* she thought *'May as well check them out now. I've got nothing better to do.'* She made herself comfortable on the bed and picked up the first sheet.

Many hours later she placed the last sheet with the others and sat back with a sigh. This would delay her return to the UK and she let out a huge sigh. Just to be sure that she had not misread anything she picked up the pile and went through them again. The deeds to the land were there, her mother's inheritance which now passed on to her, deeds to the land and apparently a house too. She sat back frustrated. The land and the property was no use to her, especially if she was

193

returning to London.

At the first sign of the family rising, Hira left her room and padded along the corridor. Down the stairs and to the room where she was hoping that she might find some help.

The door to Grand Aunt's room was shut. Hira hesitated, unsure whether she should knock. Grand Aunt may well be sleeping. Thinking twice she turned to go back to her room. As she walked away she heard the door open.

'Hira?' Grand Aunt called after her. 'Child what are you doing up so early?' Hira turned round. 'I think the question isn't what are you doing up so early but have you even slept?' Hira shook her head. Grand Aunt tutted. 'What are you doing? You will make yourself sick, if that happens what am I supposed to say to your grandfather? That I brought you here only for you to fall sick again?' Hira shook her head.

'No Grandma, no such thing will happen and you won't have to tell anyone anything. I just wanted to ask you something?' Grand Aunt ushered her into the bedroom.

'What is it that you want to ask?' She sat down on the bed.

'I have papers which relate to the land that belonged to mum which has now passed onto me. I would like to sell the land. Will you help me? I want to go back to London.' Grand Aunt looked sad for a moment.

'I can't stop you if that is what you want to do. But I was hoping that you would stay on.' Tears pooled in her eyes. 'I have only known you for a short while but I have grown so attached to you.' Hira found herself crying too.

'There is nothing left for me here,' she told Grand Aunt. 'I love you to bits and Sabina, Amara, Dadaji, Aary...' She stopped abruptly. 'It is for the best.' Grand Aunt held her hand.

'If that is what you have decided.' Hira nodded. 'Why don't we do this? Before you finalise your plans why don't we go and see the land. That way you will get a first hand look at what you have inherited.' Hira nodded.

'Sounds good Grandma, can we go today?' Grand Aunt shook her head.

'I think first of all you need to get some rest. From the looks of it you have not slept. Am I right?' Hira looked uncomfortable. She felt bad for upsetting Grand Aunt.

'I couldn't sleep and then I started to read. I must have lost track of time.' Grand Aunt patted her hand.

'We all do that at times. I think that it is better for you to have some breakfast and then try and get some sleep. In the mean time I will give this information to Hameed to check out the paperwork and make arrangements to take us there.' Hira smiled weakly. 'But on one condition.' Grand Aunt waggled her finger at her. 'That, you will spend today getting some rest. Deal?'

'Deal.'

Grand Aunt finished her breakfast and sat looking into space with a sad expression on her face. Her daughters-in-law and grandchildren looked on concerned.

'Mother, what is wrong?' Farida asked her sitting next to her.

'Hira wants to leave,' Grand Aunt replied sadly.

'She wants to go back to Dadi Soraya's?' The old lady shook her head.

'She wants to go back to the UK.' Farida consoled her as best she could.

'If that is what she wants to do. We can't stop her,' she whispered. Grand Aunt nodded, sighed heavily and got up.

'I need to speak to Hameed. Can you call him for me?' Farida nodded.

'I'll get him to give you a call. Is that alright?'

Grand Aunt opened the door to Hira's room and peered through the crack. As per her request Hira had taken to bed and was fast asleep, the sheets bunched up at the foot of the bed. Gently she stepped forward and covered Hira and sat down. Then she noticed the photographs on the pillow. After spending all her life with just herself and her mother, Grand Aunt saw how Hira had finally found a family only to have it taken away on the whims of a cantankerous old woman. Gently she stroked Hira's forehead.

'Don't worry, my child. Things may look dark just now but I will get to the bottom of this.' She whispered.

Hameed smiled as he looked up and saw Hira making her way towards him.

'Hira. Come and sit down.' He patted to the space beside him.

'I hear that you would like to go and seen the land that your mother left you?' Hira nodded and joined him. 'Excellent,' he continued. 'Grandma you join us too. Now it made good sense to ask me about this. After all, I work in the Ordinance office and have all the information to hand.' He opened up his laptop. 'Now the land that you have acquired is in Saharanpur which is just under two hours away from here.' He brought up the information on screen. 'The land mostly has been lying idle for many years. Previously its primary purpose was as an orchard.' Hira looked intently at the photos that were brought up on screen.

'May I?' Hameed nodded. Hira took over the laptop and navigated through the site taking in the information on screen. 'Are there any stipulations on the land?' She asked. Hameed looked puzzled. 'I mean are there any implications to anyone living on the land?'

'I am not sure,' Hameed told her. 'I don't have any information on that as such. Anyway, I have arranged to visit the site on my day off. It will only take us a couple of hours to get there. Do you feel up to the trip Grandma?'

'You know me Hameed. Mention a journey to me and I am already at the door, with my picnic basket, raring to go, excited as a five year old.'

'Do you also do the 'are we there yet?' questions?' Grand Aunt smiled benevolently.

'But of course.' Hameed laughed and shook his head. His grandmother would not grow up gracefully.

Chapter 46

City roads gave way to countryside as the small group made their way to Shahranpur. For ease of travel Hameed had decided that the people carrier would be better.

'Are you alright there, Grandma?'

'Perfectly fine,' Grand Aunt replied. 'Just make sure that we have enough stops when we need.' She held Hira's hand. 'Are you okay?' Hira nodded.

'You know I am actually excited. I didn't think I would be but seeing the photographs the day before makes me want to see the land for myself.' Grand Aunt patted her hand before continuing to watch the speeding countryside out of the window as they drove.

They were met by a guide on the outskirts of the land. Hameed stepped forward and introduced himself and then his grandmother and Hira.

'So you have inherited the land?' The guide beamed at Hameed. 'I am so happy. The land has been idle for so long. What do you intend to do with it?'

'The land is not mine,' Hameed told him. He indicated towards Hira. 'It belongs to Hira.' The guide gave Hira a disdainful look.

'A non-resident Indian?' he queried. 'And a young girl?' Hira's hackles rose.

'Is there a problem with that?' she stepped forward. 'Why can't I own the land? You don't have a monopoly on it?' The guide backed down. Hira on the defensive was a force to be reckoned with and she stood before him anger flashing in her eyes.

'I'm sorry. I didn't mean to offend you. It is quite a new phenomenom in these parts of a woman inheriting such property. Shall we move on? I will show you around. Just be careful.' He told them but looked directly at Hira and Grand Aunt. 'It is quite overgrown in places.'

Hira held onto Grand Aunt's arm to support her as they made their way past the gates and came upon the house. Hira looked up at the house, a reminder of a bygone age and marvelled at it.

'At one time it must have been quite a majestic house,' she said in awe to Grand Aunt.

'These houses were built in the old way. As you can see it has stood the test of time and is still sturdy.' The man continued. 'Do you want to have a look inside? I can't guarantee what state that will be in.' Hira shook her head.

'Can we see the rest of the land?' they asked him. The guide showed them to his landrover.

'The best way to see the land is by this.' He helped them into the vehicle and set off. True to his word the land was quite overgrown. However, its purpose as an orchard still remained and the trees stood proudly displaying their wares, groaning under the weight of the fruit.

Grand Aunt chatted and chastised the guide for driving too fast or too carelessly, she pointed out various things to Hira until they eventually stopped by the edge of a bubbling, crystal clear stream.

'This is where your land ends,' Hameed told her pointing at the row of trees on the other side. Hira got out of the landrover and stared. She was somewhat dumbstruck. This was more land than she had anticipated. A lot more. Silently she wandered to the water's edge, sat down and cast her eyes down stream taking in the lush open land opposite. It looked familiar. She closed her eyes and smiled. The water gave her a sense of calm, a peace that had been missing in recent days. Ripened guavas fell from the branches and splashed into the stream causing her to open her eyes. At last she got up and caught Grand Aunt looking at her. Hira now knew why she had suggested to Hira to see this place and nodded knowingly at her.

'Are you alright?' Grand Aunt asked holding her hand.

'I'm fine,' She told her, turning to take in a final look at the place. 'Shall we get back? The weather looks like it will turn any moment.' Grand Aunt looked towards the gathering dark clouds.

'You are not wrong there.' She turned to Hameed and the guide. 'It is getting colder. We should make a start.' The men agreed. Within minutes they were on their way back navigating the small dirt tracks and on to the main road.

'Are you sure you don't want to have a look around the house?' The man asked her once more.

'Another time perhaps.' Hira replied. A light drizzle was beginning to fall and she did not want Grant Aunt to get wet.

'Ishrat? Ishrat is that you?' An elderly voice called out.

Puzzled Hira turned around. The owner of the voice moved before her. 'You are not Ishrat.' He looked confused. 'But you look so much like her.'

'Ishrat was my mother,' Hira told him. 'My name is Hira.' The old man nodded. He looked at Grand Aunt and offered her a greeting.

'My name is Mukhtar Ali but everyone around here calls me Mukhti. I have been living on the outskirts of this land for many years.' He looked at Hira but saw another person in her place. 'You are so much like Ishrat it makes sense that you are her daughter. May I make one little request?' Hira looked at Hameed and Great Aunt. They nodded in unison. Mukhti pointed to a little cottage just peeping through the trees on the opposite side of the road. 'That is my little home there. Won't you come in and have something to eat?' Hira was about to refuse but there was something about this man that made her want to sit and chat with him. Hira smiled and nodded.

The guide bade farewell and left them in the care of Mukhti. They crossed the road and entered the cottage. Mukhti introduced his grandson and granddaughter-in-law to them. While the food was being prepared Mukhti sat them down and gave them blankets to warm them up.

'I was a young lad when I joined my father in this cottage,' he told them. 'At that time this place was busy and full of life. Our family has been here on this land and kept an eye on things for generations.' He passed over milky cups of tea to them, his hands shaking slightly. 'Your grandfather employed my father as a watchman and after my father passed on I upheld the tradition and kept watch. These days there is no one to give us a salary but we get by. Alas to say, I am the last of my kind.' He indicated towards his grandson. 'My grandson now works in the city. He doesn't have the inkling to continue in my line of work.' He fell silent for a while, almost apologising for the end of a tradition. Hira leant forward.

'You called me by my mother's name. How much did you know her?'

'I remember your mother when she was a young child. Your great grandfather, Shazad used to bring her here often. She would often play in the gardens and want to run off further into the orchards. I would play hide and seek with her. We would go as far as the stream and play. When she was tired I carried her back home on my shoulders. She was a breath of fresh air. Then one day she was gone. I heard that her father had taken her abroad. It was a dark day for us. Things were never the same for Shazad. His arguments with his daughter grew worse day by day.'

'My grandmother? What kind of arguments?' Hira sat forward listening intently. 'I hardly know anything about Dadi.'

'There were arguments galore,' he told her. 'From her lack of care to her studies to her behaviour towards others, by all accounts she was the epitome of a spoilt brat but the main one was that she chose to marry a man of her choosing. When Shazad refused their union she ran off and got married. Shazad was a broken man. For a few years he did not talk very much. Just holed himself up in the mansion. We hardly saw him for days but when Ishrat was born we got our Shazad back. The smile re-appeared on his face and he could not stop talking about her. Then came the fateful day when Ishrat's father took her away. She was still a babe in arms. We never saw her again after that.' Hira took the samosa that was offered to her.

'But how did you think that I was my mother?' She bit into the samosa. 'You said that she was a baby when she left?' The old man smiled.

'I saw Ishrat here in early June. She had come to see the place and make peace. She also gave me some sweets all the way from London.'

'Do you know what happened to my grandmother?' Hira asked. Her great-grandfather must have been really hurt to take the action that he did.

'Soraya?' The old man thought out loud. 'She was a nasty, nasty person. She came back here to live after her husband divorced her but she was never happy. She argued with Shazad morning, noon and night. In the end I heard that Shazad had fixed her alliance with a widower by the name of Sadiq. She fought it every step of the way and argued that she did not want to take on someone else's children but in the end she married him. After that we never saw her again although there was some talk, rumours mostly that Soraya had something to do with Sadiq's first wife passing away.' Hira reacted visibly to that piece of news.

'Was anything proved?' she asked. But the old man had not heard her. He continued reminiscing. 'Shazad passed on and that was the last time I had dealings with his family.' Grand Aunt snorted and woke up from her nap. Hira shivered involuntarily.

'Are you cold?' Grand Aunt asked. Hira shook her head.

They had stayed with Mukhti longer than anticipated. It was nightfall when they pulled up outside the house. Grand Aunt led the way greeting Farida and Janaat at the door.

'Any chance of a hot cup of tea and some nibbles?' she asked.

'Of course, Mother,' Janaat replied and headed off to the kitchen. Grand Aunt sat down and removed her shoes.

'Oh that feels good.' She leant back. 'I love going out on trips but I love it more when I can get back and take my shoes off.' Hira chuckled.

'Grandma you are not alone. Most women in London do the exact same thing when they come home after a long day or partying.'

'One of the best feelings there is.' Hameed walked by on his way to the study.

'Hameed,' Hira called after him. 'Can I borrow your laptop for a while or do you have a spare one.' Hameed handed over his laptop to her.

'Here you go.'

After an hour Hira sat back. She had surfed the internet for some time and had come up against a brick wall. Hameed noticed her disappointment.

'What were you trying to find out?' he asked her.

'Can you access birth, marriage and death certificates on the internet here?' Hameed shook his head.

'India might be competing shoulder to shoulder with the rest of the world on IT issues and development but as far as accurate records go, we still have plenty of work to do. Were you looking at birth certificates in particular?' Hira nodded. 'Can I say something? Please don't be offended.'

'Shoot.' Hameed looked puzzled. 'Sorry, I mean go ahead.'

'I know that you received some shocking news and for that I am sorry but I just want you to think about this. Would your Dadi have fixed your marriage if she knew that both you and Aaryan are closely related?' Hira sat back and thought hard. Hameed had a point.

'Dadi is so blinded by hatred and greed that I wouldn't put it past her.' Hira spoke bitterly. 'By all accounts she was not averse to using people to suit her own ends. I can't give her the benefit of the doubt Hameed. She has a mean streak that feeds on making people feel inferior.'

'Can I do anything to help you?' Hira was surprised.

'You? Why would you want to do that?'

'Aaryan and I go back a long way, almost to the crib.' He laughed. 'I have stood by him as he vented his frustrations, when he eventually fell in love with a mad girl from the UK.' His features sobered for a moment. ' ... and I have seen him in the depths of despair. If by helping you I can ease his pain then I will do what I can.' Hira looked at him with grateful eyes. Aaryan was lucky to have a friend like him.

'It would be really helpful if you could,' she told him. 'But bear in mind that what we do find out may not be what we were hoping for.' Hira sat back. The small ray of sunshine she had seen was now obscured by the thoughts of a different reality.' Hameed leant forward.

'Whatever it takes.'

Chapter 47

Hira sat at the breakfast table and suppressed a yawn. She smiled at Ghalib, the youngest member of the family, who copied her. At the age of three, he showed great promise in becoming a top police inspector when he grew up. Every question was followed by another to the point that he was driving the poor family members mad.

'Amma, why do you hide your money there?' He pointed to Farida's bust. 'Do you keep it there for the milkman?' Farida blushed and blustered, trying to give him an answer that would not lead to another. Hira chuckled. She called to him.

'Ghalib come here.' He ran to her. 'Do you want to help me make some fairy cakes?' He looked at her with big eyes.

'Caketh come from the thops,' he lisped. Hira looked at Farida.

'Do we have ingredients?' Farida nodded.

'If we haven't then Azam can go and get them for you,' she said gratefully. Being blessed with a son so late in life was quite an experience and now that he was at the enquiring stage he was wearing her out. If Hira could keep him occupied for a few hours it was a boon. Hira bent down to Ghalib's level.

'Today we will make cakes better than the ones you get from the shops.' Ghalib gave her a disparaging look as if he knew better but followed her into the kitchen anyway.

It seemed to do the trick. Ghalib yawned as the cakes were placed in the oven. Hira carried him to the little area set up for him, laid him on his side and covered him with a shawl. Farida came up behind her and handed her a glass of juice.

'You have earned this.' She told Hira. 'Not many can handle someone else's child with such affection straightaway.' Hira took the glass from her and smiled. 'Well he is such an adorable child. Who cannot fall for his charms?' She sipped the juice and immediately thought back to Mukhti's words.

'She fought with Shazad that she did not want to take on someone else's children. There was some talk, rumours mostly that Soraya had something to do with Sadiq's first wife passing away.' Hira almost choked on the juice.

Grand Aunt came upon the two deep in conversation.

'And what are you two up to?' she asked a teasing smile played on her lips.

'Hira has spent the morning keeping Ghalib entertained.' Farida told her. 'She tired him out.' Hira yawned and tried to cover it up.

'… and herself too. You should do what I do. Grab as many naps as you can. It keeps you young.' She nudged Hira and winked.

Grand Aunt turned to go to her room.

'Grandma,' Hira called out to her. 'I know that I must have made you sad with my request yesterday morning.' Hira looked at the ground and then back at Grand Aunt. 'I am so sorry. I didn't mean to hurt you.' Grand Aunt touched her cheek.

'You can never hurt me.' She smiled. 'My happiness lies in what makes you happy.' Hira was touched. Slowly she raised her hand and covered the old lady's and held it to her cheek.

'I have never met anyone like you or the people in this family. You are so giving and loving. If ever I go away from here I will take some beautiful memories with me.'

'If?' Grand Aunt looked into Hira's eyes. She nodded.

'There is some unfinished business and a couple of relationships that I need to get to the bottom of. I am not going to leave until I get some answers,' she said confidently. Grand Aunt smiled and threw her arms around Hira.

'Each and every day I see you I am proud in the way you conduct yourself. You have my prayers and blessings with you.' She stepped back.

'Grandma I would like to visit the land again, if that is alright?'

'But of course. I will get Hameed to arrange for a car and accompany you.' Hira shook her head.

'No Grandma. I don't want to put Hameed out. He has his work to do. If you have a car I can drive then I can go alone maybe spend a few days there.' The first thought that ran through Grand Aunt's mind was to refuse Hira. However she saw a determination and a light in Hira's eyes that she had not seen before.

'Are you sure?' Hira nodded. 'A compromise perhaps, instead of you driving and ending up getting lost how about I get one of our drivers to go with you. That way you can travel without any worries.

My one request is that you wait a few days.' Hira nodded and threw her arms round Grand Aunt.

'You are the best,' she exclaimed.

'I know.' Grand Aunt laughed. 'Now I should really go for a nap.' She yawned loudly. 'I will speak to Hameed and get him to make the arrangements for the car and somewhere to stay.' Hira rewarded her with a smile.

Chapter 48

'Hira. The driver is waiting for you.' Farida's voice carried to the bedroom.

'Coming Aunt,' Hira called back. She finished packing a few things in the overnight bag and rushed out. She stopped in her tracks as she saw the line of family members waiting to see her off. Hameed stepped forward.

'I have arranged for you to stay with Ajay's family and sent word to Mukhti to look out for you.' He beckoned the driver. 'Ajay will make sure that you won't have any hassles and he will be available to drive you wherever you want. Just let him know when.' He handed her a phone and charger. 'One other thing, we want you to keep in contact at all times. And remember the rains come in fast and cut the place off.' Hira took the items from him and took note of his words.

'I will call every evening, and don't worry – it will be a short visit.' She looked at Grand Aunt, reassuring her. She hugged Grand Aunt and continued down the line hugging the female members before getting in the car. She waved until they cleared the compound then sat back, hoping the rains would not come too soon.

Mukhti sat waiting at the depot for them, upon seeing him Hira instructed Ajay to call out to him. He joined them and they made their way to where they were to be staying.

'It is so good to see you back so soon.' Mukhti turned in the front seat. His brow creased. 'But what brings you back?'

'I just wanted to take another look at the land but mostly to see the house properly.' She sat forward. 'I would also like to find out a bit more about the history. Is there a library or anywhere where archive records are kept around here?'

'What!'

'Li-bra-ry?' He enunciated the words, '... and archive records? What are those?'

Ajay laughed and took great pains to explain to Mukhti what Hira was requesting. Mukhti shook his head.

'No such things here.' He claimed not to know.

'Don't worry Miss Hira. I will find out where they are,' Ajay reassured her. 'I will make some enquiries.' He pulled up outside a

206

whitewashed house with a verandah adorned with colourful saris being dried. 'Home.' He smiled, stopped the car, took out Hira's bag from the trunk and handed it to a woman in a brightly coloured sari. 'Miss Hira I would like to introduce you to my wife, Janki.' Hira greeted her warmly. 'If you rest for a while then you can tell me what you want to visit first.'

'I can rest later,' Hira assured him. 'I would like to visit the house.'

'First won't you have some tea and savouries?' Janki spoke shyly. Hira smiled at her.

'I would love to sit with you and have some tea.' She told her. 'But first I would like to visit my great grandfather's house while it is still light.' Janki nodded her acceptance. 'Do we have the key?' Ajay nodded, took a package from Mukhti and handed it to her.

'Here is the bunch of keys. Let me get a change of clothes and we will go.'

Hira unlocked the heavy metal door and pulled it open with some effort. Behind it was an intricately designed wooden door, standing sturdy and proud, protected from the elements by the outer door. Hira stood at the entrance with a little apprehension, ready to duck if, at any moment, a colony of bats made tracks for the door. Thankfully that didn't happen. Hira took a deep breath and stepped over the threshold.

She stood in the middle of huge hall and turned, looking around her. Furniture lay forgotten, covered by off-white dust sheets. Faded pictures hung on the wall. Hira walked along the walls looking up at the history. She stopped infront of a portrait. A stern face stared down at her.

'That is Shazad.' Mukhti stood with her.

'Are you sure?' She turned to see that he had donned a pair of glasses. He stepped forward and brushed the brass plate underneath it, revealing the name. She got her answer.

Hira spied even more paintings on another wall.
'Is that …?'
'That is Shazad with his daughter, your grandmother, her husband and his two children.' Hira studied the images of the children

closely. Her brow furrowed.

'His two children.' She muttered absent mindedly, more to herself than to anyone else. 'Are these the only pictures?' She asked. Mukhti nodded.

'These are the only ones that have stood the test of time.' He looked at the other canvases strewn on the floor. The images faded beyond recognition.

Hira snapped on a flashlight and investigated further into the house. She stumbled upon what she assumed to be the study. The bureau was caked in dust. As she turned towards the bookshelf she stumbled against something, reached out to steady herself and knocked a number of books to the floor. Dust flew in the air, swirling around her making her cough and sneeze violently.

'I guess we should leave now.' Mukhti grabbed her by the elbow and led her outside. He helped her as she shut the heavy door and padlocked it. She doubled up and wheezed.

Mukhti looked on in amusement.

'What do you have there?' He pointed to what Hira was holding. She looked down in confusion.

'I must have picked these up without realising.' She looked at the door. 'Guess it is too late to go back in now.'

Darkness was fast descending, bringing with it a chill in the air. Mukhti delivered Hira to Ajay's house. Janki looked horrified as she set eyes upon Hira.

'Hira Miss. What happened? You are covered in so much dust. Come I will give you some towels. You get washed and then come and eat.' She handed her a towel and bundled her towards the bathroom.

Hira dried her hair and wondered over to the dresser. Spying the phone she remembered her promise to call every evening. Picking it up, she scrolled down the host of numbers that Hameed had input and rang his number. The engaged tone beeped mercilessly, eventually she gave up and decided to send a text message instead. For good measure she sent one to Grand Aunt's number as well. That way no one could accuse her of not being in touch. Her gaze went to the pile of papers she had removed from the house. Suppressing a yawn she decided that she would check them out later. For now she wanted to sleep.

The rain beat down mercilessly. Hira stood on the verandah with her cup of tea and stared out miserably as the grey sheet shrouded the locality in its mist. It was the second day and the rain had started at the same time as the cock had crowed at an ungodly hour that morning, the joys of living out in the country. *'Stupid, annoying cockerel.'* Hira grumbled at being woken early yet again. She spied said cockerel sheltering on the verandah. *'Count yourself lucky that you reside in a vegetarian household.'* She threatened. *'If it was up to me you would have been peri peri grilled chicken long ago.'* The cockerel stared at her with its beady eye. Hira held the stare and pumped the air in victory as the cockerel wandered off.

'Hira Miss, are you alright?' Janki stood in the doorway, eyeing her as if she had gone mad. Hira blushed and smiled shamefully. Ajay ran through the rain and sought shelter in the verandah. He wiped the water from his face.

'The rains have come early. We will need to make a move sooner rather than later.' He told her. 'The rain is not likely to let up. If we stay any longer we could become stranded. The river is already swollen. Before some of the low lying roads disappear under water we must go.' He turned to Janki. 'I will be back before the end of the month and will send you money as soon as I reach. Can you pack some food to take with us? I don't want to take any chances by stopping on the way just in case we the waters rise.'

Janki nodded, disappeared inside and started to pack food for their journey. Hira packed all her belongings and bade farewell to Janki and gave her a gift by way of a thank you. Janki opened the package and beamed. The car stopped and Ajay began to come out.

'Don't worry Ajay. I'll come to the car.' She ran, getting drenched in the rain in the short distance it took to get to the car and dived in.

They made their journey back on small side roads awash with water. With extreme caution Ajay navigated the perilous roads. Hira held her breath as a few times they skidded and almost got stuck in the mud. At last they made it to the main road leading to Ambala and only then did the apprehension lift.

'That was tough,' Ajay commented.

'You coped well. How often do you get caught like that?' Hira asked.

'Never.' Hira laughed more with relief than anything else.

'You handled the roads like a real pro. I am impressed.'

'Thank you Miss. I hope your stay at my house was not too basic.' Hira smiled at his back.

'No it was nice. Very quaint.'

'Quaint?' Ajay viewed her through the rear view mirror. She racked her brains, trying to find the comparative word in hindi and failed.

'It was very nice.' She said.

Due to the rain Ajay had not been able to call Hameed or Grand Aunt that they were on their way back and therefore they were not expected. Hira got out of the car, rang the bell and stood shivering.

Chapter 49

'Hira. Oh my god. Look at the state of you,' Janaat exclaimed and ushered her in. A flurry of activity ensued as towels were brought to dry her off and hot drink was called for. Grand Aunt had the presence of mind to take Hira to her room.

'Drop all of this.' She referred the the bag. 'And go and have a warm shower. After that I shall get you some hot milk and some food and you can tell me how you got on. Now quickly, before you catch a chill.' For good measure Hira sneezed. Grand Aunt threw her hands up. 'And there we go. Now hurry. Go and shower.' She shooed Hira to the bathroom and left to request food and drink for her.

Hira pushed the plate of food towards Grand Aunt.

'Eat with me?' she requested. Grand Aunt nodded and broke off a bit of chapatti, took some curry and popped the morsel in her mouth. Between them they made light work of the meal.

'How was the trip?' Grand Aunt eventually asked.

'Rained off.' Hira smiled. 'But I did have a quick look around the house. Saw a picture of great grandfather hanging there. There was one of Dadaji and Dadi too and ... '

'Hira.' Ghalib ran in and jumped onto the bed. 'Where did you go, why did you come back, did you have a nice time and have you brought sweets for me?' Hira laughed.

'You little monkey.' She grabbed him and wrestled him on the bed. 'Did you miss me? Is that why you are asking all these questions?' Ghalib shrieked and kicked his legs. Eventually she let him go. He got down off the bed, stood before her and viewed her with serious eyes.

'You have a present,' he said and ran off. Hira watched as he ran.

'A present?' she mulled.

'Oh yes. Wait here.' Grand Aunt crossed the corridor to her room and reappeared with a small package. 'This arrived the day after you left for Saharanpur.' She handed it to Hira. Realising that it might be something personal she made and excuse and left.

Hira opened the parcel and looked in mild surprise as she

211

took out a phone. Another one, the only difference being that this was her phone. She turned it over in her hands before checking it and switching it on. It pinged, alerting her that she had received a text message.

'Call me.' The message was short and simple. Hira looked at it, wondering if she should call. She placed the phone on the bed and sat staring at it.

'Hira you have a phone call.' Farida called to her. Hira frowned. *'Who would be calling her?'* She put on her shoes and made her way to the communal area, deep in thought.

She took the phone and held it to her ear. Hesitantly she spoke.

'Hello?'

'Hello Hira. How are you?' Hira beamed.

'Amara! I am fine now. How are you? How are things at home?'

'I am fine.' Amara whispered down the line. 'Dadi is having her nap so I took the opportunity to call you. When are you coming home?' She asked sadly. 'Nobody is talking. Aaryan is quiet like before and now even Dadaji is not speaking to Dadiji.'

'I am not sure.' Hira sighed. 'I needed sometime to get my head together.'

It was late evening when Hira returned to her bedroom. She almost tripped over her holdall, which reminded her to unpack her things and pack them away. She put down the borrowed laptop and tended to the bag. Lastly she pulled out the pile of papers she had brought with her, sat on the bed and sifted through them. There seemed to be a diary, some letters and a couple of faded photographs. Curiosity abound she opened the diary then found herself frowning. The script was very faded and was written in Urdu. Hira sighed. With her knowledge of the written word it would take her a month of Sundays to read. Disappointed she put it on the bed nudging the phone and knocking it into life.

She picked it up and turned the phone in her hands a few times mulling the request she had received. She sighed. Before she got a chance to change her mind she dialled the number.

The phone lit up the dark room and resonated throughout. A hand reached out to take it.

'Hello.' Hira almost hung up. She took a deep breath.

'Hello,' she replied awkwardly then fell silent.

'How are you?' Aaryan changed position on the bed and lay back propped up against the headboard.

'I am okay. I think,' she replied.

'You aren't asleep yet?' he asked gently.

'Well no. I am talking to you.' That brought a small smile to his face.

'How did we get here Hira?' he asked her. Hira stared and made a face into the phone.

'How? Do you want me to draw diagrams?' She cradled the phone to her ear and picked up the photographs. From behind one of them a newspaper clipping fell out. Very carefully she unfolded it. It had the same picture she had seen at the house. She began to read the article underneath it.

'Diagrams won't take back what has happened. I am so glad that you called. I was afraid that you might ignore the text...'

'Son of a ...' Hira exclaimed. Aaryan moved the phone from his ear. He looked at it before replacing it next to his ear.

'What was that for?' He protested. 'I only said...' Hira stopped reading and blushed.

'I'm sorry.' She apologised to him. 'But listen to this.' She read out the article to him. Suddenly everything became clearer.

Grand Aunt looked about her bed trying to locate buzzing noise that started to irritate her. She swatted the air around her shooing away the source of the noise, imagining it to be a mosquito or a midge until she realised that the buzzing was actually coming from her phone. She answered it, listened intently then smiled.

Chapter 50

The sound of excited chatter reached her ears, the following morning, as she made her way along the corridor. Warm smiles greeted her.

'Hira come and sit with us,' Farida beckoned her.

'What are you doing?' she asked seeing the women seated at the dining table. Each busy in their task.

'We are making samosas,' Aunt Farida explained. 'All the neighbours have come to help.'

'So many and so early?' Hira noted and sat down with them. 'Why?' Farida smiled, passed her a cup of tea and some food.

'We are gearing up for a celebration. Whenever we have a wedding or a big function in the area we all gather together and help to make snacks. We are going to host a mehndi here and serve them then. It brings the neighbourhood closer.' She sat down.

'Can I help?' Aunt Farida smiled.

'I insist.' She watched as Hira put together a samosa laid it on the tray and started another one.

'Mehndi? Whose?' she asked.

'It is the wedding of the daughter of my sister's cousin's nephew's niece,' Aunt Farida blabbered. Hira looked amused.

'Aunt Farida, doesn't that mean that they are related to you too?' Everyone laughed at Aunt Farida's gaffe. Grand Aunt walked in stroking a kitten that tried its best to be somewhere else. As she walked up to the table her daughters' voices rang out in unison.

'Amma not near the table please,' they protested, rushing to shield the food. 'Please take the cat back to its rightful owner.' Grand Aunt pretended to look put out.

'I don't know why you don't like cats.' She muttered and set the cat down which in turn bolted for the garden and freedom. 'I'll just go and wash my hands.' She smiled.

'I wonder what the cat's owners must think,' Hira mused.

'What is there to think?' A brightly dressed lady with a red face joined in the merriment. 'I am just happy that my cat has such a good friend to play with.' She looked towards Grand Aunt who had returned to the fold. 'Whether it wants to or not.' Hira chuckled. Grand Aunt hugged her tight.

When will we get to see the bride?' she asked. Aunt Farida

was ready with her reply.

'On the day of the wedding I am afraid. She is flying in for the wedding from Pakistan. There were a few visa issues which is why it is so close to the wire. But never mind. We will have a smaller gathering here. We will apply the henna to our hands and feet and sing and dance the night away as if we were there at the mehndi. Why should we miss out?' Hira looked puzzled.

'Can that be done?' Aunt Farida nodded.

'No reason not to. Besides, our family never does things by the rule book. We just follow Amma's lead. She has been a trailblazer.'

'I want a henna tattoo all the way up my arm,' Grand Aunt stated and for good measure rolled up her sleeve to reveal her arm. 'I want it to go all the way to here. My outfit will be sleeveless and I want to create a statement. I want a suggestive one.' More laughter ensued.

'Amma you are such a rebel.' Another of her daughter-in-laws cut in. 'What will people say?'

'Let them say what they want to,' Grand Aunt responded. 'I am no less than any of you. I am young; full of life.' She winked at Hira. 'After all, there is no law that says I have to grow old, sit in a corner and be damp. I prefer to be out there having a good time, causing mayhem and being damp!'

'Mother!' A shocked chorus of voices echoed followed by raucous laughter.

Hira chuckled heartily. She wiped the tears of laughter from her eyes and looked gratefully at Grand Aunt.

Grand Aunt looked at the women gathered round. 'If I can make people laugh, then I feel that I have achieved something.' She cradled Hira's face in her hands. 'Keep laughing my child. Life looks so much better when there is laughter.' Hira hugged her tightly.

'Grandma, please don't change. Ever.'

Snacks had been prepared, along with the chutneys, sweets and evening meal. The neighbours had left, happy and armed with goodies. The rest of the family were sitting sipping tea, their preferred method of relaxing at the end of the day before retiring for bed. Grand Aunt appeared carrying a large number of bags and proceeded to hand them out among her children and grandchildren. She handed one to Hira who looked up confused.

'There is a wedding to go to. You need new and suitable clothing.' She smiled at her and the others gathered around. There were gasps and appreciative comments all round as each person checked their bags. Feeding off the excitement from everyone else Hira dipped into the bag and pulled out two outfits, a beautiful emerald green shalwar kameez with embroidered dupatta and an absolutely gorgeous ivory and red lehenga suit with gold embroidery. Hira gasped.

'Grandma? This is lovely.' She fingered the material between finger and thumb and marvelled at the feel of it. 'But Grandma isn't this, the outfit of a bride?' Grand Aunt quickly looked away before answering her.

'You can wear the shalwar kameez tomorrow for the mehndi and the red for the wedding.' Hira looked closely at Grand Aunt. The cogs began to turn in Hira's brain. She put two and two together.

'Grandma,' Grand Aunt realised that she had been rumbled and hid behind Farida, hoping like a child that she would find sanctuary there. They all laughed at her antics.

'I can never organise things properly.' She peered out from behind Farida. 'It is true. That is the bride's outfit. It is not any relative of Farida but you who will be getting married. Hira thoughts muddled themselves together until they were jumbled into one puzzling mess until last night's telephone conversation came to mind.

'Hira. What are you thinking of?' Tasneem and Noor deflected her line of questioning. They sat with her. 'Don't go hiding away. We need a wedding? Say yes if only to give us a chance to enjoy ourselves. Grandma has everything in hand.' Hira's eyes filled with tears, she blinked them away. Since arriving with Grand Aunt she had been shown nothing but love and concern. In some ways it was her undoing.

'No tears,' Grand Aunt told her. 'There will be no tears in my house.' Hira was enveloped in a hug.

'Pagli.' Tasneem consoled her. 'You mad thing. There is no reason to cry. We are family, yes?' Hira nodded.

'I'm sorry,' she apologised, giving her a watery smile. 'I guess I am still overwhelmed by your kindness.'

'Pfft!' They all brushed her comments aside. Noor opened a

magazine and thrust it in front of her.

'I have such a lovely hairstyle for you. See? You will look stunning.'

'Just like me,' Grand Aunt cut in. 'I shall be the belle of the ball.' She did a little dance, earning herself a playful scolding from her sons. 'Alright, alright I guess I know when I am being told off. It's getting late. I shall retire to bed. Goodnight all.' She yawned loudly, hitched up her shalwar till it reached mid-calf and headed for her room. 'I suggest that you all go to sleep at a decent time.' She called out without looking back.

Chapter 51

The singing started in the early evening. The neighbours, who had previously been to the house to help prepare the food, started arriving. Excited chatter filled the ground floor as the womenfolk gathered in the garden while the menfolk gathered to hold their own celebrations in another part of the house. Hira stood at the top of the landing and watched in awe as the women sat together and sang. Noor sidled up to her.

'I love weddings. They give me a good chance to eye up the available men and show myself off at my best,' she whispered. Hira looked at her, amazed at her frankness. Noor giggled. 'It is what all our mums and aunties do. We are looking at hot marriageable material and they are looking for good sons-in-law and perfect matches. Come on. Let's go down and join in. What are you like singing?'

'Ermm the less said about that the better,' Hira replied.

'You will join in even if brides normally don't. Mostly they sit in the corner and blush,' Noor insisted. 'But you will be the bride and the guest. I guarantee that you will have a blast.' Hira turned to her.

'You are so sure? Bring it on. I have no qualms of not sitting blushing in a corner.' She laughed. Noor grabbed her hand and dragged her down stairs.

They gathered up plates of snacks and headed into the crowd. Finding a place amongst other family members they sat down and tucked in. Hira looked around her. The majority of women sat and sang songs while a few others sat around chatting. They had all come together for a pre-wedding ceremony and at the same time were using the occasion as a means of networking. Hira guessed that what Noor had earlier said was true. Such an event was used to everyone's benefit. The sound of laughter and cat-calls drew her attention to the centre of the circle. Grand Aunt stood in the centre balancing an earthenware pot on her head and was shaking a few moves. She completed a couple of circuits then passed the pot to the next person.

'Hira. Come and join in,' Tasneem called out. 'There is plenty of singing and dancing to be done and you have to take an active part. There is no shying away.' Noor and Hira joined her. Tasneem reached up, grabbed Hira's hand and pulled her down to sit with her. 'If there is anything you don't understand or know tell me and I shall explain.'

Hira leant forward.

'How about all of it,' she whispered. Tasneem looked surprised.

'Really? Well we start with this.' She handed her a sheet of paper with song words written on it. 'We start with this and then play by ear. There will be songs and dances with role playing too. You have to take part,' she told her. Hira shrugged and smiled resignedly. 'When in Rome...' she thought to herself.

For some reason her attention was drawn towards the door and at the last remaining guests arriving. Her eyes lit up and she got up to greet them.

Sabina and Amara stood smiling. Since Grand Aunt had taken Hira away Dadi, in a foul mood had ensured that they did not have much time to dwell on the past events and kept them busy all the time. As they spied Hira, Tasneem and Noor walking towards them, they squealed and ran forward, hugging each other like long lost friends.

'Oh my god Hira how good is it to see you. We are missing you so much.' Sabina and Amara hugged her tightly before turning their attention to Tasneem and Noor enveloping them in a group hug.

'I am missing you too,' Hira told them. Noor coughed. Hira laughed and hugged her tighter. 'But my sisters here are looking after me really well.' Sabina and Amara were dragged to join in with the mehndi celebrations. They greeted the elders and took their blessings before joining in with the singing.

'How is Aaryan?' Hira whispered.

'He is doing better than before,' Sabina told her, 'but he has missed you a lot.'

'The house is not the same without you and Aaryan too. We feel we have lost two members of our family. You are here and we hardly see Aaryan.' Hira quickly changed the topic.

'For now let us put those things aside. This is a mehndi. Let us enjoy ourselves.'

No sooner had she said that then she felt a strange tingle go down her spine.

Dadi stood at the threshold with Akilah at her side, eyes blazing, seeking out the object of her displeasure.

'See, I told you that something was being planned,' Akilah leant in and whispered. 'All this is happening and they did not tell you.' Dadi adjusted her dupatta and glared at the gathering. Grand Aunt stepped forward.

'Appa, so you have graced us with your presence...' Dadi stared at her icily and cut her short.

'What is going on here Zehra? Am I right in thinking that you have organised the wretch's mehndi ceremony?' Grand Aunt's demeanour changed. She looked at Dadi with undisguised anger.

'No. Not just the mehndi, but the wedding too.'

'How can you possibly get her married off? She is not divorced.' Grand Aunt brushed her comments aside.

'If you are here to join the mehndi you are welcome. If not I shall appreciate it if you leave. I don't want any upset. Not in my house.' She walked back to the watching guests.

'Where are the drums, the music? I want to see dancing. Come on.' She cajoled a group of young girls to start dancing.

Dadi and Akilah made their way to Hira. Hira stared at Akilah. It was the first time they had met since the accident.

'What are they doing here?' Hira asked.

'They tagged along with us. Akilah turned up and whined that if she could not attend then neither could we,' Sabina told her. Hira stood up.

'If you would excuse me for a moment?' She walked towards Dadi and Akilah but instead of offering a greeting she stared at them indifferently and walked past, greeting Mrs Desai who had arrived behind them. The two ladies stood fuming at the snub they had received. Hira felt their eyes on her back throwing a million sharp daggers at her and smiled.

'Mrs Desai. So good to see you here is it possible that I can have a brief word with you?' Mrs Desai smiled back.

'Of course.'

'I have acquired some land as part of my inheritance and I thought that maybe we could discuss some things?' Dadi turned with a mixture of surprise and anger on her face. As Hira and Mrs Desai spoke Dadi moved nearer, straining to hear what was being said. Just at that moment the drums and trumpets started up dashing any hopes she had of eavesdropping. Dadi cursed inwardly and went off to find women of her own age-group to sit with. Akilah had already made a bee-line for the food.

Despite her reluctance and the appearance of Dadi, Hira joined in whole-heartedly with the celebrations. She danced and sang with the best of them. The role playing with Tasneem and Amara reduced her to tears of laughter as they dressed like a young married couple singing of love, romance and stolen kisses while Noor donned male attire as a patriarchal figure and chased the young lovers from place to place, all narrated in song.

There was silence for the briefest of moments. Grand Aunt stood up.

'Now that we have danced, laughed and worked up an appetite we shall eat. Please help yourselves to food. We will then apply the mehndi afterwards.'

Hira took her place with Sabina and Amara while Tasneem and Noor sat with their friends.

'How is Dadaji?' She asked them taking a morsel of food.

'Dadaji is surviving. But he and Dadiji haven't spoken properly to each other since he returned from visiting Grandpa Hafiz.' Amara fiddled with her glass. 'If anything Dadiji has become worse she is in a constant bad mood,' Hira grimaced.

'Don't feel bad.' Sabina reached over and held her hand. 'Dadi has been back and forth to Akilah's in-laws. Every other day there is a call. If it is not Akilah complaining and moaning about the way her in-laws are treating her then it is them threatening to send her back. Dadiji has to go and smooth things over. Looks like Akilah has met her match. They are not putting up with her hysterics and neither is Dadaji. When she turned up on the door step he got to the bottom of what happened and sent her back with a flea in her ear. Apparently she had a dispute with Riaz's brother, mother and sister. Tried to create issues between them and Riaz but it hasn't worked in her favour. Riaz got wise and tore a strip off her. She is not used to being treated harshly. She keeps ringing up and asking to come back. Dadiji tried to get her back but Dadaji said it would be over his dead body.' Hira choked and spluttered. Tasneem and Amara slapped her on the back while Noor handed her some water.

After a few sips and a dozen slaps she settled down.

'Food went down the wrong way.' She explained brushing aside their concern. Amara finished her meal and pushed the plate away.

'I don't think that I could have coped with her being back with us. Even with Dadiji in her mood it has been somewhat peaceful.'

'What are you three doing sat here chatting?' Aunt Farida came up behind them and leant on the back of the chairs. 'Get ready to have the mehndi applied. There are so many beautiful designs to choose from.' She handed them a file full to bursting with designs. Sabina smiled.

'Thank you Aunt.' They poured over the designs.

'Yes dear. Come and sit down. Have you chosen your design?' The beautician smiled as Hira took her place.

'We have,' Sabina told her. 'Hira will have this one and Amara and I will have this one and this one.' She pointed the designs out.

'Beautiful choices if I may say.' The woman smiled. 'Especially this one, it is very intricate.' Hira looked at the next few seats and saw Grand Aunt sitting patiently with her sleeve rolled up while her chosen design was applied. True to Grand Aunt's wishes the design took up all of her arm. Thankfully the promised suggestive tattoo had not been applied. Hira had seen quite a few that raised her eyebrows.

'Grand Aunt,' she called out to her. 'You do realise that the design will be ruined if that sleeve does not stay up?' Grand Aunt looked at the design and then her sleeve.

'I didn't notice that. Good job you told me. What am I going to do now?' she wailed, looking about her. Hira removed a safety pin which held her dupatta in place and handed it over.

'You can pin the sleeve with this.' The beautician took the pin and secured Grand Aunt's sleeve.

'Much better.' Grand Aunt smiled. 'You get your good ideas from my side of the family.'

The beautician drew Hira's attention. She held up the file and studied the design.

'You will stay still won't you? You're not ticklish are you?' Hira shook her head and presented her hands.

222

The early hours of the morning finally saw the ladies disperse and head off home. Singing wedding songs as they made their way to their cars. Hira watched them go and yawned. Her hands were already caked with the dried henna but even so she was careful not to ruin the designs.

'Let's see your design,' Sabina asked her. Hira held out her hands. The colour of the henna was already coming through strong. Sabina scrutinised the hands and smiled to herself.

'That looks so beautiful. She did a good job.' Hira nodded her head.

'She did, didn't she?' Sabina looked towards the door and spied Amara making her way towards them.

'We have to go now,' she told her sadly. She stepped forward and hugged her.

'Already?' Hira mirrored Sabina's sad look.

'I will call you,' she assured her. 'Dadaji would love to speak to you.' Hira nodded silently.

'I'll be waiting,' she told her. After bidding farewell to both girls Hira's thoughts turned to sleep. For the first time in weeks she felt that she would sleep well.

Chapter 52

In the depths of her dreams she imagined that she was a small child once again. She saw both herself and her mother on the beach. It was a vivid dream and she saw herself jumping on the trampolines that fringed the beach. The dream was becoming too vivid. With her eyes still closed she emerged from the dream and frowned. The bouncing still continued. Opening her eyes she was greeted by Noor and Ghalib, both jumping on the bed excitedly. Thankful that she was not losing her mind, Hira sat up.

'What are you two so full of beans about?' Ghalib continued to jump up and down.

'Dadiji thaid that I am going to be a therwala,' he lisped, bringing about a smile on Hira's face at his excitement. So, he would be accompanying the groom during the ceremony. He would look so cute she concluded dressed exactly like the groom. He would be the groom's right hand man.

'He is going to be the serwala,' Noor continued 'so he will be leaving shortly to go to the bharatis' house. Once we have the little irritant out of the way we will spend a leisurely morning relaxing and then in the afternoon we are going to the spa to be pampered.' She linked her arm through Hira's. 'We will be all calm and refreshed for the wedding.' She lay down with her. 'Go on pipsqueak. Go to mum. She will get you fed and ready. Remember you have a very important job. Don't let us down.' Ghalib got down from the bed and shot her a serious look.

'I am a big boy,' he told them. 'I will not be scared of getting on the horse.' He mimicked the sounds and movements of a horse. Hira laughed as she watched him canter off.

'He is going to tire himself before the day is out.'

'That is the plan,' Noor replied and laughed.

A call for Noor came drifting along the corridor and into the room. Noor pulled a face.

'Looks like I have got breakfast duty for the little monkey.' She moaned, getting up from the bed. She stopped at the door. 'We are leaving for the spa at 11 time to get pampered and defuzzed,' she told her. 'Comfortable clothes, absolutely no make up. See you in a while.' She shot off down the corridor.

Hira stood in front of the mirror and touched her face. Her skin tingled, she watched her face glow and her mind was on a different plane. Taking the opportunity she relaxed fully as she was massaged, pampered and introduced to the many aromas that assailed her senses. For the first time she allowed herself to succumb to the treatment being offered.

'It wasn't everyday,' she told herself as she looked across the parlour and saw that her cousins, aunts and even grand aunt had thrown off the cares of the impending wedding and had surrendered to the bliss that soothed them.

They emerged hours later, massaged, pampered and refreshed, walking as if they were on air. High even. Hira smiled at the scene, a group of totally spaced out women waiting on the pavement for their cars. The nearby beggars and hawkers soon realised that the women we getting ready for a big occasion and descended on them offering them blessings at a cost. The jostling was becoming uncomfortable and a few times she felt hands on her which had no right. Not that they stayed on her for long. A few words and they were soon gone. Hira was relieved when the drivers arrived to take them home.

'Hira. Don't stay up too long.' Grand Aunt appeared in the doorway. 'Have an early night.' She came to her and placed her hand on her head, blessing her. 'Everyone else is going to bed early tonight. Tomorrow is going to be quite a big day. Sleep and conserve your energy. Is your outfit ready?' Hira nodded. 'Excellent.' She smiled and shuffled off. Hira watched her go.

Chapter 53

She slept through the early morning call to prayer and the subsequent alarm that she had set herself. Hira opened her eyes to bright sunshine and an eerie quiet. It was then that she realised that this morning Ghalib, the whirlwind was away. She sat up and smiled to herself. The excitement on his face was so adorable. She wondered what he was doing at this time. Throwing the bedcovers aside she swung her legs over the edge, placed her feet into her slippers and headed for the bathroom.

Hira felt as if she was aboard the Mary Rose. Wherever she went not a soul was to be seen. Eventually she grabbed some breakfast pulled up a seat and ate. There was a certain peace in the house; a still and relaxing ambience that went well with the pristine white walls and lightly coloured furnishings.

After breakfasting she busied herself before heading towards the courtyard and the flowers that beckoned her. After seeing the sorry state of some of the pots from the night before she set about arranging them. Only when she was satisfied that they were at their best did she water them.

Knocking on the front door invaded her thoughts. She opened the door then stopped in her tracks. She crossed her arms.

'I didn't expect to see you here. What do you want?' Dadi stepped in looking to see if anyone else was around. She checked the nearby rooms and the kitchen before advancing towards Hira.

'You, listen to me. I want a word, somewhere private.' Hira made no move. 'Don't give me that attitude. Do as you're told.'

'I am not going anywhere. Whatever poison you need to spout, spout it here.' Dadi grabbed her by the arm and dug her fingers into her.

'Don't think that just because you are here you can disrespect me. Now listen to me.' She held onto Hira to stop her from walking away. When she was sure that Hira would stay, she reached into her cloth bag and pulled out an important-looking document. Hira looked on, curious as to what the old lady was doing now.

'You want to make a life with Aaryan, right?' She smoothed the papers out and produced a pen. 'I have had these papers drawn up.

Sign the land over to me and I will not stand in your way.' She held the pen out to her. Hira took the pen, picked up the papers and read the contents. 'Well, what are you waiting for? Sign them.'

'I don't understand. Why would you stand in the way if the relationship in the first place was 'unclean'? Why give your permission now especially as you were the one who instigated the alliance in the first place?' Dadi quickly looked away. Hira leant forward and whispered. 'Or is it that you weren't entirely truthful, with me or the family.' Dadi sucked in an impatient breath.

'Are you going to sign it or not?' she snapped. Hira stood in front of her, tore the papers into tiny pieces and theatrically let them flutter to the floor.

'No. I can't sign this land over to you. I won't,' she declared. 'I already have plans for it. I have spoken to Mrs Desai and have decided that the land will assist the women of the refuge in Saharanpur branch.'

'What?'

'Yes. The women will be employed to tend the orchards and the refuge will get a percentage of the proceeds.'

Dadi seethed. 'You fool. I will not allow it. You are going to use such low, disgusting and fallen women? They are not even worthy to set foot on my father's land.'

Hira was incredulous. She looked on as the old woman ranted, 'As for you marrying Aaryan still deluding yourself I see. What makes you think that he will want to marry you? I have filled his ears so much that he himself wants nothing more to do with you. The ceremony will not go ahead. It will stop before you will have had the chance to retake your vows. I have made sure that it won't. You know what is said about girls who are rejected by their grooms on their wedding day?' She sneered.

'They have had a lucky escape?' Hira replied. 'If a groom is not man enough to step up then she is better off without him.'

'Don't act smart,' Dadi warned. 'You still have time. What is your answer?' Hira stood up.

'I gave you my answer. I won't change my mind. No matter what carrot you dangle in front of me. I will not budge and it is not up for negotiation. The land is mine and I will do with it as I will.' Dadi's face darkened in anger, she waggled her finger close to Hira's face.

'Sign it. If need be I will leave you in no state to even stand on your feet,' she threatened.

'I don't doubt that you would spare me,' Hira lowered her voice a fraction. 'Just as you didn't spare my mother … or Aaryan's grandmother come to that.' As soon as Hira uttered those words she saw Dadi's features change from surprise, to shock, to anger.

'You wretch.' Dadi lurched forward and reached for Hira grabbing her arm and swung her round. 'You think you are so clever. There is only one person who knows what happened and that person is me.' She dug her fingers into Hira's arm so hard that she was sure that she would carry the bruises for days afterwards, before pushing her away causing her to trip and fall forwards. She put her hands out in front of her to break her fall.

Hira landed at a pair of feet. Slowly she looked up. Strong hands helped her up.

'Are you alright?' Aaryan supported her. Hira nodded. The feet belonged to Dada. He stepped forward.

'Is that true, Soraya?' he asked.

'I came to see Hira. I wanted to see if she needed anything?' Dada narrowed his eyes.

'I asked if what I had heard was true? As for Hira, you have never cared for her before? Why now, all of a sudden?' Dadi wiped her perspiring face with her dupatta.

'Hira is a child. She will say anything.' She refused to make eye contact with him.

'Soraya!' Dada took a few steps towards her. His face red and contorted with rage. 'Are you possessed or something? You made your choices in life. If they did not work out then why are you blaming everyone else and making their lives hell? Why? Why are you hell bent on ruining these children's lives, everyone's lives? Are you that bitter?' He wheezed and swayed a little. Hira and Aaryan propped him up and took him to sit down.

'Dadaji, please calm down.' Hira pleaded with him. Dada sat down and began to regulate his breathing.

'You even resorted to … to violence.' He could not bring himself round to say murder. He gasped and rubbed his chest in some distress. Hira did her best to calm him down and reassure him.

Car horns and shouts heralded the family's arrival. Grand Aunt came in and stopped in her tracks. The sight of Dada in obvious pain scared her and she rushed forward.

'Sadiq Bhaijan. How have you got yourself into this state? Calm down.' Dada focused on them and controlled his breathing. They watched expectantly as his breathing became normal.

'Hameed, Aaryan. Take Sadiq Bhaijan to the hospital.' Hameed nodded. Together with Aaryan he pulled Dada to his feet and helped him towards the car.

Coming alongside Dadi he asked them to stop.

'Get the driver to take you home. When I get back I want you gone. I don't care where you go. If I am feeling generous I will call for you but for now stay away from me and my family. Free us from your poison.' Dadi gasped. All eyes were upon her. Grand Aunt held the door.

'I think you'd better go now.' Dadi held her head high, with a parting shot she stormed out.

'You will do as my brother says.' Grand Aunt shouted after her. 'You are no longer welcome in my house.'

Hira began to shake. Grand Aunt consoled her.

'Your Dadaji will be fine. He is made of sterner stuff. I am sorry we left you alone. We had to go out and pick up a few more provisions and then we went on to the cemetery and offer a prayer at the grave of my late husband. It was long overdue. Leave this.' She said referring to what had happened. 'I want you to spend all your energy in getting ready. I have warned your grandmother to keep away. If she does come tonight I want you to show her that you are strong. She cannot wear you down. I want you laughing and carefree. Understand?' She schooled her.

By dinnertime they still had no word on Dada's progress. Hira declined her food. Farida sat down with her.

'Hira try and eat. We will hear shortly and I am sure that your grandfather wouldn't want you to be morose like this.' Hira shook her head.

'I can't eat, Aunt even if I wanted to. I can't swallow. Maybe I should have just kept silent.' Farida shot Grand Aunt a look. Grand Aunt shook her head. She reached out and held Hira's hand.

'Hira everything will be fine. I am sure of it.' Just then the phone rang. Hira picked up the call.

'Hello.'

'Hira.' A relieved Aaryan's voice carried down the line. 'Where have you been? I have been trying your phone for ages.' She reddened.

'It is in my room.' She mumbled. 'How is Dadaji?'

'Dadaji is fine. He just got stressed out and hyperventilated. I am waiting for the doctors to discharge him and then I shall take him home to rest.' Hira sighed with relief.

'He is definitely ok?'

'He is.' Aaryan reassured her. 'You get some rest now. I shall see you tomorrow at our wedding.'

'Even after the altercation with Dadi?'

'Especially after the altercation with Dadi. You stood your ground against what is yours and your idea for the orchard is worthy. I am proud of you. See you tomorrow.' Hira wished him goodbye.

'Dadiji is ok.' She bounded back and relayed the news to the family. 'Where is that food? I am starving.'

Chapter 54

Hira laid out her outfit on the bed and admired it. From the day she had taken it out of the bag she had fallen in love with it. Tasneem told her that the beautician would be doing her make up so until everyone was done she had to wait. Feeling bored, she decided to go and see what everyone else was up to.

At the exact moment she reached the door and opened it Tasneem and Noor bounded in. Both had their outfits in their arms.
'Where do you think you are going? We thought you might start wandering,' Tasneem began. 'So we thought that we would come to your room and dress. Afterwards we will help you dress. The beautician is here too? She will do our make up as well.' Noor put down her outfit. 'We are paying for a service, may as well make use of it. No?' Hira nodded. She could see the logic in that. Patiently she sat and waited her turn as she watched the beautician work.
At last they stood before each other made up and glowing.
'You look gorgeous,' they chimed in unison. The beautician had brought out the very best in them.

Their complimenting was cut short by the sound of drums and trumpets heralding the arrival of the bharatis and the groom. Tasneem and Noor squealed in excitement and headed out to see the arrival of the wedding procession.
'Hira, you stay here until we come to get you,' Tasneem called back. 'We won't be long, promise.'

Hira paced the length and breadth of the room. Eventually she sat upon the bed.

***

When the wedding party comes from the boy's side everyone rushes to see the procession. The bride is not supposed to see them enter the house. So she sits in her room alone and thinks about her journey ahead. Hira lay in bed and yawned.

231

'Tell me more Maman. Why does she think about the journey ahead? Is she going to a faraway place?' Both mother and daughter lay in bed. Hira had her mother's red and gold wedding dupatta over her.

'Not always a faraway place. Sometimes the bride will wonder what type of life she will have. Whether her husband will love her, if she will get on with her in-laws, what her children will be like?' Hira sat up and looked down at her mother.

'When I get married will I have to sit in a room by myself? Her mother shook her head.

'No. I will be there with you. I will allay your fears.'

***

Hira brushed away a tear.

'Where are you now, Maman. We spent so many nights speaking about this, the rituals, the dress, a beautiful wedding. I have all that but where are you?' Her heart ached and she closed her eyes, willing herself not to cry.

Tasneem and Noor had been gone for some time. Tired of waiting she picked up the heavily embroidered chiffon dupatta and arranged it hastily over her shoulders and turned to go and find Tasneem and Noor. Not seeing Grand Aunt in her rush she almost ran straight into her.

'Grandma I am sorry,' she apologised breathlessly. Grand Aunt placed the bag she was carrying on the the bed and looked at her wistfully.

'You look so beautiful.' She reached up and touched her cheek. 'That colour suits you but it is not quite finished yet.' She reached down and pulled a jewellery box out of the bag. 'No one attends a wedding without wearing accompanying jewellery, least of all the bride.' She opened the box. Hira gasped. 'You put these on, quickly.' Grand Aunt helped Hira put on the intricately designed necklace, earrings and bangles. 'Perfect.' She took the dupatta draped it over her shoulders and head, bringing it forward to the point of hiding her face. Hira looked confused. 'You will appear before the groom with your face hidden. Tasneem and Noor will be doing the same. We are going to play a few games with the groom. His shoes have already disappeared.' She chuckled. 'You wait here. When it is time you will be escorted downstairs. Everything else is going exactly the way you wanted it. I have to go down now. I will send someone up to keep you company.' Moments later Tasneem and Noor appeared, their faces covered.

'Come on Hira,' Noor called to her. 'Let us go and give the bridegroom and run for his money.'

Despite herself Hira began to feel nervous and her legs began to feel like lead. Walking along the landing she slowed down.

'Hira what are you doing?' Tasneem grabbed her arm and whispered in her ear. 'Come on.'

They both flanked her and led her along the corridor to the top of the the staircase and stopped. A second red and gold rectangular length of chiffon was unfurled and held above Hira's head.

'Hira?' Tasneem and Noor stood each holding a corner of the veil above her head. They had been joined by Sabina and Amara. 'Shall we go?' Hira nodded.

'It's now or never.' She declared. Slowly they descended the staircase with Hira under cover of the heavy red and gold cloth and made their way down the stairs to where Aaryan sat on the dias with his family and stopped before him.

Aaryan got to his feet, followed by Dada, Aiden and Alman. All four of them smiled.

Aaryan reached forward to lift her veil. Noor was too fast. Before he got close she moved Hira away, stood before him and held her hand out, demanding money for the luxury for the face revealing. After much haggling Noor got the amount she wanted from Aaryan, and lifted her own veil before thumbing her nose at him and ran off happily while her place was taken by Tasneem who demanded more money but this time with menaces. She was handed money also for the privilege but did not comply. Aaryan stood wagging his finger at her. Tasneem poked her tongue at him and laughed before helping Hira to take her place on the dias with Grand Aunt and Farida. Aaryan sat next to her. She smiled at him. Hira then leant forward and made eye contact with Grand Aunt.

'Thank you,' she mouthed. Grand Aunt nodded and smiled.

Grand Aunt beckoned the imam to come forward. Nodding he stepped forward, took the microphone and spoke to the gathered guests.

'I understand that the nikaah had been undertaken previously and does not necessarily need to be performed. However at the behest of the elders I am happy to preside over a second nikaah.' Aaryan covered his head with a scarf while the imam recited the sunna khutba (sermon). After the khutba he called on the bride's representative if he has the bride's permission to enter her into the marriage. Grand Aunt's son stepped forward.

'I accept ... I mean, I do,' he flustered. Grand Aunt palmed her forehead and shook her head. Imam asked the question to Hira.

'Hira Malik, daughter of Nawaz Malik, do you on this day accept Aaryan Dajani, son of Qadir Dajani as your husband? Do you accept his gift of mehr to you?'

'I accept.' He then turned to Aaryan.

'Aaryan Dajani, son of Qadir Dajani do you accept Hira Malik, daughter of Nawaz Malik as your wife?

'Stop this nonsense at once!' The words brought the proceedings to a halt and a hush descended in the house. Dadi stood at the door. As she made her way to the dias. Dada stood up.

She stood a few feet away from Aaryan and shot him a murderous look. 'Reject her,' she ordered him. Dada glared at her.

'Say anything further Soraya and you are gone forever from my life.' He warned her. She looked at Aaryan.

'You can't do this! I do not give my consent,' she ranted. 'You won't disobey me,' she said with conviction. Then her tone changed. 'Remember how I used to take care of you? You owe me that much at least.' Aaryan thought back to his childhood. Of Dadi spoiling him, feeding him sweets and showering her affection upon him. He also saw the other side of Dadi, the mean, cruel woman who had tormented and reduced his mother to tears so many times for the smallest of things.

He looked into her eyes and felt nothing. She no longer held any importance for him or any relation and he knew that nothing she could say or do could change his mind now or in the future. He

reached for Hira's hand, kissed it and held it to his chest.
'I accept.' Aaryan's answer was loud and clear.